A NARROW
TRAJECTORY

A NARROW TRAJECTORY

FAITH MARTIN

ROBERT HALE

First published in 2016 by
Robert Hale, an imprint of
The Crowood Press Ltd,
Ramsbury, Marlborough
Wiltshire SN8 2HR

www. crowood.com

www.halebooks.com

British Library Cataloguing-in-Publication Data
A catalogue record for this book is available from the
British Library.

ISBN 978 0 7198 1998 8

Typeset by Catherine Williams, Knebworth

Printed and bound in India by Replika Press Pvt Ltd

CHAPTER ONE

HILLARY GREENE GOT OUT of her old Volkswagen Polo, Puff the Tragic Wagon, and closed the door quickly behind her as a blast of cold November air tried to snatch it from her fingers. She put the hood up on her green parka coat and all but power-walked towards the entrance to Kidlington's Thames Valley Police HQ, trying not to shiver under the icy onslaught.

She made her way down into the bowels of the building where, although a retired Detective Inspector, she now worked as a consultant for the Crime Review Team, taking a second look at cold murder cases. Giving the desk sergeant a friendly salute as she passed him, he responded in kind, barely breaking stride as he dealt with a gaggle of traffic cops who seemed to have some sort of grievance and were clearly set on trying to get him on side.

This week her new boss, Detective Superintendent Roland 'Rollo' Sale formally took over the reins of the CRT from Acting DCS Steven Crayle, who'd been promoted to head a new team operating at St Aldates, in Oxford. As she headed through the labyrinth of corridors in the basement towards her office – which had once, literally, been a stationery cupboard – she glanced at her watch a shade nervously, relieved to see that it was still well before eight a.m. She was hoping to catch Steven before her new boss arrived, since there were two important things that they needed to discuss in private. One was work related, but the other was very much more personal.

She hastily slung her bag under the desk and shucked off her coat, then retraced her steps, noting that the small shared office where she worked with her team was also empty. Jimmy Jessop, the old former sergeant who acted as her right-hand man would probably be in soon, though.

The CRT was a low-priority department and thus more subject to budgetary constraints than most; the brass had recently taken to recruiting young civilian consultants who would be content to be paid peanuts in exchange for an apprenticeship of sorts, thereby freeing up fully trained police officers for more active duties. The two currently assigned to Hillary, young goth Wendy Turnbull and wealthy whizz-kid Jake Barnes would probably also be in early, since both were keen and eager to work.

Hillary's lips twitched slightly as she contemplated Jake Barnes's ulterior motives for such diligence, and sighed. Ever since he'd joined them in the CRT, she couldn't help but wonder why a good-looking young guy, who'd made so much money so fast, should be interested in a second career in the police force. Right from the start she'd doubted him, and had since been proved right to do so. But before the day was out, they were finally going to get some answers from that young man. And she could only hope that they were going to be ones that they could all live with.

The top brass, not surprisingly, regarded him as their golden boy and something of a PR coup. And Hillary wasn't looking forward to being the one to disabuse them of that fond notion.

She tugged down the navy blue jacket of her two-piece suit, and smoothed back her cap of dark chestnut brown hair before tapping on her boss's door. Her lips curled into a slight smile as a familiar voice called for her to enter.

Acting Detective Chief Superintendent Steven Crayle looked

up as she opened the door and stepped in. What he saw was a woman who had just celebrated her fiftieth birthday, with an intelligent, pale oval face, large, sherry-coloured eyes and an old-fashioned hourglass figure. It was a figure that he knew very well indeed.

As she approached his desk he could see that her eyes were sparkling, and a small tug at her lips let him know that she was probably up to some kind of mischief.

With a sense of pleasant anticipation, he leaned back in his chair and smiled back at her. A tall, lean, dark-haired man, he wore his own elegant navy suit with a casual nonchalance that somewhat belied his sharp mind and steely competence.

'Hello, beautiful,' he said.

Hillary Greene raised one dark eyebrow. 'Hello, gorgeous.'

'Now that we've both established that we could be had up on sexual harassment charges, what brings you in so early?' he wondered aloud. As a former DI Hillary had, of course, worked all hours, but as civilian consultant, one of the perks she enjoyed was a regular (and strictly no-overtime) nine-to-five regime.

'I wanted to talk to you,' Hillary said seriously, settling into the seat opposite his tidy desk and only then admitting to herself how truly nervous she felt. Her heart was beating slightly too fast, and she could sense a little flutter in her chest that told her that she hadn't got her breathing quite under control. She swallowed compulsively. 'It's about that question you asked me a little while ago.'

Steven Crayle felt his own mouth go suddenly dry. 'Oh?'

'Yes. Look, first, let me say that I'm sorry I've kept you waiting this long for an answer. And thanks for being so patient. It's just that I needed to think it through carefully,' she said, keeping her eyes firmly fixed on his face. He was nearly six years her junior and, it was, she had to admit, an extremely attractive face.

Steven was divorced with two grown children and was

clearly a man of significant ambition. Hillary hadn't been exactly enamoured of her new boss when she'd first been persuaded by Commander Marcus Donleavy to return to work.

And, it had to be said, Steven Crayle hadn't been best pleased to have a new lead investigator foisted on him either, without even being given the courtesy of interviewing her himself.

So it was funny, Hillary thought philosophically, just how quickly things could change – and in ways that you'd never expect.

'And the answer to that question is yes. And no,' she said.

Steven blinked, his dark chocolate coloured eyes showing a moment of utter confusion.

'How can it be yes and no?' he said, doing his best to keep his voice level. For nearly two weeks now, he'd felt his nerves being stretched to the limit, waiting for her response. And only his own resolve to be patient, and to remember that she was well worth the wear and tear on his nerves, had kept him outwardly calm. Now he felt totally confused and just a shade angry. What sort of a run-around was this?

'Either you do want to marry me, or you don't,' he stated flatly.

Hillary sighed gently at the – not unexpected – bite in his voice. She certainly didn't blame him for the ambivalence. They'd been lovers for nearly a year when he'd stunned her by, seemingly out of the blue, asking her to marry him. It had been the last thing that she'd expected, and it had given her a serious dilemma.

Hillary had married relatively young and had had a long, bitter time to regret it. Ronnie Greene had turned out to be a serial womanizer and a bent policeman as well, but he had died in a road traffic accident before he could be prosecuted. She herself had been investigated, but cleared of any complicity in his scams; not surprisingly, the experience had left her very wary of men indeed, and of the state of marriage in particular.

Steven, of course, had known all this. He had never been in any doubts about the nature of his growing feelings for this woman, and now he echoed her sigh. He'd always walked a very fine line in this relationship, but was determined to win her trust.

'OK. So, what exactly does "yes and no" entail?' he asked with a grin, attempting to lighten the mood. He wasn't sure that he'd completely succeeded in hiding his disappointment, however, because she left her chair and came to his side, propping her delightful derriere on top of his desk, and leaning over him.

Although it had always been tacitly understood between them that they didn't show their affection for each other at work, Hillary Greene now broke that rule by reaching out and pushing the dark hair from his forehead. He was, technically, no longer her boss, and soon he wouldn't even be working in the same building. Besides, she wanted to kiss him. A state of affairs that had been fairly routine just lately, she mused wryly.

As she proceeded to do so, and raised her face from his, she saw that he was watching her somewhat warily, and again her lips twitched.

'Yes, I want to be with you, and live with you, and let every-one know that we're together as a proper couple and all of that,' she explained. 'But no, I don't think we need to get married to do all of that. And I can't be doing with all the hassle of going through a wedding and what not. Besides, it's not as if we really need a piece of paper to make it official. Is it?'

Steven slowly nodded. It was pretty much as he'd suspected, and he tried to ignore the little niggle of rejection that he could feel worming its way into his guts.

'So, what, you want to move in to my place?' he hazarded tentatively.

Hillary grinned. 'Well, you could move into mine, but it would be a bit cramped, don't you think?'

When she'd left Ronnie, who had contrived to keep control

of their family home, Hillary had moved onto a narrowboat, *The Mollern*, that had belonged to her uncle. She had always intended her new accommodation to be strictly temporary, but she had found, to her surprise, that she had grown to like life on the canal, and had later bought the boat outright. It was now home to her, and she wasn't quite willing to give the old girl up yet.

But she had a plan.

'I thought, since your back garden practically runs down to the canal, I could bring the *Mollern* up from Thrupp,' she said, mentioning the nearby village where she'd been permanently moored for the last few years, 'and tie her up at your place. That way, we could take the boat out for weekends away and holidays and what have you. Makes sense, doesn't it?' she asked, with just a shade of worry in her voice. It was important that she sell this compromise to him, because she didn't quite know what she'd do if he vetoed it. Whilst she didn't feel able to marry the man, she didn't want to lose him, either.

'I know you're going to be as busy as hell with your new job, so it'll probably be some time before you have anything as luxurious as time off. But with the boat available, we can just slip the moorings and be off alone together at a moment's notice, which will help you cope with the stress.'

Steven was to head up a new unit dedicated to bringing down the gangs of men who targeted young girls and women, and she knew that such an enterprise could prove exhausting. 'Also, since you'll probably have no end of nights when you don't come back from the office at all, I'll be able to stay overnight on the *Mollern*, instead of rattling around in the house alone. So that's an added bonus, too.'

Steven nodded a shade wearily. 'You seem to have it all worked out,' he said quietly.

Hillary felt her hands become cold and sweaty. 'Is it really such a bad plan?' she asked, a shade gruffly. She knew that he wanted marriage for the security and the sense of permanence that it represented, and she felt undeniably guilty for not having the guts to give him that. So if he rejected her compromise, it was going to hurt like blazes, because she simply had no idea where they could go from there.

So she found herself holding her breath as she waited for his verdict.

Steven caught the glimmer of fear in her eyes and bit back a groan. 'It's not a bad plan at all,' he said softly, and reached out for her as she kissed him again. And the relief she felt was obvious in the strength of the grip of her hands on his shoulders. Slowly, he could feel the tension ooze out of her. And he was glad.

But he still couldn't help but feel disappointed.

He tried to admonish himself for being too greedy. After all, living together was definitely a step up from where they'd been, and he could work on that, right? And as the woman in his arms began to laugh gently, he felt the tension in his own shoulders slowly begin to ease. So what if he'd hoped for more?

He wanted to be the one to exorcise the ghost of Ronnie bloody Greene forever, but hadn't that been an unrealistic and somewhat juvenile ambition? He'd known from the outset all the baggage that Hillary Greene carried around with her, and yet in spite of that, he'd watched this gifted copper solve cold case crimes that even he had believed to be impossible. He'd watched the professional detective at work and marvelled, and later, had been lucky enough to find his way into the private life of the woman behind the high-solve rate and all-but-legendary reputation.

So he'd damned well take what he could get, and be grateful.

'Steven?'

'Hmmm?' He was leaning right back in the chair now, his silver and blue tie somewhat askew, and he straightened his shoulders imperceptibly as he saw and recognized the look in her eyes. In a flash, she'd gone from pleasure to business.

'About Jake Barnes,' she said.

Steven sighed, but nodded. One thing they'd always had in common, right from the start, was a strong work ethic and his response matched her abrupt change to the professional. 'Right. You're ready to bring Rollo into the equation?'

Hillary nodded. 'I think so, don't you? We really do need to get this sorted out before you leave. I know I'll have Donleavy's backing come what may, but it'd still be better if we present him with a united front. And it'll be fairer to Rollo, too,' she added wryly. 'Poor sod, he's coming in today thinking that he knows what's what, and that all he's got to do is keep the ship on course and balance the budgets, when actually, there might be a big fat fly in the ointment.'

'Have you any idea at all what Jake is playing at?' Steven asked.

Hillary shrugged and shook her head. 'Not really.'

For the past few months, she and Jimmy had been keeping a careful eye on their new recruit, ever since they'd discovered that the technically proficient dot com millionaire had been hacking into Hillary's computer.

And what they'd learned since had hardly been reassuring. He'd hired a private investigator, been in contact with a high-level fixer who provided documents and other sundry services to high-end criminals, and, just two nights ago, had met with an extremely dangerous enforcer for their local bad boy, and Thames Valley's most wanted, Dale Medcalfe.

'Whatever it is, it isn't good,' Hillary said, in classic understatement. 'And it's about time we tackled him, before things really get out of hand. I think we've given him enough rope to play with now.'

'OK,' Steven said, more than willing to go along with her judgement. 'Just what are you hoping to get out of him?' he asked curiously.

'Everything,' Hillary said grimly.

'And if it *is* something criminal?' Steven said. 'Something *really* criminal, I mean – something that we can't fix internally. Won't we have tipped our hand?'

Hillary sighed. 'Perhaps,' she acknowledged slowly. 'That's always a risk, but the man's already made so much money – legitimate money – that I just can't see him wangling his way in here simply to make even more illegally. No, I have a feeling this is going to be something personal. I get the sense the boy's on some sort of mission or crusade. But...' She shrugged.

Steven sighed. 'We might end up having to arrest him nonetheless.'

'I know.'

'The brass will have a hissy fit,' he pointed out glumly.

'I know.'

Steven couldn't help but grin at her flat, unimpressed tone. 'Well, aren't we the cavalier ones? I suppose, as a mere civilian, having to weather the fury of the powers-that-be no longer worries you.'

Hillary thought briefly of Commander Marcus Donleavy, the shark in the grey suit, and laughed somewhat hollowly. 'Yeah. Right! Well, there's no point in putting it off. I'll go and see if Jake's in. If he is, I'll take him down to my office, and give you a bell.'

'OK.'.

He watched her leave, not sure whether to laugh or cry. She'd refused to marry him, but had kissed him silly and was going to move into his house. And she might be about to drop a very nasty and smelly mess right in his lap, just when he needed to keep his mind clear for his new job.

But that was Hillary Greene for you, he supposed.

He had no idea what their future together might hold, but he doubted if boredom would feature in it much.

*

As it turned out, all three of her team had arrived and were settling down in the small office in anticipation of Rollo Sale handing out their latest cold-case murder file. Wendy Turnbull, dressed like a Hell's Angel in motorbike leathers, her eyes heavily lined in black, looked up and gave Hillary a happy smile. She always felt wired at the beginning of a new case.

Jimmy Jessop also looked up at her – his grey hair thinning fast now – and shifted a shade uncomfortably on his chair. In the last few days or so his back had been giving him jip. He was closer to seventy than sixty, so he supposed he would have to accept that bits would start seizing up on him, or wearing out. Better that than dropping off, he supposed.

There was nothing wrong with his eyes, though, and they sharpened perceptibly as he saw Hillary turn and look thoughtfully at the third person in the room.

At thirty-three, Jake Barnes was older than most of the new recruits, who tended to be youngsters still trying to find their ideal career, or old-timers, like himself, who'd retired and then found themselves longing to return to the work place.

Jake was a good-looking lad, tall, with green eyes, and was dressed in a suit that Jimmy suspected cost more than his old jalopy. And he looked surprised as Hillary said quietly, 'Jake, can I have a word in my office?'

'Course, guv,' he said, getting up and reaching automatically for the mobile tablet that he carried with him everywhere.

Hillary caught the old man's eye and gave such a slight nod that Wendy didn't even notice it. But Jimmy, who'd been keeping Jake under observation for the last month or so, watched the two of them leave with interest. Clearly things were going to come to a head. And he could only hope that whatever mess the youngster had got into, Hillary would be able to get him out of it.

In her office, which only had room for a tiny desk, a single chair and one set of old tin filing cabinets, Hillary sat down and reached for the desk phone. She punched in Steven's extension and watched as Jake, with literally nowhere to sit, leaned a shoulder casually against one wall.

He was expecting her to fill him in on their new case assignment and consequently looked slightly surprised when Hillary asked Steven Crayle to join them instead. Because of her joke of an office, normally if they had meetings, they were held in either the boss's office, or the communal space.

A moment later, Steven knocked and entered, closing the door firmly behind him.

'Thank you for joining us, sir,' she said, nodding and smiling politely at him. And it was only then, when Hillary Greene turned and looked at him with the stone-flat look that she usually reserved for her prime suspect, did Jake Barnes realized that he was in trouble.

Deep trouble.

'OK, Jake,' Hillary said. 'Suppose you tell us just what the hell is going on?'

For a moment, he went utterly still, and she could almost hear that very clever brain of his going into hyper-drive. Obviously he was desperately trying to read the situation, but in the meantime Hillary could almost see the shutters come down firmly. He made some attempt to relax his shoulders by shifting slightly against the wall.

'Sorry?' He sounded almost genuinely baffled, but Hillary could see that his body language was screaming alarmed caution, and she had no doubt whatsoever that he was going to start lying to her. And nor did she particularly blame him. In his place, she'd want to find out exactly what the situation was before committing herself.

'Come on, Jake, remember who you are talking to,' Hillary said. 'And don't start insulting my intelligence,' she added, almost as an afterthought. 'Did you really think you could just waltz in here and help yourself to my computer and who knows what else, and I wouldn't twig?'

Jake shot Steven a quick look, but the Acting Chief Super's face gave literally nothing away. He wasn't even looking at Jake, but at some point over his shoulder and seemed, if anything, slightly bored.

As the silence lengthened, Hillary waited with growing impatience for Jake to weigh his options, and was relieved when he evidently decided that outright denial was pointless. Instead he went for the shame-faced, but no real harm done approach, by spreading his hands slightly and giving a rather cheesy grin. Nevertheless, she could clearly see the growing panic at the back of his green eyes.

'OK, OK, you've caught me,' he admitted briefly. 'Look, what can I say?' He gave a graphic shrug. 'I was curious, and computers are my thing. I just wanted to learn more quickly, you know, get a head start on things.' His eyes flickered between them, to see how they were reacting, and when they simply stared back at him, he rubbed one eyebrow worriedly with the back of his thumb. Clearly, a lot more explanation was needed. 'Wendy can be pretty competitive and, although I know it's not a competition exactly between us, I still wanted to do—'

'Stop it,' Hillary interrupted his woeful diatribe. 'You're just embarrassing yourself now and – even worse – wasting my time. You've got ten seconds to start to spill your guts, or Steven will just have to read you your rights and take you across to Holding, where you can find out first-hand what the inside of a cell looks like.'

This was news to Steven. They hadn't discussed the possibility of arresting Jake right then and there, but he was willing to let her have her head, so he merely sighed slightly and continued to stare at the wall just above Jake's head.

'And you're a bright boy, Jake,' Hillary swept on remorselessly. 'You must have researched just how many laws you were breaking before you went ahead and broke so many of them, so you know exactly what kind of penalty you can expect.'

At this, Jake glanced down at his hands and seemed slightly surprised to see them clenched into fists. Carefully, he spread out his fingers and took a deep breath.

Hillary was fairly sure that getting arrested wouldn't worry the boy wonder all that much – after all, he had the money to buy the best lawyers. And besides that, he might even be willing to bluff it out in the hopes that the top brass would rather hush things up than be humiliated by the fact that their golden boy had been shafting them all this time.

So she was almost certain that it wasn't the thought of having to face criminal charges that was making him look so damned unhappy. This realization only reinforced her belief that the man had come here in order to do something that was vitally important to him – something that would definitely get screwed up if he should be arrested and charged.

'Look, I'm really sorry, OK?' he pleaded. 'And I'll sign any-thing you want, and pay any fine, but I really want to stay and continue working here. I think …'

'And why should we let you stay? So that you can go on paying mysterious visits to our local Mr Fixit?' she shot at him grimly. 'Mr Gordon Tate is well known around these parts for being the go-to man for any dodgy bastard who wants to get things done. So just what was it that you wanted from him, Jake? Funny money that needs laundering? Dodgy papers? An introduction to some high-ranking, usually shy villain?'

Jake's mouth literally fell open as he gaped at her. Then, slowly, the look of shock morphed into one of wry amusement – to think he believed he'd been so clever. Had he really thought that things had been going to plan, when all the time … He gave a little grunt and smiled bitterly. 'I should have known, shouldn't I? Just how long have you suspected me?'

Hillary shrugged. 'From the moment I got back from holiday and found you with your feet already tucked so firmly under the table, I knew that something was off,' she informed him.

Since she had nothing to do with the hiring and firing, when she'd returned from her annual leave and found Jake had been allocated to her team in her absence, his presence wasn't a particular surprise. But when she'd read his personnel file, alarm bells had definitely started ringing.

'Self-made rich boy wanting to give something back to his community? Please!' She smiled dryly. 'The PR department and top brass might have swallowed that bullshit whole, but it only sent me cross-eyed.' She sighed and shrugged. 'It was only a matter of time – a game of wait-and-see – until I figured out what you were really up to. And once I realized that you'd been sniffing around my computer, I put Jimmy up to following you.'

She wouldn't have been human if she hadn't felt a certain sense of satisfaction in seeing him go slowly white with the realization that she knew far more than she was letting on.

'Yes,' she agreed, although he hadn't actually spoken. But then, they both knew that he didn't need to. 'Which leads us nicely on to the crux of the matter, and your interest in a certain Mr Darren Chivnor, doesn't it?' she said quietly. 'The main suspect in umpteen assault cases, pimp, thief and all round bad boy. So tell me, Jake, given that you've met this scumbag at least twice to our knowledge, just why shouldn't we sling your duplicitous backside to the media wolves and just wash our hands of you?'

He swallowed hard. 'Look, it's not what you think,' he began nervously. He was openly sweating now, and the look of panic was back in his eyes.

Hillary smiled over at Steven. 'Hear that? It's not what we think.'

Steven sighed heavily. 'If I had a penny ...'

Hillary shook her head sadly.

'I wasn't after drugs—' Jake flashed hotly.

'Never thought you were,' Hillary shot back, ruthlessly

interrupting him before he could work himself up into a lather of righteous indignation. 'You're a clever boy, Jake, you could score whatever poison you fancied in much easier ways than that. No, our Darren and his boss specialize in a different kind of merchandise altogether,' she continued, watching him like a hawk. She was satisfied to see the white lines around his mouth turn to red as he realized just what she was implying, and he flushed angrily.

Good, Hillary thought. It was just as she thought. Now, all she needed was one more nicely placed insult and it should have him erupting nicely. Then they could start to get to the bottom of things.

'So what did you fancy, Jake, hmm? An underage girl, perhaps? A cross-dresser? Tranny? What's your fantasy?'

Pushed beyond his limit, Jake launched himself from the wall and took a single step towards her. The fact that was as far as he got was due to several things. Firstly, the office was so tiny, that that single step took him right up to her desk. Secondly, as he moved, so too did Steven Crayle, who looked ready to grab him and slap on the cuffs without a moment's hesitation.

But mostly, it was the look on Hillary Greene's face that stopped him dead.

She looked at him like she'd look at a dog turd on the pavement. On her face there was contempt, and impatience, and maybe a touch of wry disappointment. And it was that more than anything that made Jake Barnes feel like crying.

Because he'd worked with this woman on several murder cases now, and had come to respect and admire her enormously. She'd won a medal for bravery in the past by taking a bullet meant for a superior officer. She had a solve rate that was literally second to none. The brass ranked her as one of their best detectives, whilst the rank and file respected her for different reasons. Her reputation was for looking after her own, even in the face of a real shit storm. In the short time he'd known her, Jake had never seen her back down from anything. And for her to be looking at him as she was now, made him feel sick at heart.

'No! It's nothing like that,' he denied passionately. 'That's not what this is about,' he added hoarsely. 'In fact, you've got it so far wrong it's almost ludicrous!'

Hillary's lips twitched slightly. Damn if he didn't look like a little whipped puppy. 'So, you gonna keep it to yourself, Jake?' she asked him wearily.

'No,' Jake muttered eventually, slumping back against the wall and sighing heavily. 'It's about Jasmine.'

Hillary nodded. Out of the corner of her eye she could see Steven smile slightly. 'Tell me about her,' she said softly. Although she could already make a bloody good guess as to what was coming next. 'She was someone in your life who got mixed up with the wrong people, and you want to get her out of it. Right? Pay her pimp off maybe? Get her out of the life? Into rehab, if she needs it? You're gonna be her knight in shining armour, is that it?'

Jake's lips twisted wryly. 'Seen it all, know it all, done it all. That right, guv?' he asked a shade bitterly.

Hillary sighed heavily. 'Sometimes it feels like it,' she surprised all three of them by admitting just as bitterly. Then she nodded. In truth though, she wasn't feeling nearly as world-weary or cynical as she sounded. Her manner was mostly for show, to get Jake to open up. In reality, she felt for him. She knew all too well – hell, what copper didn't? – how life could make a victim out of anyone. And when you loved someone, you were willing to do all sorts of crazy things to try and put things right. 'OK, give it to us straight, from the beginning, and don't mess us about and we'll see what we can do for you. All right?'

She looked across at Steven who nodded his permission for her to go ahead. He was already looking relieved that the worst-case scenario had been avoided. Jake clearly hadn't been out to set himself up as some kind of criminal mastermind. He was just an idiot with a big cheque book and a super-hero complex.

'Jasmine is my sister,' he began flatly, then immediately contradicted himself. 'Well, not my sister really. After my dad died when I was little, my mum married my stepdad, Curtis. He had already had a little girl by his first partner, and this partner had something of a drink and drugs problem, as we later came to realize. Since they were never married, Jasmine's surname was the same as her mother's – Sudbury. I think Curtis, even at the beginning, doubted that…. Oh, hell, hardly any of that matters now.' He paused to collect his thoughts, and leaned his head back wearily against the wall.

'Jasmine came to live with us when Curtis and my mum got married. By then her mother was judged unfit to care for her, and Mum had always wanted a daughter. And Jasmine took to her right away – she was such a loving, needy little thing. So in spite of the odds being against us, it all seemed to work out. And even though she was littler than me, and could be a bit of a clingy pest, instead of resenting her, I loved her right away as well. I was an only child and, I suppose, was probably lonely. Besides,' he grinned a bit at the memory, 'she idolized me, and for a young lad, that did my ego an enormous amount of good.'

He paused and shrugged.

'Anyway, as I said, at first everything seemed to be fine. Her birth mum was in and out of rehab and barely bothered to visit her, which was something of a relief, as you can imagine. Curtis had always worried about what influence her mum's behaviour was having on her. We grew up in a council house, as you know, and although we didn't have much money, both Curtis and Mum worked, and Jas never had to go without. She got the pretty dresses, and the toys she wanted at Christmas. She made new friends and she was happy. Or so we all thought.'

Steven and Hillary exchanged glances, knowing just where this was going, but knowing that Jake needed to tell it anyway.

'When I went off to uni, Jasmine was barely fourteen,' Jake carried on sadly.

'And it was only when I came back home in the holidays, that I first began to notice stuff. She'd go out drinking with her mates, even though she was underage. She started cheeking Mum and defying Curtis. Being rebellious. Stuff like that. It didn't seem like a big deal at first, you know? Just the usual teenager playing up. But….'

'It got worse,' Hillary said. 'She ran away from home?'

'Several times,' Jake confirmed. 'Once, I managed to find her and bring her back. And I was really appalled when I realized she was on drugs. We got her into rehab right away, of course. But it didn't take. And it didn't help that, around then, I began to make all my money. Jas seemed to think that that meant I would bankroll her habit. Of course I didn't – that was the worst thing I could have done. In spite of all her pleading, I wouldn't enable her to carry on being a junkie. It made me feel so guilty, but both Mum and Curtis and her counsellors agreed I was doing the right thing. Tough love.' He grunted softly, a bitter bark of laughter. 'So she began to resent me. And she ran away again.'

He sighed and ran a hand through his hair.

'All traces of the sweet, happy girl we knew seemed to vanish. Once, she got pregnant and lost the baby. That seemed to scare her for a bit and she sobered up for a while.'

'But it didn't last,' Hillary said.

'No. Then, a couple of years ago, she went missing and just didn't come back. She just – well, stayed missing. And this time I couldn't find her. None of her friends knew where she might have gone, either. Mum and Curtis were going out of their minds imagining the worst. Well, you know – I don't have to tell you how girls like Jas can end up.'

He didn't. She and Steven shared a long, level look.

'So I hired private investigators, and eventually they got a lead.'

This time it was Steven who spoke. 'You found out she'd become a prostitute?' he said gently.

Jake swallowed hard. 'Yes. They tracked her down to Oxford. But then they refused to stay on the case. I had to pay them off. I think the pimp she was working for scared them off.'

'Yes. He would,' Steven said. 'You're talking about Dale Medcalfe now, right?'

Jake nodded. 'Apparently, Jas had been a girl in one of his stables for a few years. The investigators thought she was working the S&M circuit.'

Hillary winced. That was bad news. Very bad. Only girls that Medcalfe was willing to throw on the scrap-heap got hired out to the kind of risky John who was into sadomasochism.

Jake caught the look and swallowed hard again. 'Yes. I know,' he all but whispered. He looked so miserable that she had to fight the urge to get up and go and put her arms around him. But right now wasn't the time for that.

'Go on,' she said instead.

'I found out that she dropped out of sight nearly a year ago. She had been living in a squat in Cowley, but … she just vanished again.'

Hillary slowly leaned forward on her desk, she intended to say something like, 'Jake, that probably only means one thing,' but she was saved from actually having to say the grim words.

'I know. You think she's dead,' Jake said, his voice as dead as the look on his face. 'You think that some sick John got too aggressive and killed her. Or the drugs got to her. Or perhaps AIDs or who the hell knows what else. I know that. I know she's probably dead.' His voice had been growing steadily louder and harsher, but now he fell abruptly silent. And then he took a long, shuddering breath. 'But I have to find out for certain. I need to know. Mum and Curtis need to know. We can't go on living in limbo like this. So that's why I joined the police as a civilian consultant. That's why I went into your computer. I needed to get access to police records. I needed data. I needed to get a foot in the camp that could help me find out what happened to her.'

Hillary nodded.

'And that's also why I approached Darren Chivnor,' he added.

At this, Steven stirred a shade restlessly, since Jake was straying into the remit of his new job.

'I hired another top-notch PI team, and they gave me as much intel as they dared on this Dale Medcalfe character. So I know a lot about the set-up that he runs. His gang consists of mainly family members or long-term friends and people from his old neighbourhood. They take the fall for him, as well as acting as his enforcers. He's never even been inside a prison cell,' Jake swept on, sounding disgusted.

But Steven didn't need telling any of this. It would be part of his new job to put men like Medcalfe away. It wasn't going to be easy – it never was. Men like that ruled by fear and intimidation and casual, gut-churning violence. Who would testify against a man if they knew that their daughter could be raped on her way home from school? Who would lodge a complaint against one of his thugs, when doing so meant you could end up kneecapped, or worse? Silence and acceptance became the norm, and the police, more often than not, were helpless to offer a viable alternative. You couldn't be everywhere at once. But how could he explain these very hard facts of life to a man like Jake?

'So I started looking for a weak link in his chain,' Jake swept on, unaware of the Acting DCS's angst. 'And that's why I met Darren Chivnor.'

Steven now felt his blood running a little cold. 'There's nothing weak about Chivnor, Jake,' he interrupted harshly. 'The man's very handy with a knife, and is one of Medcalfe's main boys. He runs the girls, and enforces the rule on anyone who gets out of hand.'

'Yes, I know all that,' Jake said, a shade too casually for Hillary's liking. 'But he's also a man with ambitions beyond working for Medcalfe for the rest of his life. He's got a girl he wants to marry, and a lifestyle away from Oxford that he dreams about. So I approached him with an offer – forged documents for himself and his girlfriend, a cash-bribe for a sweetener, plus the promise of enough money to start abroad somewhere, well out of Medcalfe's reach.'

'All in exchange for information about Jasmine?' Hillary put in sceptically. 'Jake, you know he won't grass on his boss.'

'No, I know that,' Jake said a shade impatiently now. 'I'm not *that* stupid. I told him outright that I wasn't interested in bringing his boss down. The thing is, I thought that the negotiations were going well with him, but something went wrong.'

Hillary grunted. 'I'll say. You ran out of that gent's lav like the hounds of hell were after you.'

Jake's eyes widened. 'You saw that as well?'

Hillary smiled. 'Jimmy and I were following you. So you arranged to meet him at night in the gent's loo in the park. What happened? Why did he pull a knife on you and chase you out?'

'I don't know!' Jake said, sounding almost comically aggrieved now. 'I had the bribe money on me, and the forged documents, and I showed them to him. I swear he was genuinely excited and up for it. Everything seemed to be going OK. We had just started – I hadn't even mentioned Jasmine's name and what I wanted him to do to earn the real money, when everything suddenly changed.'

'Perhaps he was just playing you,' Steven put in reasonably. 'He kept the documents and the cash, right?'

'Yes.'

'So perhaps he decided just to take that, and forget about the

25

rest,' Steven hypothesized. 'He never intended to risk upsetting Medcalfe by talking to you anymore. Perhaps he even planned to cut you in order to prove his loyalty.'

'Don't think I haven't been wondering about that,' Jake said wryly. 'Believe me, I have. But I really don't think so. Chivnor was really interested in hearing more, I could tell. About how much exactly I was willing to give him. And, yes, I could see he was also nervous and on edge, but if he'd already decided just to take the money and run, he wouldn't have been so jittery, would he?'

Steven shrugged at this bit of logic.

Jake sighed. 'Look, I still maintain that he was hooked enough to want to find out exactly what it was that I was pro-posing. But then, in a flash, everything just seemed to change.' He was clearly frustrated by the memory of that night, and Hillary shot Steven a back-off look.

He nodded.

'Exactly what happened?' Hillary asked, turning back to Jake. 'Tell me every little detail that you can remember.'

'Well, we were alone in the loos. He'd seen the £20,000 in cash and the documents. And then I heard someone come in.'

'Did you see who?' Hillary asked.

'Just a bloke. He had ginger hair, I think.'

'Did you know him?'

'No.'

'Was he a member of Medcalfe's gang?' Hillary pressed. 'Your PI firm gave you photos of them, right?'

'Yeah. No, he wasn't another of Medcalfe's people. I'm sure of it. In fact, I'm sure he only came in to use the facilities. He looked surprised for a moment.' Jake laughed grimly. 'Which probably wasn't all that surprising, seeing as Darren had a fistful of money in his hand at that point. And then suddenly Darren pulled a knife.'

'Perhaps Darren thought the newcomer might try and take

the money from him,' Hillary mused.

Jake shrugged. 'It would take someone with nerves of steel to try to mug Darren! Anyway, I just ran as fast as I could,' he admitted, looking a little ashamed. 'I just panicked, I suppose.'

'You had an attack of common sense more like,' Hillary said bluntly. 'If someone like Chivnor pulls a knife, anyone with two brain cells to rub together would run. You did the right thing,' she assured him. No doubt he felt as if he'd acted cowardly, and she needed to knock that idea right on the head.

'It sounds as if it was definitely the visitor who startled him,' Steven contributed. 'Chivnor was bound to be nervous in the first place, meeting you behind Medcalfe's back. He would have been hyper-alert to danger. Did the man who came in after you stay?' he asked Jake sharply, but it was Hillary who answered him.

'No, he didn't. He legged it, the same as Jake,' she said shortly. 'I agree with Jake. I think he was just an innocent caught up in it. Let's hope so anyway.'

Steven nodded. 'And this all happened three nights ago?'

'Right,' both Jake and Hillary confirmed together.

'Then I think we're safe in assuming that Medcalfe doesn't suspect anything yet. And he certainly can't have any idea that Jake and Darren are in contact.'

'Why do you think that?' Jake asked curiously.

'Because Chivnor's corpse hasn't shown up somewhere yet,' Steven said succinctly. 'And neither has yours.'

Jake gulped, then forced a smile. 'It's as I told you. I'm sure Darren is still thinking things over. He knows I can offer him an out, and I still think he's willing to play along, if I can convince him that the risks are worth it.'

'So Jake still has, potentially at least, a source in Medcalfe's camp,' Hillary said almost to herself, and with a growing sense of excitement that she could clearly see echoed in Steven's eyes.

And who could blame him? At the end of the week, he'd be

taking up his new job, trying to bring down the sexual preda-
tors on his patch. And it would be one hell of a bonus if, on his
very first day in the job, he could pull a top-class informant out
of his hat. Maybe one who even brought with him a chance to
bring down Medcalfe himself.

'So you're going to help me then?' Jake said hopefully. 'You're
going to look for Jasmine?'

Hillary looked across at Steven, then at Jake.

'Is she officially listed as a missing person? Because if she is,
then we can make an argument that hers is a cold case. And
that her disappearance falls under our mandate.'

'I made Mum register her as a MisPer when I got the job
here,' Jake said eagerly. All along, and especially after learning
how good Hillary Greene was at her job, it had always been
Jake's hope that he could somehow persuade Hillary and the
team to take on Jasmine's case.

Hillary's lips twitched. 'That was very far-sighted of you,'
she said drolly.

Jake had the grace to blush. 'So are you going to arrest me?'

'Probably not. Not right now, anyway,' Hillary said deadpan.

Jake grinned. 'So I can stay?'

'We need to tell Superintendent Sale everything,' Steven
warned him. 'Since he's taking over, it'll be up to him whether
he lets you keep on working with us or not. You'll have to do
your best to reassure him you're not a loose cannon.'

Jake nodded tensely.

'I'll talk to him first,' Steven said. 'No promises, but I think
we can probably work something out. He won't want to make
waves any more than the top brass will.'

'And while you and Rollo are talking about what to do with
the boy wonder here,' she said, nodding to Jake, 'I'd better bite
the bullet and go and have a word with Commander Donleavy.
Explain how things are, and that he needs to give us a little
leeway here.'

Steven shot her a wry look. 'Yes. You do that,' he said neutrally.

Everyone at HQ knew that Hillary Greene and Commander Marcus Donleavy had always been tight. And that if there was anyone who could handle the Commander, whilst ensuring that she got her own way, it was Hillary.

CHAPTER TWO

Iᴛ ᴡᴀs ᴍɪᴅ-ᴀꜰᴛᴇʀɴᴏᴏɴ ʙᴇꜰᴏʀᴇ all the explanations had been given, and all parties had approved a plan of action.

Marcus Donleavy, although busy, had agreed to see Hillary at once, since his secretary had long-standing orders that she should be slotted in to even his most hectic of work schedules.

A tall lean man, with grey hair, grey eyes, and dressed in his trademark silver grey suit, he'd greeted her with his customary wariness. They both knew that she wouldn't be in his office unless something unpleasant needed sorting out.

Naturally he had not been pleased to hear of Jake's extra-curricular activities, but had merely raised an eyebrow when it became clear that Hillary had been keeping it under her hat for some time. He didn't bother to reprimand her for it. For a start, he knew that it wouldn't have done much good anyway. Hillary was now a civilian, and as such, didn't have as much to fear from the top brass. Besides, what could he do about it? Sack her? That was never going to happen and they both knew it. He'd had to connive, threaten and cajole her into coming back to work in the first place. No, they both knew her place was here, solving cases.

But mostly, Commander Marcus Donleavy had always approved of her tactics anyway. Plausible deniability was one of his favourite phrases, and he knew that Hillary Greene had always been very good at watching both of their backs. So he was always willing to let her head off trouble before it landed in his lap. So he listened with growing interest, and with gradually less and less alarm, as she related that morning's events.

And after thinking it over in silence for all of a minute, he sighed softly. 'And I suppose you already have some idea of how you want to deal with all this?'

'Yes, sir,' Hillary said promptly. 'But I'd like your input and I'll need you to run some interference, should anybody start questioning what we're up to down in CRT. Not that I expect they will. If we're lucky, I think there's a way that we can keep this from blowing up in our faces and turn it to our advantage. Things could get tricky, but this is what I had in mind.'

An hour later, Rollo Sale looked up from his desk as Hillary Greene tapped on the door and walked in. Since Steven was in the act of moving out at the same time as he was moving in, the two men were temporarily being forced to share the same office. At that moment, though, it was going to be more of a convenience than a problem, since it meant that they could liaise more easily.

He smiled briefly and somewhat sardonically as Hillary shot Steven a questioning look. 'Come in, Hillary, and take a seat. It's all right. Steven's explained everything.'

Roland 'Rollo' Sale was fifty-eight, and whilst not exactly looking forward to retiring with his pension just yet, he was well aware that this posting would be his last. And he was content with that. Of medium height, with light brown hair that was going grey rapidly, he was uneasily aware that he was just beginning to get a bit of a belly on him. He'd been happily married for over thirty years, and had three grown boys, none of them having joined him in the police force. Living and working all his life in Aylesbury, he'd had a varied career, but not too much experience of murder cases, so when the opening for a new head of the Crime Review Team had come up at HQ, he had had no hesitation in applying.

And he'd quickly learned that Steven Crayle had done an excellent job of getting the whole scheme up and running, but it came as no surprise that the ambitious Superintendent – now Acting Chief Superintendent – was heading on to higher things.

Rollo was no tyro when it came to office politics, and he'd always understood that all that was needed, post-Crayle, was for a safe and steady pair of hands to keep the CRT on course. And he fitted that description perfectly. He had no illusions about himself, or how others saw him, but that didn't mean that he wasn't going to do things his way. And make a damned good job of it.

So he'd spent the last month learning the ropes from Steven, a man he'd quickly come to like and admire and now Rollo felt confident that he could handle the job. He'd also become aware that in Hillary Greene he had an excellent criminal investigator who could be left, more or less unsupervised, to manage the cold murder cases, leaving him free to deal with the admin side that constituted the rest of their remit. This was, in fact, mostly computer and forensics based. Following recent advances in both DNA profiling and IT, the CRT's work focussed on matching DNA samples from old cases to those found in new cases. The vast databases they now had at their disposal were useful in finding these links between crimes stretching back for years; robberies and rapes that were years old and which had previously been regarded as beyond conclusion, could now be re-visited with more modern eyes. And more often than not, closed.

Rollo had to admit ruefully that he hadn't expected the blinder which the Jake Barnes scenario represented, and this even before he'd officially taken over as the new head. He felt deeply uneasy about what the fall-out might be. And just who would be in line to take the flack.

'How did Donleavy take it?' asked Steven, typically getting right to the heart of the matter.

Hillary smiled slightly and gave a somewhat weary shrug. 'You know the Commander,' she said, somewhat cryptically.

Roland Sale, who didn't, shot Steven a quick look. Steven smiled crookedly in response. 'I'll fill you in later,' he promised, before turning back to Hillary. 'So, what's the official line then?'

'OK.' Hillary settled down at Rollo's desk and Steven pulled up a chair as they began their council of war.

'Tomorrow morning,' Hillary began, 'the PR department is going to announce that the CRT is doing a review of all MisPer cases from the last twenty years of women between the ages of sixteen and forty. As you know, the vast majority of missing persons turn up again eventually.'

Rollo nodded, as did Steven.

'They either simply went off on holiday and didn't tell anyone, or shacked up with a man their family didn't approve of, until the relationship hit the buffers and then they come back home with their tails between their legs. Some are found in morgues, others in hospital or abroad.' Hillary paused and glanced at her new boss. 'But of course, hardly anyone ever thinks of telling the police about it when they turn up again. So officially they're still listed as missing.'

'Right. Which plays havoc with our crime statistics,' Rollo grumbled.

Hillary nodded. 'Exactly. So the PR department are going to call a press conference and explain all this, and to put out an appeal for anyone who's reported a missing relative or friend, but who now knows that that missing person has turned up. Such friends or relatives will be encouraged to contact us.'

'Well, that should close umpteen cold cases right then and there,' Rollo said happily. 'But I take it that's not the point?'

'Hardly,' Hillary agreed. 'But what it *will* do is give us a plausible reason to start looking into MisPer cases of young women whom we know, or suspect, ran foul of our friend Dale Medcalfe. Which would include, of course, Jasmine Sudbury.'

'Ah,' Rollo said. 'So young Jake is going to get his way after all? We *are* going to take on his sister's case?'

'Yes. Donleavy insisted on this, since it'll keep Jake quiet and happy. And a happy Jake is less likely to spill his guts to the media about what he's been doing, and thus prevent us all from looking like a right load of wallies,' Hillary said wryly.

'Which is all the top brass cares about,' Steven put in.

'Yes. But it'll also play right into our hands. Well, your hands more than ours,' Hillary pointed out reasonably. 'Your new job has bringing Medcalfe down at the top of its list of priorities, right?'

'Him and others,' Steven confirmed grimly.

'Right. Well, let's consider this.' Hillary settled more comfortably into her chair. 'Imagine for a moment that you're Dale Medcalfe, and you hear on the news that the Thames Valley Police are doing a review of MisPer cases of women. Now, he knows that some of those missing women are going to be down to him. And that the police will soon be poking around, asking questions about them. So, what's the first thing that you do?'

Steven blinked, then slowly began to smile. 'You know, I always suspected it. But now I know. You're a genius.'

'True,' Hillary agreed deadpan. 'But please answer the question.'

'I would summon my cronies, thugs, and assorted enforcers and tell them to get out and about, and start reminding any witnesses that they need to keep their mouths shut if they know what's good for them,' Steven said.

'Which helps us how?' Rollo asked bluntly. He could see how well these two got on together, both in their private and personal lives, from the way that they seemed able to read each other's mind. And he could only hope that, given time, he would be able to follow Hillary Greene's thought processes as easily as his predecessor.

'Well, this is where Jake comes in, and starts to earn some brownie points to compensate for the mess he's got us into,' Hillary explained. 'We're going to have to brief him thoroughly, but basically it goes like this. He gets in touch with Darren again, and Chivnor learns what it is that Jake wants in exchange for all that money he's been promising. News about his sister, Jasmine Sudbury – is she alive? And if she's dead, where's her body? And, providing Medcalfe wasn't personally responsible for it, the name of whoever it was in his gang who killed her.'

'But surely he's not going to play ball with us now? Not when his boss will be on high alert, what with the news that we're looking into missing girls again,' Rollo said.

'Yes, but there are two things that will help with that.' Hillary leaned forward slightly in her chair. 'The one thing we're all agreed on is that Darren would be normally very wary indeed of meeting Jake again in case his boss finds out and wonders what he's up to. Right?'

'Right.' Rollo nodded.

'But if he *is* seen talking to Jake, he's now got the perfect cover for that. He can either say that Jake had approached him to talk about the missing girls. Or, if he prefers, he can tell Medcalfe that, as the *brother* of one of the missing girls, he was attempting to find out how much bother Jake would be to them and was trying to warn him off.'

'Got it. Yes, that's clever.' Rollo nodded again and followed the thought through. 'All Chivnor has to say is that he was threatening Jake with a knife in his ribs one dark night to warn him off co-operating with the police.'

'Right,' Hillary said. 'Plus, when Medcalfe finds out that Jake's working as a civilian here at HQ, it will instantly make him a high-priority threat. In which case, he'd probably send Darren to sort him out anyway – he's one of his most trusted and experienced enforcers. He sure as hell won't want to get his hands dirty himself.'

'OK. So that's one reason why Chivnor might feel brave enough to risk re-establishing contact with our boy. And since I understand that Jake's already offered to give him a fortune, greed will also have been eating away at him all this time. And let's not underestimate good old greed.' Rollo smiled wolfishly. 'But what's the second thing? You said there were two things in our favour.'

Hillary nodded. 'The other is pressure. Before, Darren wasn't in any hurry. He could afford to take his time. But as soon as Medcalfe hears about our MisPer review he's bound to get nervy. And a nervy boss is an unpredictable boss. So if Darren is going to get his pay-off and get out of the country, he's got to do it fast. In other words – he's now motivated.'

Steven shifted slightly in his chair. 'This is beginning to sound a bit iffy to me, Hill,' he said tersely.

'Oh yes. It is,' Hillary agreed, making no bones about it. 'And we're going to have to warn Jake and play strictly fair with him. Drum it in to him that he'll be playing a dangerous game. That Chivnor could turn on him at any moment. You've seen him,' she said to Steven, 'He's hell bent on doing whatever it takes to get answers about his sister, he's that desperate. And it's not as if he hasn't already put himself in the firing line already. And, quite frankly, this is the best shot we've had of getting Medcalfe in quite some time. Even Donleavy can see that.'

'Look, I'm not saying it's not tempting, believe me,' Steven said, looking between the man who was shortly going to take over his old job, and Hillary. 'It'll be one hell of a feather in my cap if, right from the start, I can deliver Medcalfe. But I'm not happy about putting Jake at risk.'

Hillary nodded. 'Me, neither. But Jake's *already* at risk,' she said. 'He's been meeting Chivnor at night and nearly getting stabbed. He's been flying by the seat of his pants all this time, and it's sheer dumb luck he's got through it so far with his skin intact. So what we'd be doing now is giving him proper backup, and actively improving his chances of survival. When you look at it that way, we're doing him a favour.'

Rollo Sale sighed. 'She's right, you know. Things have probably already gone too far now to back out anyway. And who knows – if we don't follow through, maybe Chivnor will be tempted to offer up Jake to Medcalfe as proof of his loyalty anyway.'

'In which case, we'll be fishing the boy wonder's body out of the Thames before the week is out,' Hillary said.

'OK. So we announce the MisPer review. We brief Jake on what he's going to say in his next meeting with Chivnor. What else?' Rollo demanded.

'We start investigating several of the missing women cases,' Hillary said. 'Which is just what Medcalfe will be expecting us to do. Not that we'll let Jake anywhere near his sister's case, of course,' Hillary said quickly and firmly, reaching into her briefcase and extracting several buff-coloured files that she'd collected from Records. 'I'll be taking on that one, and perhaps one other, personally. The rest I'll divide up between the rest of the team. Commander Donleavy and I have been sorting through the old cases, and have come up with a number of missing women whose disappearance was almost certainly down to Medcalfe and his gang.'

She distributed the files between Steven and Rollo, but they all knew that it would be Rollo who would oversee them. Steven had enough on his plate starting his new job and running the Jake/Darren scenario, without adding that to his list.

'So, along with Jasmine Sudbury, we have Rebecca Tyde-Harris, Amanda Smallwood, and Lydia Clare Allen,' Hillary began. 'There are others, and Wendy and Jimmy will have their hands full with them as well, but these four are our best bets. I'll leave these copies with you. Steven, you're going to want to talk to Jake right away, I take it?'

Steven nodded. 'Best get it over with, and start planning our strategy,' he said grimly.

'OK.' She got up and picked up her briefcase. 'I'll send him down to you. In the meantime, I'm going to tell the troops about the MisPer review and allocate them their cases. We'll meet up again later, after you've had a chance to see how things go with Jake, and make sure we're all clear on what's what? Yes?'

'Sounds like a plan,' Rollo said, a shade hollowly.

Hillary could tell that her new boss wasn't particularly happy with the speed at which things were happening, nor with the way that he'd been presented with a fait accompli by the Commander and herself, and she could hardly blame him for that. After all, the poor sod had been expecting a gentle, easy slide into his new job and instead he'd been landed with a potential disaster.

Still, Hillary supposed philosophically as she walked down to her office to brief her team on their new cases, it was as good a way as any to find out just what her new boss was made of.

The moment she walked into the communal office, she looked across at Jake. After he'd confessed what he'd been up to, she'd ordered him back here to catch up on his paperwork, and with strict instructions not to talk about his situation to anyone. And under no condition was he to call his mother and stepfather with the latest developments. She was confident that, in spite of evidence to the contrary, he knew better than to disobey a direct order. Besides, he must have been as aware as anyone that until she'd had a chance to clear things with the Commander, he could still face legal action.

And she could see, from the way he looked anxiously back at her, that the time must have dragged for him whilst everyone had been deciding his future. It had probably been good for him – in her opinion a salutary lesson or two would do him no harm at all.

So her face gave nothing away as she said calmly, 'Jake, I think the new boss wants a quick word with you.'

Over in her seat, Wendy Turnbull grinned and blew him a raspberry. 'And just what has the boy wonder been up to then, to get called to the headmaster's office?' she goaded cheerfully.

Today, her short black hair was standing up in tufts, the tips of which had been dyed turquoise, which matched her nail polish and eye shadow. She was wearing a black leather bustier and a pair of skinny blue jeans that had been hand-stencilled with skull and crossbones. A pair of skull and crossbone earrings dangled from her ears.

Jake shot the goth a flippant finger and a carefree shrug, but Hillary could see that his eyes were troubled as he went past her on his way out.

Hillary could only hope that both Steven and Rollo read him the Riot Act for his past misdemeanours, and also managed to get it through his thick head just how incredibly lucky he'd been so far.

But it worried her that they then had only a short amount of time to start briefing him in what he would need to do in order to handle Chivnor safely from now on. Well, as safely as it was possible to handle someone as violent and unpredictable as one of Dale Medcalfe's enforcers. Normally, such training lasted months – not days.

It wasn't a task that she envied either of them.

When he'd gone, she looked across at Jimmy and gave him a very slight wink, and saw him smile faintly. No doubt the old timer had quickly figured out what had happened, and had been wondering which way the brass was going to jump.

But in truth, once she'd learned Jake's story, there really hadn't been much doubt that she would take on his sister's case. After all, that's what they were all there for, wasn't it? To try and protect the gormless, innocent and unlucky, whilst at the same time, doing their best to heft the villains out of circulation. At least for a while. And she knew the old man had agreed with their decisions when she'd put him in the loop earlier.

'OK, troops, apparently the PR department have come up with a good wheeze,' she began, and totally for Wendy's benefit, since she knew that Jimmy would be far too wily to believe a word of what she was about to say. 'They're going to do a big publicity blitz about missing persons, in an effort to massage our crime figures.'

She launched into a quick explanation for Wendy, whilst Jimmy continued to look thoughtful. When she'd finished, the young woman looked visibly disappointed.

In her early twenties, Wendy had already gained a sociology degree, but was humming and hawing about whether or not to take the plunge and become an actual social worker. She'd joined the CRT team to gain more experience, but mostly, from what Hillary had been able to gather, because she was hooked on detective novels and crime shows on the telly and saw herself as a detective.

She had a winning way with her, and there was no doubt that she enjoyed working with Hillary – especially when she got to go out and about interviewing witnesses, but Hillary was yet to be convinced that she'd make a good police officer. It was not her outrageous personality that concerned Hillary so much, since a lot of people responded well to her. It was more to do with the softness of her heart which would be an asset in social work, if only Hillary could just knock some of the harder realities into her head.

She could understand why Wendy was hesitating. Recent cases in the media had tended to sling mud at social workers, more often than not casting them in the roles of incompetent do-gooders or neglectful dupes. But Hillary, like every good copper, knew that good social workers were an absolute necessity in modern-day Britain.

'So, no murder cases then?' Wendy said now, all but pouting

her disapproval. Since she'd started here, she'd helped work on several cold murder cases, and had been thrilled to watch and learn as Hillary Greene had solved them all.

After that, a review of MisPer cases seemed rather tame.

Over at his desk, Jimmy hid a grin at the youngster's petulance, then winced as he twisted in the chair and a lance of pain shot up his back.

'Oh, I wouldn't say that,' Hillary said, taking out the files. 'I've cherry picked several that I think look interesting, from our point of view. As I've just explained, most missing people turn up. But some don't. And some don't because they can't.'

At this, Wendy visibly perked up. It was not that she was particularly ghoulish – despite her dress sense. Nor was she immune or oblivious to the pain and misery that violent crime inflicted, not just on the victims, but on their friends and family.

Hillary knew that she enjoyed the thrill of the puzzle, and the satisfaction it brought when they were finally able to expose a killer. And who could blame her for that? Didn't they all feel the same way? But so far, things had all been a bit remote for the girl, cushioning her to some extent from the punishing reality of what life in the police force was all about. Not only had the crimes they'd worked on been years old, taking off the edge and rawness to some extent, they had all been of the domestic or private and personal kind. What's more, working cold cases meant that you dealt with people who had had time to get over the worst of the shock, and to adjust and adapt: all of which allowed them to do the bulk of their work without really getting their hands dirty.

Hillary knew, though, that things were going to be very different with these new cases. This time they were all going to get very dirty indeed. And she wondered just how the girl was going to cope, tackling head on the sordid underbelly of prostitution, drug addiction, and wrecked, lost lives.

Then again, perhaps it would give Wendy the wake-up call

she needed to get her priorities sorted out.

'So, there are four main cases,' she began crisply. 'Jimmy, you and Wendy can take two, whilst Jake and I work on the others.'

Jimmy's eyes sparkled as he detected yet another lie drop from his guv'nor's lips, because he knew damned well that she wouldn't let Jake Barnes anywhere near his sister's case. Besides, he had no doubt the boy wonder would soon have his plate full tackling the fall-out from his activities with Darren Chivnor.

He understood why Hillary wanted to keep Jake's activities – and the truth behind all these MisPer cases – a secret from Wendy; for whilst he didn't doubt the girl's loyalty, he did wonder about her discretion. And the last thing they needed now was for anyone to start talking out of turn – especially if the media should get a hold of it.

And he didn't doubt that right now Steven and their new boss would be giving Jake a proper roasting and letting him know in no uncertain terms what would happen to him if he didn't have the sense to keep his mouth firmly shut as well.

'Jimmy,' he heard Hillary say his name, and instantly became attentive. 'We have a list of eleven women here altogether, and you and Wendy will need to check them all out at some point and in your own time, but I want you to concentrate on these two.'

She handed him two files, smiling as Wendy shot up to hover over the old man's shoulder in order to speed read the case notes.

'First up, Rebecca Tyde-Harris—' Hillary said, looking at her own copy.

'Hell, that sounds like a posh bird type of name to me,' Wendy interrupted.

Hillary smiled, but ignored the comment – which had been rather perspicacious. 'Aged twenty-eight when she went missing in April 2010,' she continued seamlessly. 'As you can see from the photograph, Rebecca was five foot nine or so, with brown hair and green eyes.'

'Pretty,' Wendy said.

'Shush,' Jimmy said a shade impatiently. 'Haven't I told you before about not interrupting a senior officer's briefing?'

'She did indeed come from an upper middle-class background,' Hillary continued doggedly, pretending not to see the clenched-fist salute Wendy pulled behind Jimmy's back, 'and attended college in Oxford as an English Literature student. Unfortunately, she seems to have gone off the rails pretty quickly, no doubt due to the usual mixture of finding bad friends, good booze, and an easy supply of the recreational drug of her choice.'

Jimmy sighed. 'Let me guess. The parents were supportive at first, loaning her money and trying to get her into rehab, before realizing, in the end, that they were only enabling her drug habit, at which point they were forced to cut her off.'

Hillary nodded. 'And we all know what happens next.'

'What?' Wendy asked eagerly.

'She went on the game to feed her habit, what do you think?' It was Jimmy who spoke, and again, a shade testily. This was uncharacteristic of Jimmy, he was normally very patient with the youngsters, but he was finding it hard to get into a comfortable position in his chair that didn't set his back aching, and for some reason, Wendy's sometimes naïve outlook on life grated on him today.

'Oh,' Wendy said flatly.

Jimmy glanced at the name of the missing woman's pimp at the time of her disappearance, but he already knew what he'd see. Unless he really was losing his touch, all of Hillary's so-called MisPer review cases would have Dale Medcalfe's dirty fingerprints all over them.

'Right,' Hillary said crisply. 'So, you know the drill, Jimmy. Contact all her old friends from college that you can find, question her family again, and see if any of the girls on the street will talk to you. Streetwalkers have a limited shelf life, so most of the girls she would have known are probably long gone by now, but there'll probably be one or two who still remember her,' Hillary said.

Jimmy nodded but gave an unhappy sigh. 'Not that anybody in that line will want to talk to us,' he said, and again, strictly for Wendy's benefit.

'Well, in this case, you might have struck lucky,' Hillary said. 'When she disappeared, the parents put up a substantial reward for any information that led to her whereabouts being discovered. As far as I can tell, that money's still unclaimed and up for grabs. You might want to confirm that with the parents before mentioning it to any witnesses.'

Jimmy flipped through the case file until he found the relevant information, and Wendy whistled between her teeth when she saw all the zeros. Then she blinked. 'Hey, guv, if Jimmy and I can find her, can we claim the reward ourselves? Even my half of that much would let me put down a deposit on a decent mortgage somewhere.'

Hillary grinned and left it to Jimmy to put her clear on that later.

'Your second vic,' she swept on, 'is Amanda Smallwood.' They all turned to the second file, and Hillary once again summarized the bare details. 'Amanda was thirty-five, divorced, and a single mother of two. As you can see, she too was an attractive woman, petite with red hair and green eyes. That's another bonus for you two, because a MisPer with a striking physical appearance is more likely to remain in people's memories. And pretty women in particular, tend to stick in people's minds for longer. She went missing in December 2013 – her children are now being raised by their grandparents.'

'The father of the kids must have been a prime suspect, guv,' Wendy said eagerly.

'Normally yes. In this case, no,' Hillary said, and she saw Jimmy tap a relevant page for the goth's attention.

'Oh. She was another prostitute then, guv,' she said.

'You'll find a lot of female MisPer cases fall in that category,' Jimmy said. 'For obvious reasons. Most are drug addicts, all are vulnerable to attack, and when they've been in that life for some time, they're almost estranged from friends and family. They lose their support network. So if their bodies do show up, they often lay unclaimed in morgues.'

Wendy sucked in a breath. 'That's harsh. And it's not fair, either, what you said about pretty women being more memorable. It shouldn't matter,' she insisted.

Hillary sighed heavily, and felt about a hundred years old. Had she ever been that young and idealistic? If so, she could no longer remember it.

'Nobody said it was fair,' she said flatly.

When Jake came back an hour later, he found them all hard at work.

Hillary told him to help Wendy, who was busy sorting through the bulk of the other MisPer cases that they were going to review, and gave him a long, hard look, just daring him to make a fuss about it. It was grunt work plain and simple, demanding painstaking patience and hours spent on the phone and on the computer, checking and re-checking facts. She knew he must suspect that she was probably in the very process of reviewing his sister's case, and feel desperate to be included.

But Steven and Rollo would have hammered it into him now, though, and that he wasn't going to be allowed anywhere near it. And that his main job was to do everything that he could to help Steven and his new team hook Darren Chivnor so thoroughly that he would never be able to wriggle free.

Without a word, Jake went over to Wendy and accepted the pile of folders that she gleefully thrust into his hand. Then he returned to his own half of the desk and began reading.

But for all his silence, he was, in truth, not feeling particularly unhappy. After all, he'd got what he wanted – sort of – in that Hillary Greene and the CRT team were now going to start looking actively for Jas. And whilst, naturally, he so very much wanted to be a part of that, since working here he was becoming enough of a realist to know and accept that that simply wasn't going to happen.

He was feeling excited about getting in contact with Darren Chivnor again. After all, it was more than possible that Chivnor might be able to lead him to Jas, or to Jas's body, faster than Hillary Greene's more painstaking investigation.

At least things were *progressing*. When he'd come to work that morning, he'd had no idea that so much could change for the better, and so fast. And Steven had given him permission to warn his mum and Curtis that Hillary Greene would be calling on them soon to interview them, so at least they'd have the comfort of knowing that something was finally being done.

And yet, at the back of his mind, a dark realization was slowly taking shape – sometime soon, he might actually have to face the fact, once and for all, that his little sister was dead.

Over at her desk, Hillary Greene was, in fact, not reviewing Jasmine Sudbury's case at all, but the other case that she and Donleavy had selected.

Lydia Clare Allen had been twenty-nine when she'd disappeared in the winter of 2014. Strictly speaking, this case wasn't particularly cold, but neither was it being actively investigated, either, so nobody was going to cry foul. A local girl, she'd lived in the town of Wantage all her life before leaving home at the age of sixteen to share a place with three other girls in Oxford. Like their other cases, she had quickly spiralled down the usual route of drink, drugs, and finally prostitution. Photographs of her were few and far between, but one blurry shot of her taken at a party when she was nineteen or so, revealed that she had been about five feet ten inches tall, with long – almost certainly dyed – blonde hair and big pansy brown eyes.

Her mother had reported her missing when she had failed to return home for the Christmas holidays. From the case files, it was clear the officers who'd taken the original complaint had quickly concluded that she'd either fallen foul of one of her Johns, or had just legged it for sunnier climes with a sugar daddy.

Hillary hoped that was the case. But Dale Medcalfe wasn't well known for taking it kindly when one of his girls tried to leave his control, thereby trying to rob him of his immoral earnings; the likelihood that they'd track Lydia down to some Greek island, enjoying her happily-ever-after, seemed somewhat remote.

She sighed, and glanced at her watch. Already the day had got away from her.

'All right everybody, it's nearly five. Get off home, and we'll start fresh tomorrow.'

Wendy needed no second bidding and was off like a shot, but Jake looked as if he might want to linger and make another plea to be included in his sister's case. After one look at Hillary's set face, however, he too collected his jacket and tablet, and left quietly.

When the youngsters had gone, Jimmy looked across at Hillary and sighed.

'So what are they going to do about Chivnor, guv?'

Hillary quickly filled him in on the finer details of what had been decided. When she'd finished, it was clear that Jimmy too had his doubts that Jake was up to the task of running someone like Darren. It wasn't as if Chivnor had earned his reputation as a knife-man by whittling images of Pudsey the bear.

'I know. Steven's not happy about it, either,' Hillary confided. 'But since the idiot's already on Darren's radar now, we don't really have much choice but to go with it.'

'You'll be in on it though, guv? When Jake and Chivnor meet up, I mean,' he asked uneasily.

Hillary smiled across at the old man wryly. 'You know me, Jimmy,' she said. 'Every time those two meet, I'm going to be right there, watching and listening.'

Jimmy gave a short grunt of laughter. 'Does the guv – I mean, Steven, not the new man – know that?'

'If he doesn't, then he really hasn't been paying attention all these years, has he?' Hillary said.

And this time, Jimmy Jessop laughed until his back started to hurt all over again.

CHAPTER THREE

THAT EVENING DARREN CHIVNOR sat slumped in his favourite chair ostensibly watching the football on telly, but more often than not watching his girlfriend Lisa as she sat on the sofa and painted her toenails.

The sight made him happy.

Lisa was a pretty, blonde-haired, blue-eyed babe, and he'd always known he was lucky to catch her eye. They'd both grown up in the Leys, both attended the same squalid, useless comprehensive, both came from broken, working-class homes. But still, he'd always felt Lisa was a cut above the rest and way out of his league.

Perhaps because she worked part time at a beauty salon and always looked like a million dollars. Perhaps it was just the way she'd always tried to dress well. She might not have been able to afford designer labels, but she'd always had style. Real class, not like some of the skanks he knew.

He shifted slightly in his chair and sighed slightly. He knew that he himself was no oil painting – a shaved head, a few tats. He was in good physical shape, true, but even so, he always felt that she could have done better. That was why he'd worked so damned hard to give her everything she'd never had.

Growing up where he had, he'd always been aware of Dale Medcalfe and his gang – there was no getting away from them.

And his mum had always warned him off them, telling him to stay away from them and go straight. His dad probably would have said the same, had he hung around long enough to bother. He hadn't, though, and as the oldest, Darren had always felt the responsibility of looking after his mum and younger brothers weighing heavily on him. And much as he wanted to please her, and do well at school and get a job, and all that stuff that she wanted for him, he'd always known deep down inside that it was never going to happen. At a very young age, Darren had come to grips with reality on the estate.

The teachers at the school had been so dispirited by the grinding inevitability of it, they were often out sick. And if not absent, they were dead scared of the older pupils, who came to school carrying knives and razors. So what chance had he got of getting enough of an education to get through exams and try for uni? Bloody none. Not that he'd had the brains for all that stuff anyway. And even if he had, and got a degree, everyone knew that nowadays that was no guarantee of getting a good job. You saw people with fancy diplomas serving you Big Macs at the local McDonald's every day.

Nah, he'd long since realized that that particular game was for losers. So when, at the age of just eleven, he'd been approached by one of Medcalfe's lower-rankers to do a spot of running and fetching for him, he'd jumped at the chance. And simply hadn't told his mum. Not that she noticed – she was too busy being worn out working three jobs and trying to placate the truant officers, who were always coming round.

And from those humble beginnings, Darren had tirelessly worked his way up the ranks. He'd even joined the local gym, where they were giving out free martial arts classes in an effort to keep the city's disaffected youth off the streets. And in the alley-ways behind the public-funded sports centre, he'd been given lessons of other kinds, by different kinds of masters – lessons in how to use a knife, baseball bat, and other sundry items.

And the pay in Medcalfe's outfit was good. Very good. Before long, and as he took on more and riskier higher-level responsibilities, he managed to save enough for a deposit and a mortgage on a former council house just outside the Leys, for his mum and brothers.

Of course, by that time she knew, or suspected, what he was up to, but had become too worn out by life to object.

And it was around then that he'd reconnected with Lisa. At school she'd gone out with the school 'stars', such as they'd been. A kid slumming it from one of the outer burbs that everyone knew would go on to work in his dad's estate agents in Summertown. And, ironically enough, a younger brother of another of Dale Medcalfe's gang, whom everyone expected would go on to uni and the chance of a fabled 'good, steady job'.

Back then, of course, he'd never have dared to ask her out, fearing the inevitable rebuff and the taunting from his mates that was bound to follow. But after leaving school at sixteen, just three short years had seen his circumstances change dramatically. Not only that, but Lisa's dad had died, and her mum had hit the skids. The landlord had tossed them out of their home and Lisa had taken to sleeping on friends' sofas or floors, forced to shift from one crash pad to another.

And it was only then that Darren had decided to risk making his move.

He had been only a mid-level man in Medcalfe's outfit then. And all he could offer her was the sofa at his mum's new house. She'd been glad to take the offer, though. And, after a little while, had been glad to take all his other offers as well. Because by then she'd had the chance to see how things could be for them, and Lisa had always been a bright girl.

Darren was coming to the big man's attention more and more, and was making a bit of a name for himself. He was streetwise, brutal, and hard-working, and his star was definitely on the ascendant. He was fast becoming just the kind of trust-worthy lieutenant Dale was famous for looking out for, which meant that it could only be a matter of time before he started earning serious money.

And so it had turned out. Since then he'd bought a second place outright – a nice flat in a converted Victorian house in Botley. He had a view of some trees and everything. They had satellite telly, a good car, went on holidays abroad.

And Lisa had flourished. With money to spend, she got class-ier and classier. No kidding, he reckoned she could be a model or something. They'd been together for five years now, and were even starting to think about having kids of their own.

And therein, lay the rub. Things were going to change soon, and although this life was great for a young guy on his own, as a family man … forget it.

He looked outside as a gust of wind-driven rain pounded on the windows and sighed heavily. He was getting heartily sick of grey, cold, broken England. They should be abroad somewhere now – in the Caribbean sun maybe, for a winter break. Or even, long term, further afield. Australia maybe? Why not? He cer-tainly didn't want to be stuck here in bloody Oxford, forever at the beck and call of someone like Dale. The thought made him squirm even more. Such thoughts, he well knew, were danger-ous. Dale didn't tolerate dissatisfaction in the ranks.

He wasn't quite sure when he first started thinking such thoughts. For a long time, he'd been contented enough – running Dale's girls, transporting the overseas merchandise, slapping back in line anyone daft enough to try to skim the profits, or grass to the coppers. And he'd always been careful, and unlike a lot of Dale's firm, had never been nabbed or spent a day of time inside. He knew Dale liked that about him. Dale was a careful man himself. Very careful. He now had more mil-lions than the taxman believed, and led a life of insulated ease in his mansion in Headington.

It was the sort of life that Darren envied and coveted for himself – or, at least, a lesser version of it. He wasn't greedy. Just enough to get out of this life and set himself and Lisa up somewhere nice would do him well.

This was why he'd been so intrigued and tempted by Jake Barnes's offer.

The man had appeared on the horizon quite unexpectedly and offered him just what he craved most. Money; a way out; the promise of finally making all his dreams come true. And he could still hardly believe it. He was still, in fact, half-inclined to wonder if it was all some sort of trap. Dale's trap perhaps – setting him up, testing his loyalties. Or, far more likely, a copper's trap.

Over on the sofa, Lisa shifted around and started to paint the nails on her other foot. Occasionally she'd hum softly under her breath, the latest pop tune, or a golden oldie. He wondered what she'd say if he told her that a total stranger had handed over twenty grand in cash, along with a slew of first-class forged documents for both of them. Because that alone would provide enough spending money for a month or so.

But that wouldn't be nearly enough, of course – as that millionaire bastard Barnes well knew. They'd need more. Proper seed money to set up some kind of business – holiday lets, a bar, something like that. But then, Jake Barnes had even promised that as well.

And Darren was tempted. Extremely tempted.

The trouble was he still didn't know what it was that Barnes wanted in return for all this bounty. And the last time they'd met to discuss just that, things had gone badly pear-shaped, and he'd probably scared him off forever.

Or maybe not. Maybe he should just stop poncing about and call him? Set up another meeting. Explain what had gone wrong. Because the bloke definitely wanted something from him all right – Darren could almost smell the need and desperation on the man.

And Darren had had the chance to do his homework on Barnes now – the internet truly was a wonderful thing. Like himself, Barnes had grown up in a working-class family, and on a large housing estate. But unlike Darren he'd had brains, and luck on his side. He'd made his fortune young, something to do with IT, and then bought up tons of real estate when the bottom fell out of the market.

And now he worked as a civilian at Thames Valley Police HQ.

Just the thought of that made him go cold all over. It didn't even matter that he wasn't a real copper, because if Dale ever found out they'd been in contact … well, that would be it. The very least he could expect would be a severe beating, with major hospital time afterwards. And a demotion right back down to scut work. And that was only if he was lucky, and Dale was feeling in a generous mood. Because if he weren't – well, his mum would just have to arrange a funeral for one of her sons.

And Lisa would look really beautiful in black.

He gave a brief snort at his own bleak humour and when he sensed Lisa look up at him, pretended to be sneering at the antics of the Arsenal team on the telly.

But he continued to think.

On the plus side, Jake Barnes had been up-front right from the start about where he worked. He'd shown good faith by turning up at their meeting with the documents and the money. And after having tried to chase him across the dark, Oxford park, he was confident that Barnes had been at the meeting alone.

But best of all, Barnes had sworn that he didn't want Darren to grass Dale up and that this had nothing to do with his day job. Of course, he could have been lying, but Darren didn't think so. And for sure, coppers didn't use civilians in under-cover work – the media and insurance people would have hissy fits if they did, and got killed or injured because of it.

Besides, Darren had always been a good judge of character – it was one of the reasons he'd risen so fast in Medcalfe's organization. If people owed Dale money, Darren was good at sorting out the bullshit from the truth. And reading someone, with an eye to seeing just where to apply the right pressure, had become second nature to him.

It was the same with the girls. He knew which ones were trying to hold out on them, or pull a stunt, and which ones were genuinely in trouble or failing. And, likewise, how to deal with both situations.

No, over the years, he'd developed a good nose for scenting trouble – picking up on the slightly off; the dodgy; the dangerous. And he'd got none of those vibes from any of his encounters with Jake Barnes.

In truth, the millionaire whizz kid intrigued him. He was obviously out of his element, and scared witless by what he was doing, but he'd gone through with it anyway. But just what the hell did the guy *want*? What was so important to him that he was willing to be so generous with the incentives? And if the twenty grand and the documents were just the sweetener, what might the true pay-off be like?

Darren could feel his chest go so tight it was hard to breathe, and his mouth all but watered at the thought of it. He could almost feel the prize in his hand: leaving Oxford for a new life in the sun somewhere with Lisa. It was only something he'd agree to if it didn't involve crossing Dale – because, for sure, his mum and brothers wouldn't be safe if he did. Even if he and Lisa got away, he knew Dale would take it out on his family.

Jake had intimated that Dale didn't even need to know anything had happened.

Still. He could just be a lying little toe-rag.

And even if he wasn't, it was still playing with fire.

But then, something worth having always involved risk, didn't it?

Shit. He felt stupid, humming and hawing like this. It was time he grew some balls, and at least find out what it was Barnes wanted. And then make a decision.

'I'm just going down to the pub, Liss. Won't be long.' He grabbed his coat, car keys and mobile, but in fact, didn't head for the car at all. Instead, he walked to the end of the street, deserted because of the cold and the rain, and then called a number that wasn't listed in the phone's digital memory.

He wasn't about to leave any traces that Dale might stumble over.

The phone rang four times before it was picked up.

In his study in his north Oxford mansion, Jake Barnes picked up his phone and took a deep, sharp breath, as he immediately recognized the voice on the other end.

Both Steven and Rollo had coached him extensively in what he was supposed to say to Darren Chivnor should he make contact, and he knew that his phone now recorded everything that came in, just in case.

They had all anticipated that it would be Jake who would make the first move and they were due to meet in the morning to finalize the best and safest way for him to do this. So now he found himself perched nervously on the edge of the chair, praying that he didn't blow it. Despite the tension Jake felt, which was making him feel slightly sick, he remembered the drill. Let Chivnor do the talking. Don't be confrontational. Keep mentioning the money. Say nothing yet about Jasmine.

They had to get Chivnor on tape, and with full photographic evidence to back it up, if they were to have any hope of getting him to turn on his boss. And for that to happen, they needed major leverage.

'Hello, Jake. Remember me?' Chivnor's voice sounded faintly ironic, as well it might.

'Hard to forget you, man,' Jake replied, his mouth dry, his

words sounding faintly breathless. 'I thought you were going to kill me.' Then he winced. That could definitely be said to be confrontational, and he could have kicked himself for his stupidity.

Darren laughed uneasily, and felt like swearing himself. He was grimly aware that he needed to persuade Barnes that he could trust him again, otherwise he'd never get his hands on the man's money. The trouble was, apologizing or explaining himself had never come easily. In fact, having to crawl to anyone made him tingle with rage, which was why it was beginning to grate, having to lick Dale's boots so constantly.

But in this case, it had to be done. Reminding himself to keep his eyes on the prize, he forced himself to sound contrite. 'Yeah. I know. Sorry about that. I only drew the knife because of that bloke who came in. Do you remember him? I thought he was one of the boss's men. He's a ginger nut, too, like that guy was. It was only when I saw him in a better light, that I could see it wasn't him. But by then, it was too late. You'd already legged it. Like a bloody whippet you were, man, I've never seen anybody run that fast.'

Jake laughed himself now. 'Can you blame me? I thought you'd decided that the documents and the twenty grand were enough. I should have said that there was another cool million in it for you.'

There, he'd made his first mention of the money that was up for grabs.

When they'd discussed it that morning, both Rollo and Steven had decided on the amount – and he could understand why. It was a nice, round figure. And even in today's market, was still a lot of money. Enough, surely, to hook someone like Darren.

And, as if in confirmation, he now heard a swift intake of breath from Darren, and he grinned, feeling a moment of hot, happy triumph.

'So, what are we gonna do about it then?' Darren asked cagily. 'What do you want for it?'

Jake's grin vanished instantly. 'Not over the phone,' he said quickly. 'You never know who might be listening nowadays. We need to meet again, but this time, not in the dark. It's not that I don't trust you…. Well, hell, yes, actually it is,' Jake continued, sticking to the script that he'd been given, 'I don't mind telling you, I nearly shat a brick last time. I'm not cut out for all that rough stuff,' he added.

It had been Steven's idea – to play up the impression of Jake as a harmless innocent-abroad and make Darren feel even more in control and give him something to sneer about. He suggested they reinforce the image that Jake was just another victim, and Dale the big bad wolf. Make him think he held all the aces.

'OK, fair enough,' Darren said, a shade reluctantly. 'But we've got to be careful. If I think that Dale even *suspects* I'm up to something, I'm out. Like a shot. Million or no million – you can't spend it if you're dead.'

'OK,' Jake agreed quickly. And told him where and when and how they could meet. Just as Steven and Rollo had coached him.

When he hung up a few moments later, he let out a long gust of breath then was straight on the phone to report back to Hillary Greene.

He felt elated. And scared. And utterly determined to make the meet and find out, once and for all, just what had happened to his baby sister.

The next morning, Hillary tuned in to the local radio station as she drove the short distance to work, and sure enough, the MisPer review being carried out by the local police was item three on the news bulletin.

As she pulled into the car park, she thought about Jake's phone call the previous night. Not surprisingly, when he rang her Jake had been totally hyped and talking far too fast and she'd had to calm him down and talk him through it. It sounded as though it had gone as well as they could have hoped.

As she climbed out of her car, she glanced at her watch. By now, Jake, Rollo and Steven should be listening to the recording, and making detailed plans for the forthcoming meet. She'd already made it clear to both of the bosses that she wanted to be one of those watching and listening in when the time came.

But just at that moment, she had other priorities.

Once she'd checked her emails, touched base with Steven, and made sure that Jimmy and Wendy were clear about their assignments, she went back to Puff and headed to the north of the county.

It was time she met Jake's parents and began to learn all that she could about their daughter: the good, the bad, and the ugly.

Jake had done right by his parents when he'd come into his first fortune, and they now lived in a very pleasant, detached modern house in Middleton Cheney, not far from the market town of Banbury, where he'd been brought up.

As Hillary parked in front of the large and still colourful garden, she mused on what Jake's mother, Rosemary, must have made of her only child making such a success of himself at such a young age. Had she worried that earning all the money would go to his head? And had her stepdaughter's descent into drug-use caused her to worry that Jake, too, might go off the rails?

She shrugged and emptied her mind of all preconceptions as she walked up a flagstone path which had been lined by a mixture of evergreens and other coloured-foliage plants that looked good even in the cold, grey, November light.

The house, though new, had been built of the local pale stone and an electric lamp, set in an ornate black iron and glass case, was burning a welcome above a neat porch. Hillary rang the bell and waited, knowing that not only had Jake told them to expect her, but that he had also filled them in, to a certain extent, on what they were doing. They had been told nothing about Medcalfe of course, or the intricacies and breadth of the police brief – only that Hillary had agreed to look into Jasmine's missing persons' case herself. Jake had reassured her more than once in the last twenty-four hours that this agreement was all that his parents had hoped for. The boy wonder freely admitted that he'd been singing Hillary's praises ever since getting his job with the police, and that both his stepfather and his mother were more than happy to co-operate fully with her. He'd also told her they would willingly answer any questions she might have, no matter how personal or potentially painful.

All this was good in one way, Hillary supposed, but in another, it only served to pile the pressure onto her shoulders. Although she knew that she'd had more than her fair share of successes, failure was always an option. In any case you investigated, if luck was against you, then it didn't matter how good your interview technique was, or how clever your deductive reasoning, you could still come up with zero. Experience could take you so far, but if the proof wasn't there to be found, then you were left with nothing you could take to court.

She only hoped that Jake hadn't built her up too high, and that his family didn't expect miracles.

When the door opened and Hillary found herself face to face with Jake's mother, she could see at once that Jake had inherited his striking green eyes and his good looks from her. For the woman in front of her stood at just a little over five feet tall, and had naturally fair hair that was just turning silver. She was dressed in a pair of warm black trousers and an intricately knitted cream jumper. She wore no make-up, perfume or jewellery, and instantly smiled and held out a long, well-shaped hand.

'You must be Mrs Greene,' she said, and as Hillary tried not to flinch at the little-used and unwelcome title, swept on. 'Jake's told us so much about you. I can't tell you how much we appreciate what you're doing for us. Please, come on in.'

Before Hillary could respond, she'd already turned and was leading the way into a large, modern sitting room with an expensive mock-fire and indicated a pair of sweeping brown leather armchairs. As she did so, a man in his mid-fifties rose from the matching sofa and turned to face her.

'Curtis, this is Jake's boss.'

Jake's stepfather was about a half a foot taller than his wife, but that still put him just an inch or two shorter than Hillary herself. He was running a little too fat around the middle and his dark hair was thinning, but he had soft, rather gentle brown eyes and a pleasant face which currently wore a slightly anxious expression.

'I hope Jake hasn't got himself into too much trouble with everyone at work, Mrs Greene,' he began, forcing Hillary to nip all the *Mrs Greene* business in the bud quickly in the only way that she could.

'Please call me Hillary,' she said. 'And don't worry about Jake. From what I've learned of him so far, he's well able to take care of himself,' she added, not seeing any point in pretending that she condoned their son's behaviour. And saw the couple exchange a quick, rueful look.

It was Curtis who laughed slightly. 'Sorry. It's just that Jake warned us you wouldn't sugar coat things for us, and that you were something of a tough nut. And I mean that in a good way,' he hastened to add as his wife shot him an appalled look.

Hillary smiled to show there were no hard feelings, which there weren't; in her life she'd been called far, far worse.

'What Curt means,' Rosemary put in quickly, 'is that Jake really respects you, for your worth ethic, experience and intelligence. He's told us as much as he can about the cases you've worked on, and how clever and tenacious you are and how much you've always impressed him. So—'

Hillary smiled, but held up a hand, intent on stopping the woman in mid-flow.

She understood why these people were anxious to get her on their side, of course, but she didn't need her ego stroking. 'Please, let's all sit down, shall we?' she suggested. Once they had all settled, she began to take control of the interview. 'I know that the circumstances in this case, and how we came to be investigating it, are a little unusual, but believe me, it won't affect how I do my job. So, to get a few things clear – yes, we're not pleased with Jake and what he's been up to,' she nodded to Curtis, 'but no, he's not in any real trouble.'

She didn't add that trouble was almost certainly coming Jake's way in the form of Darren Chivnor, because she knew that the boy wonder hadn't kept his parents informed about that part of his campaign to find Jasmine. As far as they were concerned, his only misdemeanours had been in joining the Thames Valley under false colours, and poking about in data that wasn't in the public domain.

And Hillary, for one, was happy to keep them in ignorance.

'And so there's no need for any more awkwardness,' she swept on. She needed these people to feel less wrong-footed and to be more focussed on giving her what she needed. 'When I finally learned the reasons behind what Jake was doing, I was happy to help – we all were – both Acting Chief Superintendent Crayle, and our new boss, Superintendent Sale: We're all dedicated to finding out what happened to Jasmine.'

This had the effect that Hillary hoped for – both of them seemed to relax slightly.

'So, I know the basic facts of what happened,' she went on swiftly. 'Jake's filled me in on your family history and given me his version of things. What I need now is your input. I take it her biological mother is out of the picture?'

'She is.' It was Curtis who spoke, flatly and firmly.

Hillary nodded. 'I understand you might not want to talk

about her, Mr—'

'Curtis. Call me Curtis.'

'Thank you. Curtis. But I need to cross her off as a possible link to Jasmine's whereabouts. Would Jasmine have contacted her mother, either with a view of getting money or as someone she might live with when times got rough, for instance?'

Curtis snorted. 'No and no. For a start, Jas would know that her mother wouldn't have a penny to toss in the pot – and if she had, she certainly wouldn't share it with anyone. Everything she ever got went up her nose or in her veins. And secondly, we – and this includes Jas – don't even know where she is anymore. We haven't done for a number of years. She might even be dead by now. In fact, she probably is.'

Hillary nodded and made a mental note to check the databases to see if that was, in fact, the case. Not that she seriously expected Jas to have gone to her mother for help. From the sounds of it, it seemed pretty clear that the woman had never played a large part in her life.

'She never was interested in Jas even when she first came to live with us as a little girl,' Rosemary put in sadly. 'Never visited at Christmas or remembered her birthday or anything,' she added, shaking her head. 'I don't know how she could do that, do you? I mean, not even to care how your own child was faring.'

Curtis sighed, but said nothing.

'Did Jas resent that?' Hillary asked gently.

'Oh no. Right from the start, she was happy here, wasn't she, Curtis?' Rosemary said, looking across at her husband for confirmation, which was quickly given. 'I was a little nervous when she first came to us,' Rosemary confided. 'I was frightened she would resent me, think that I was trying to take her mummy's place, or take her daddy's love away from her. You know how difficult it can be with young children. But that didn't happen. Instead, she really took to me. She was such a loving little girl.'

Rosemary's voice faltered a bit, but she quickly swallowed back any sign of weakness. 'And I'd always wanted a daughter. Who knows, perhaps she sensed that. We did all the things mothers and daughters did – we went shopping for a pretty dress whenever she got invited to a birthday party. We took her out to the zoo, and we baked cakes together. She really was happy.'

'You gave her everything she could have wanted, Rose, I keep telling you,' Curtis added, glancing over at his wife with a kind of sad resignation. 'It was nothing you did, or said, that made things turn out as they did.' And then, turning to Hillary, added unnecessarily, 'Rose blamed herself for what happened. But it wasn't her fault. It was growing up for those first, formative years with her real … I mean, with her biological mother that did the damage. No, if anyone's to blame for how things turned out, it was me. I should have insisted that Jas come and live with me the moment I realized how things were and left home. But she was only two then, and I thought … well, you do, don't you, that if you take a little kiddie of that age away from their mum, it's not good psychologically.'

He shook his head. 'But if I had it to do all over again, it'd be different, I can tell you. Because watching her mother booze and drug herself up to the eyeballs – even if she wasn't old enough to really understand what she was seeing at the time – well, it has to register in here, doesn't it?' he demanded, tapping the side of his temple with his finger.

Hillary said nothing. She could tell that she was witnessing something that this couple must have struggled with for years, but there was very little in the way of comfort or consolation that she could offer them.

Instead, she shifted them back on track.

'I understand that the trouble began when she was a teenager at school. Jake told me that he was away at uni then, and when he came back for the holidays, he realized she was drinking.'

'Yes. That's how it started,' Rosemary said quietly. 'At first, we didn't realize. She was fourteen, and going out with a gang of other girls and boys that age. And you expect teenagers to be a bit rebellious, don't you? To start having secrets, to stop wanting to be so tight with the old parents. They think they're all grown up and know everything – and that's all perfectly normal. I remember thinking the same things, at that age.'

'Me, too,' Hillary added with a smile.

'Unfortunately, the gang she was hanging out with had older friends who'd go into shops and buy cider for them. And six-packs of beer,' Curtis took up the story. 'And then we found out that they were going to one of the kid's houses, whose parents were always away, and raiding their liquor cabinet. And then it wasn't just shandy or cider they were drinking, but the real hard stuff. Whisky, brandy, gin, vodka, you name it.'

'And those horrible alcopop things,' Rosemary put in quickly. 'They look so pretty in their coloured bottles and so harmless with their cool brand names and what have you. Jas used to drink them like she used to drink cans of Pepsi.'

'And not even Jake could get her to stop,' Curtis said bitterly.

'Not even Jake?' Hillary pounced. 'Jas usually listened to Jake, did she? I know he said that they were close, but I wasn't sure how much of that was just wishful thinking on his part.'

'Oh no, he was right. Jas adored him, didn't she, Rose?' Curtis said promptly.

Hillary turned to see that Rosemary was also nodding her head emphatically. 'It started off as hero-worship of course,' she said, with a fond smile. 'Do you remember how she used to follow him around like a hopeful little puppy?'

'Jake said he found it flattering, rather than annoying,' Hillary prompted.

'Yes, he was always very good with her. Very patient – some boys would probably have reacted badly to being saddled with a little sister. But he never resented her and she could tell that and adored him for it. When she was ten, she even made him promise to wait for her to grow up so that they could be married. Very serious about that, wasn't she, Curt?' Rosemary laughed. 'She'd researched it and everything. I can remember them now, sitting on the sofa together, and Jas solemnly explaining that, just because they were legally stepbrother and sister, it didn't mean anything, because they weren't related by blood.'

Curt laughed. 'I'd forgotten that. She'd talked to a vicar about it, hadn't she or something.'

'A biology teacher, I think it was,' Rosemary corrected. 'Anyway, she'd got slightly confused about blood groups, or something, but she'd got the gist of it right. Because they didn't have the same genes, they could marry.'

'And what did Jake say to that?' Hillary asked, her lips twitching in amusement.

'Oh, he was very good about it,' Rosemary said instantly. 'He didn't laugh at her, like I was worried that he might. Children's egos are so fragile, aren't they? Instead, he said that he found it all very interesting, and that of course he'd wait for her to grow up, but he tried to point out that by the time she had done so, she might not be quite so keen. And that she'd probably have found a really cool and good-looking boyfriend for herself by then, and would turn her nose up at her old-fogey brother. And he promised her that he wouldn't hold it against her if she did.'

'That made her so angry – as mad as a hornet if I remember,' Curt cut in with a laugh of his own. 'Ten years old, pigtails down to here,' he indicated a spot about mid-thigh on his own body, 'and as ferocious as a hunting lioness. She stamped her foot and insisted that she wouldn't change her mind and that he'd better wait for her, or else.'

Hillary nodded. 'She sounds like someone who knew her own mind. I take it that strong sense of self only made it more difficult to reason with her later on about the drinking?'

'Yes. She defended her friends to the death, saying that we

were all just jealous of them because they were young and having a good time. And she laughed when we tried to use what happened to her own mother as a warning. She scoffed and said she'd never do drugs. She had far more sense.' Curtis shook his head. 'And like a fool, I believed her. At first.'

'We all did. Jas was so bright, Hillary, you see,' his wife cut in anxiously. 'She was clever at school and pretty and popular and seemed to have the world at her feet. She was fascinated by Jake's success and seemed so inspired by it and also determined to do well herself. As you know, she was nearly seventeen by the time Jake sold his company for all that money and started investing it in real estate and what have you.'

Hillary nodded. 'She wasn't jealous of him then?' she probed carefully. 'After all, he was the famous young entrepreneur, the hot-shot, IT whizz-kid. The golden boy. Most teenage girls would have resented all that.'

'Oh yes, I know what you mean,' Rosemary said at once. 'And of course, I do think she was a bit envious. I mean, how could she not be? Jake was buying himself a Jaguar, and that big house in Oxford and what have you. What young girl wouldn't dream of that kind of lifestyle for herself?'

'But,' Curtis put in quickly, 'she didn't resent Jake having it. She was genuinely pleased for him.'

'Oh, yes,' Rosemary was quick to agree.

Hillary nodded, sensed they were becoming a little uneasy, and decided to move on. 'And it was around this time that you noticed she was into drugs?'

'Yes.'

'Yes.'

Both of them spoke almost at once.

'Did she ask Jake for money?'

'Yes. But he wouldn't give it to her. Not when he realized why she wanted it,' Rosemary said. And for the next hour or so they went over the same ground that Jake had already covered

– charting the girl's slow, inexorable slide: the pregnancy that ended so badly; the futile stints in rehab; the leaving home, being found, the coming back and then the promises to go straight and keep clean. All ending, of course, in her final disappearance, when even Jake's PIs couldn't find her.

'I don't know what more we could have done,' Rosemary finally said. By now, she was tearful, and had cried softly off and on into a steadily disintegrating piece of tissue. Her husband was white-faced and equally despondent.

'But Jake was generous to her in other ways,' his mother continued. 'He wouldn't give her cash to feed her habit, but he took her places – swanky restaurants and nightclubs. He took her out in the jag to rock concerts and even abroad – to places that she'd always wanted to go. Monte Carlo, where he taught her how to play roulette and blackjack. He even rented a yacht and took her across the Mediterranean in it. That was a reward for staying clean for six months. And for a while, it seemed to distract her.'

She paused and then shook her head. 'But always, she slid back down into her old bad habits. We all tried everything we could to make her see how good life could be away from constant highs and lows. But nothing seemed to work.'

In the silence that followed, Hillary sighed a little. 'Did Jake tell you that I'd need a list of the names of all her friends?'

'Yes, we have it here,' Rosemary said, rising to pick up a piece of paper from the mantelpiece. 'But these are the friends she had in school, mostly. The others, the ones she knew as an adult … in that world … we just don't know who they are or where they live.'

Hillary took the information with a small smile. 'That doesn't matter. They'll either be in the system, in prison, or, more likely than not, dead.' She hesitated delicately, but knew from Jake that they had already discussed the harsher realities of drug addiction. 'You do realize that people who live as Jas has been living...' She trailed off, already seeing that she didn't need to spell it out.

Rosemary paled, but nodded bravely.

'You don't have to tell us,' Curtis said harshly. 'She's probably dead. We haven't heard from her for more than two years. Not even begging letters for money. We know that this,' he waved a hand helplessly in the air, 'new investigation you're following probably won't end well, but we just need to know. It's the not knowing that kills you. And the worst thing of all is thinking that she might still be alive somewhere, and desperate for help, but we just don't know about it. You understand?'

Hillary did. Hope was a bitch. It tormented you far more than pain or grief ever did.

'I don't know what Jake's promised you,' Hillary said gently, 'but I'm not a miracle worker. I can only do what can be done. I'll work on this to the best of my ability, and I *can* promise you that I won't give up looking for Jas until either I find out what's happened to her, or I'm convinced that there's nothing else that can possibly be done. But I have to warn you – sometimes, the families of missing people never do get answers. You should be prepared for that possibility.'

Rosemary was still staring down at the tissue in her hands. Her lips trembled, but Hillary saw her nod.

Curtis said nothing.

Slowly, and grimly feeling that she'd brought enough misery to their lives for one day, Hillary rose and let herself out of the house.

Once inside the cold interior of her car, she thought for a long while about what she'd learned thus far. As she did so, she became increasingly aware of her lowering mood. The truth was, she didn't have a good feeling about Jasmine Sudbury's case. She didn't have a good feeling about it at all.

Eventually, she turned the ignition key and Puff the Tragic Wagon coughed apologetically and stalled. She swore at him softly, and tried again, without success.

It took her another couple of minutes to coax the old Volkswagen into life, and then she headed back to HQ, trying to think of something besides the Sudburys.

It wasn't hard to find a distraction.

There was nothing stopping her from starting the process of moving into Steven's house permanently now. At least that wouldn't be so hard. It wasn't as if she'd need a removals van or anything. All she'd have to do was cruise the *Mollern* a little further down the canal to her new private mooring, and bit by bit, transfer the bulk of her belongings through Steven's overgrown back garden.

The thought of their lugging her bits and bobs to and fro from the canal under the watchful eyes of his neighbours made her smile.

With all that they had on their plates – the stress created by Steven's new job; the dangers Jake would face when dealing with Darren Chivnor and her growing unease about the Jasmine Sudbury case – she was beginning to suspect that smiles were going to be hard to come by for quite some time.

CHAPTER FOUR

WENDY DIDN'T MIND THE drive to the south coast and to Hayling Island, even though it was a grey, cold and miserable day. No doubt in the summertime the road would be clogged with sun-seekers and holiday makers, but the goth in her loved the misty, murky atmospheric days of winter. And not even congested roads, bad drivers and water spray from passing artic lorries pricked her pleasantly gloomy mood.

Beside her in her beloved Mini, Jimmy Jessop had a very different view of the proceedings. For a start, the low-slung, cupped seats were playing havoc with his back, and the dreary weather was giving him a severe case of the doldrums.

But Rebecca Tyde-Harris's parents had retired to the coast last year, and over the telephone had sounded more than keen to be interviewed. Something about their desperation and gratitude that their daughter's case hadn't been totally forgotten made him decide on the spur of the moment that the interviews would better be done face to face.

He'd have been even more disgruntled if he'd realized that the bright youngster beside him – and who'd been listening in on the telephone call – had twigged straightaway the true reason for the road trip. And that now Wendy knew that, really, he was nothing but a big-hearted softy under his stern and grizzled former-sergeant exterior, she wouldn't be so much in awe of him.

They had to rely on the Mini's sat-nav to guide them the final half-mile or so to the Tyde-Harrises' residence, which was isolated on the very outskirts of the town. Wendy for one wasn't disappointed by the Tyde-Harrises' choice of residence for their retirement.

Set at the end of a short and gloomy laurel-lined drive was what had once been an old rectory. The rain had turned its uncompromising grey façade even darker, and a number of higgledy-piggledy steeply pitched grey slate roofs ended in leaking guttering. Add to that a multitude of small leaded windows that looked as if they hid a hundred Victorian secrets, and the goth was in her element.

'Wow,' she said, looking at the dripping evergreen foliage that was climbing up one of the walls towards a round window set under the eaves. 'Can't you just imagine some poor lunatic uncle, who'd been locked away in the attics by his relatives to starve to death, just haunting the place and plotting his revenge? This place is way creepy,' she said enthusiastically.

Jimmy, who had far more of an eye for the practical cost of real estate prices these days than architectural aesthetics, looked at the large edifice and instantly concluded that the Tyde-Harrises certainly wouldn't miss the reward money they'd offered for news of their daughter. Should they ever have to award it.

'Tyde-Harris was something in banking, wasn't he?' he grunted. 'Retired just before they frazzled the economy?'

'Yeah,' Wendy agreed absently, still fantasizing about what it must be like to live in a genuine, haunted Victorian vicarage.

Swearing under his breath and wincing, Jimmy climbed out of the car with some difficulty and straightened his recalcitrant spine. He'd already taken a couple of aspirin that morning, but he supposed wearily that he'd have to take two more later. Not that he liked taking pills as a rule, but this backache which had been coming and going for weeks now, seemed to be suddenly digging in with a vengeance.

Old age was a bitch.

He regarded Wendy, who was already skipping like a spring lamb towards the house and craning her head upwards, with a jaundiced eye.

'Bloody hell, that's an actual gargoyle,' she said happily, pointing up towards a piece of sculpted stone. 'See? It's supposed to be a face.'

Jimmy grunted something that might have been appreciative. And then again, might not. He rang the bell.

It was answered suspiciously quickly by a tall, flabby, white-haired man, dressed casually in dark navy trousers and an expensive-looking, diamond patterned jumper in tones of dark blue, grey, white and sludgy-green. The fact that he'd got to the door so quickly told Jimmy that he – and probably his wife – had been awaiting their arrival for quite some time. Probably, Jimmy thought with a pang, they'd both been standing at the window for the last half an hour or so, watching for a car to come up the drive.

He swallowed back a familiar feeling of rage and helplessness, one that always assailed him when meeting the family and friends of victims of violence, and gruffly displayed his ID and introduced himself.

'Mr Jessop, I'm Richard Tyde-Harris. Miss Turnbull, please come in.'

Jimmy saw the elderly man look Wendy over with a briefly bemused expression, and was glad that today, the goth wasn't dressed particularly outrageously. Instead, she'd confined herself to a long black granny dress that looked as if it had been used to mourn the passing of Queen Victoria, and had added a cracked black biker's jacket for warmth. She still had all that black muck caked around her eyes, Jimmy noticed fatalistically, but her hair, for once, was free of any strikingly coloured dye and lay in a fairly well-behaved blob around her face.

'Come into the drawing room. Margot's laid some tea. I hope you like ginger cake,' the old man said, leading them into a dark hall with original tiles on the floor and a dark wood panelling.

Jimmy didn't like ginger in any form, but gave a pleased smile. 'One of my favourites, thank you, sir. But you needn't have gone to any trouble.'

As they stepped into a room that was dominated by a large stone fireplace, he sensed Wendy tense and turned to follow her wide-eyed gaze.

Margot Tyde-Harris was rising from a large, richly brocaded sofa and was watching them anxiously. Like her husband, she was probably now well into her sixties, but looked much older. Although even Jimmy – no expert when it came to women's fashion and accessories – could tell that she was immaculately well-groomed, he felt himself wither a little inside as he took in her appearance.

The woman was so thin she looked anorexic. She had wonderful bone structure, and was still very handsome, but her cheekbones stood out like razors. Her eyes had sunken back into her skull, but blazed out at them with a dark blue fire that could almost be physically felt.

He sensed Wendy shiver with pity, and understood why.

It might have been more than five years since Rebecca Tyde-Harris had last been seen, but for this woman it was probably only yesterday. And what's more, as Margot moved towards them, offering a hand festooned with diamond, emerald and ruby rings, one look in that ravaged face told Jimmy that this woman was in no doubt at all that her daughter was dead. There was no hope in her expression, only a savage kind of grief and helpless rage.

Her husband introduced them, watching her anxiously all the time.

'Mr Jessop,' she said, and her voice was both upper class and melodious. Her hair was pure white and arranged in a simple, elegant chignon. Diamonds studded her ears. Her hand, in his, was so bony he felt like he was shaking hands with a skeleton and he nodded mutely, at that moment unable to speak, and carefully disengaged his hand.

She turned and looked at Wendy with much gentler eyes. 'Hello, my dear. Please sit down and have some cake.'

Jimmy knew from the files that Rebecca had been their only child – and clearly having a young woman in their house again had struck a chord with the grieving mother. And Wendy, who was no slouch when it came to reading situations either, smiled at her tremulously. 'Thank you,' she said meekly. 'I'd like that.'

They all sat, and Jimmy cleared his throat in the awkward, momentary silence that followed. Margot graciously began to cut the cake and poured tea from a large china teapot into Spode cups so delicate they were almost see-through.

'Have you any news of Becky?' It was Richard Tyde-Harris who broke the ice first.

'No, sir, nothing specific,' Jimmy responded at once. 'But as I said on the telephone, we work for the Crime Review Team. It's our job to take another in-depth look at cold cases. And at the moment, Thames Valley are doing a review of missing persons, specifically those of missing women, and our boss, DI Hillary Green, has passed on Rebecca's case to us.'

'Ah yes. We did some research on the inspector. I hope you don't mind,' Richard said, with a quick glance at his wife. 'The internet is such a useful tool, in spite of all its shortfalls. I have to say, we were rather relieved and reassured by what we learned—'

'Oh, yes, Hillary is fantastic.' It was Wendy who couldn't help interrupting. She knew she shouldn't have and she sensed Jimmy's displeasure even as she did it, but Wendy didn't care. Her eyes were fixed on those of Margot. Her every instinct was screaming at her to do everything she could to try to heal some of the damage that had been done to her. 'Every cold case she's worked on so far, she's always solved.'

Margot nodded solemnly. 'I'm very glad to hear it. I have to say that neither my husband nor I were particularly happy with the original investigation into Becky's disappearance. Please don't think that we're complaining, or take what I'm saying personally, it's just that we sensed the police officers we spoke to were not committed to finding our daughter. That's why we felt obliged to offer the reward, which is still on offer, by the way.'

Jimmy coughed.

Wendy, for once, had the good sense to open her mouth only to put a piece of ginger cake into it.

'I'm sorry you felt that way, Mrs Tyde-Harris,' Jimmy said, but wasn't about to defend his colleagues. In point of fact, there was very little that he *could* say in mitigation. Prostitutes and junkies went missing all the time – sometimes with tragic results, but far more often than not, they'd simply moved on, or were having a stint in hospital, or had simply lost touch with their families and so-called friends. As such, they were never a top priority with investigators.

'But we're very thorough in the CRT, and as Wendy has said, DI Greene is an extremely competent investigator. We just have a few questions we need to ask you,' he began gently.

Over in his seat by the fireplace, Jimmy saw Richard Tyde-Harris stiffen with tension. His wife, however, didn't react at all, and Jimmy supposed that whatever cold and distant place she now inhabited left no room for such emotions as anxiety or dread.

'So, tell us all you can about your daughter,' Jimmy Jessop said carefully.

As Wendy and Jimmy were interviewing one set of grieving parents about their missing daughter, Hillary drove from Middleton Cheney to the more southerly boundary of the county to talk to another grieving parent in the small market town of Wantage.

But unlike the baroque, spooky splendour of the Tyde-Harris residence, Diana Allen lived in a cramped, terraced housing association residence overlooking a rather dispiriting street of shops, industrial units, and a county council car park. When she answered Hillary's knock, she was wearing a puce-pink, fleecy jogging outfit, with pink and white trainers, and was busily smoking a cigarette. Her fingers were stained yellow with the nicotine, and her long, brown hair was fast turning grey. Her small brown eyes looked slightly myopic, making Hillary wonder if she wouldn't be better off with glasses.

But perhaps a trip to the opticians was beyond her budget right then.

'Yes? Sorry, luv, if you've come about the dog barking, I told her next door ...' She began to point, with her cigarette to the house next door, 'that he's just excitable....'

Hillary produced her ID and Diana Allen paled slightly.

'Bloody hell, he's only a Jack Russell, not a Doberman. He don't make that much noise, they've got to stick the roz ... They didn't have to call you lot in.'

'This isn't about a nuisance call, Mrs Allen.'

'Thompson. I ain't been Mrs Allen in years, luv.'

'Sorry, of course. My fault,' Hillary said, and meant it. She'd meant to re-read Lydia Clare Allen's case file in the car after parking up, but she'd forgotten to. She was still pondering her grave doubts about Jasmine Sudbury when she should have been concentrating on the job in hand. Now she remembered that her second missing girl's mother had remarried when Lydia was about to become a teenager.

'That's all right. I don't mind, only Trev Allen was a bit of a bastard. Used to knock me about, see, so I like to forget that I was ever called that.'

'I'm sorry. Can I come in for a quick chat, Mrs Thompson?'

'What's this about then, if it's not about our Chester?' she asked warily.

For a brief moment, Hillary Greene wondered if she really was losing her marbles, since she had no idea who Chester was, then realized that the woman must still be talking about her noisy canine.

'It's about your daughter, Lydia Clare, Mrs Thompson,' she began, then could have kicked herself as the other woman went as white as milk and began to sway alarmingly on the doorstep. She took a staggering step to the side and leaned heavily against the doorframe.

'You've found the poor mare, then? She's dead, isn't she?' she wailed. 'I always knew it. Where…? When…?'

'No, Mrs Thompson, it's nothing like that,' Hillary quickly reassured her, and stepping forward, helped the other woman down a slightly dirty hallway and into an equally dirty kitchen. There she sat her down and made her a cup of tea, as well as a mug of instant coffee for herself, as she explained who she was, and what she was doing there.

Five minutes later, Diana Thompson had a bit more colour in her cheeks, and was industriously puffing away on her third cigarette of the encounter. Her tea went largely ignored.

'So, you haven't found her body then? Hell, I don't know whether to be glad about that, or cry.'

Hillary regarded the woman opposite her thoughtfully. They were sitting around a small Formica-topped table that was peeling at the edges, with an excitable Jack Russell terrier cross, barking around their ankles.

'You're sure in your own mind that Lydia is dead then, Mrs Thompson?' she asked quietly.

The other woman grimaced, shouted at the dog to shut up – which it didn't – and then sighed heavily.

'Yeah, course she is,' she said fatalistically. 'I know my Lyd. She was a good girl. She wouldn't have left me hanging this long, even if she was mad with … She would know I'd be going out of my head with worry, and she wouldn't want to think of me suffering, like. She was soft, like that. Oh, I know what they all say about her round here,' she added, with a bitter glance out of the window at the street outside, 'but she had a good heart, my Lyd. Too good, if you ask me. People took advantage of her. Not that anyone would admit it. No, their precious boys and menfolk are all saints,' she snorted bitterly, and took a vehement drag on her cigarette.

Hillary nodded. She didn't have to ask what Diana meant. She could already see it all. Lydia Clare Allen, according to her file, had been a pretty girl. Originally with long brown hair like her mother's, she'd dyed it blonde. It spoke of a girl who relied on her looks to get what she wanted. Not particularly bright at school, a girl who looked to men to fulfil her dreams. And of course, such a girl would soon earn a reputation, and would not be looked upon kindly, especially by wives and mothers who found their menfolk flocking around the honey pot like so many randy bees.

'I understand you reported her missing when she didn't come home for Christmas. That would be Christmas of 2012?' Hillary tactfully changed the subject.

'Yes. She was supposed to come home Christmas Eve and stay till Boxing Day. *He* was going up north to see his family that year, so I invited her to spend a few days with me. Stop me being lonely, like. My other girl, Shirl, she has kids of her own, and so had her hands full. And I didn't want to be alone.'

Hillary nodded, picking out the relevant bit of information. 'You say "he" was going up north. This would be…?'

'Danny,' Diana said shortly. 'My better half.'

'I take it he and Lydia didn't get on?'

Diana grunted a grim little laugh. 'Like chalk and cheese them two. Trouble was, Lyd had always been a bit of a daddy's girl. And she had always been Trev's favourite of the two. So she took it bad when I'd finally had enough of the beatings and kicked the bastard out. I threatened to have him put away if he didn't leave us alone. Anyway, when I met Danny later, Lydia was never going to take to him, was she, the man who took her daddy's place?'

She shrugged, stubbed out the cigarette and lit another one. 'To give him his due, he tried hard with her, at first. Danny, I mean. But let's face it, you can't really expect a bloke to put up with the constant cheek and backchat for very long, can you? And Lyd was a stubborn little tyke. Once she got something into her head, she wouldn't let it go. She was only twelve, but she'd decided she was going to hate Danny, and so she did.'

She sighed heavily and stared out of the grimy window. A kind of weary drizzle had started outside and fitted the mood in the room perfectly.

'Is that why she left home when she was just sixteen?' Hillary probed delicately.

'Yeah. Course. The moment she could leave school and get a job, she was off. For the bright lights of bloody Oxford! I ask you!' Diana laughed harshly. 'Still, at least it wasn't London,' she said bleakly. 'I remember thinking, at the time, how glad I was that it *wasn't* London. That's where girls always run off to, innit? But Oxford's just up the road by comparison, right? So I thought she'd be safer there, somehow. Being closer.' Again the woman gave a harsh bark of laughter. 'And look how wrong I was about that.' Again she took a vehement draw on her cigarette, as if she couldn't get the nicotine into her system fast enough.

Hillary stirred her mug of instant coffee and fought back the urge to cough and wave the cigarette fumes out of her face. Then she said, 'How did Danny react to her leaving home?'

Diana shrugged one puce-pink shoulder negligently. 'Good riddance to bad rubbish, I expect. Not that he said so. But I could tell ... and to be fair, the atmosphere in the house did get better after that. I mean, when you live in a small place like this and two of you are always at loggerheads and nit picking over every little thing ... Well, it was a relief to me, too. Not that she was gone, you understand? I missed her like crazy.'

'Yes. But not to have the constant tension must have been an improvement,' Hillary said.

'It were wonderful, to be honest,' the girl's mother admitted guiltily. 'But I still missed her, like I said. She was always bright and sunny with me. She was the sort of kid who always saw the bright side of things, know what I mean? Even coming from round here, with nothing to look forward to. She always thought things were gonna get better.'

'She was an optimist?'

'Yeah, that's it. Optimist. That was my Lyd. She was gonna meet Mr Right, who would take her off to the Ritz or something. That was her dream – like in one of those James Bond films, you know, where this beautiful bird steps out of a fancy sports car and goes into some posh place.'

For a moment, Hillary had a fleeting vision of Jasmine Sudbury, being escorted by her handsome stepbrother onto the deck of a yacht about to sail the Mediterranean, and abruptly shook it off. But the eerie meeting, even if only in her own mind, of two lost, pretty, young girls, left her feeling vaguely uneasy and slightly dizzy. One who'd been given the dream, and thrown it all away. And one who would probably have sold her soul to visit a casino in Monte Carlo. And both of them had ended up working the streets.

Hillary sighed and forced her mind to focus. 'Lydia got a job in Oxford, I understand? She was sharing a flat with some other girls?'

'Yeah. A flat. Right.' Diana echoed dryly. 'More like a doss house. I only went there once – a gloomy old place that was empty and about to be made into flats or something. Big place, dank and water damaged. Peeling wallpaper. They were obviously just squatting there before the builders could throw them out, but Lyd showed me to "her" room, pleased as punch she was by these big sash-window things and a view of some toffee-nosed college or other. All she had was an old mattress on the floor and her clothes hung from some nicked rail-rack from Debenhams.' One puce-pink shoulder shrugged again. 'But she was pleased with her life. Said she was living in Oxford with the vibe and the buzz. I can see her now – wearing a white dress with pale blue flowers. She looked pretty as a picture. She told me that Oxford was full of rich, posh boys, and that all she had to do was nab one for herself. She'd got this part-time job in a coffee shop, waitressing, washing dishes, whatever. She seemed to think that some Brad Pitt lookalike was going to wander in any moment and order a café latte and take one look at her and swoon at her feet. Take her home to meet Mummy and Daddy in some Sloane-Ranger house in Chelsea or on their country estate in the Berkshire Downs.'

She shook her head and gave another bark of laughter. 'What could I say?' she appealed to Hillary, waving her cigarette helplessly in the air. 'I couldn't tell the dozy mare that life wasn't like that, could I? 'Sides, why should I? She was sixteen, pretty, and living away from home for the first time in the city. I was glad she was happy. I was glad she was a … what did you call her?'

'Optimist.'

'Yeah. Right. Optimist. Why not? What was to keep her here, in this place, anyway?' she added bitterly, looking across at the blacked-out façade of the betting shop opposite, where an old man had just entered, no doubt intent on blowing his pension.

'And who knows. If she'd had just the littlest bit of luck, something nice might have happened to her.' Diana Thompson sighed wistfully, and then shook her head, as if sensing the extent of her folly.

'Can you give me a list of her friends, Mrs Thompson?' Hillary broke the silence gently.

'Why? What for? The friends she had here are all either married or have moved away, or still living at home with their parents 'cause they can't afford a place of their own. They won't know nothing about anything. They lost touch with her when she left. And as for her so-called friends in Oxford …'

Diana Thompson grimaced.

'Well. You know what they led her into. Lyd was a good girl, before she left home. Yeah, boys had been paying her attention since she hit puberty, but she was still a good girl. Didn't drink, neither, not like she got to doing later. Or any of that other stuff.'

Hillary decided there was no point pressing her on the 'other stuff'. Why rub salt into the wound?

'Besides, I only ever met that one cow – her so-called flat-mate. And she was no friend of Lyd's, I can tell you that. That Chinese bitch,' she added tartly.

Hillary ignored the racial slur, guessing from her tone of voice that Diana's antagonism came from something more personal.

'You're referring to Sasha Yoo?'

In Lydia's file it had been noted that, at the time of her disappearance, she'd been living in one of Medcalfe's many properties. A between-the-wars terrace that had been converted into four tiny flats, she had been sharing the top floor flat with another girl in Medcalfe's stable.

'Yeah. Her. You want to find out what happened to my Lyd, you should talk to her. She hated Lyd. I could tell, even though I only met her the once,' Diana Thompson spat. 'I'd gone to Oxford one summer for the sales, and me and Lyd met up at one of the open air cafés near the old bus depot. We were having this lovely cream tea, for a treat like, and then Lyd's face sort of dropped and I turned and saw this girl coming towards us. All smiles and poison, that one. Pretended it was a coincidence that they'd met, and all that, but all the while she's angling for Lyd to introduce us. So she does, and I learn she's the flatmate.

I could tell that the tall, skinny cow was looking down her nose at us, laughing behind my back and such.'

She paused, then flushed slightly, as if aware that she was losing her temper.

'Sorry. I dunno why I'm going on about her. It isn't as if what she thought about us mattered, is it? She was just another pro.' Then she suddenly pinched her mouth shut, as if realizing what that said about her own daughter.

Hillary tactfully steered the conversation into a different vein. 'Why do you think she might have had anything to do with your daughter disappearing, Mrs Thompson?' she asked briskly, careful to keep her voice professional and crisp.

Diana sighed heavily and finally took a sip of tea from her cup. 'Oh, I don't know. I'm not saying that she would have hurt Lyd. Or maybe she would. I don't know. She was just … vicious, you know? Oh, she was beautiful, and like I said all smiles. But there was something about her that gave me the creeps.'

She stubbed out her cigarette and rubbed her hands restlessly along the tops of her legs. 'And I don't think the coppers at the time talked to her properly. Not leaned on her like. Let's just say that I wouldn't be at all surprised if it turned out that she knew something, but kept quiet about it. She would have looked out for number one, let me tell you. She wouldn't have given a damn about what might have happened to Lyd.'

'I'll be certain to check that out,' Hillary said gravely, and when the other woman raised her tear-darkened brown eyes to look at her doubtfully, said flatly, 'and believe me, Mrs Thompson, I'll talk to her properly. And if I think she knows something, we'll find out what it is. The Crime Review Team will do our best to find out what happened to your daughter.'

For a moment, Diana Thompson's lips wobbled, as if she was going to cry, but then she looked away again, back out of the grimy window, to the grimy street outside, and simply nodded.

'Good,' was all she said. Then lit herself another fag.

Under the table, the dog began to bark again.

Once Hillary was back in the driving seat of her car, and yet again trying to coax her car's engine to turn over, she knew that she would have to talk to Daniel Thompson at some point.

Just because Lydia had been one of Medcalfe's girls, and had probably come to grief at the hands of some punter, didn't mean that a hostile stepfather could be overlooked.

But not everyone on her team was at that moment engaged in the heart-breaking business of trying to reassure the parents of missing girls that their children hadn't been forgotten.

Jake Barnes was too busy trying to convince himself that he wasn't scared. And he was only partially succeeding.

He, Steven Crayle and his new boss were at that moment seated around Rollo's desk, coming up with the next step in their plan to coax Darren Chivnor into taking their bait. And the more he thought about the moment that he would have to come face to face with the knife-wielding thug again, the more Jake's heart rate accelerated uncomfortably.

He could still see in his mind's eye that cold, dark toilet block in the park and the wicked flash of the blade that Darren Chivnor had seemed to produce out of nowhere. He still had nightmares about it – nights when he'd wake up with the sensation that he'd been running for his life, a cold sweat running down his spine, his conscious mind not quite able to recall the dream that had awoken him.

What if he bottled it? What if, after all his big talk about what he'd do to find Jas, when the time came to play Chivnor, he messed it all up?

And then, into this frenzy of self-doubt, one word his bosses were saying seemed to break through the paralyzing cold fist clenched around his stomach and made him blink in surprise. Almost, in fact, made him want to laugh out loud.

'Library?' he repeated, staring at Rollo Sale blankly. 'You

want us to meet in the *library?'*

But it was Steven who spoke. 'When you've had some time to think about it, Jake, you'll realize that it's ideal. Chivnor will know, after your last meeting, that you'll want to meet in a public place, somewhere that you'll feel much safer. And for his part, he'll want that meeting place to be somewhere where he can be pretty sure that he won't run into any of his fellow gang members, or anyone else in his life. On the streets or in cafés or bars he might run the risk of one of his string of girls seeing you, or a dealer, or one of Dale's runners. But the last place any of them will be is in the Central Library in the middle of the day.'

Jake took a long slow breath. The Central Library was Oxford's big public library at the entrance to the Westgate Shopping Centre, which in itself was soon to be torn down.

'Well, that's for sure,' Jake heard himself say faintly. 'But won't it … I mean, could we actually *talk* there? You know, without being conspicuous to others?'

'They don't have big signs saying "silence" anymore, Jake,' Rollo said patiently, but hiding a grin. Secretly he wondered if the young man in front of him had ever set foot in a public library in his life. Why would he? Everyone now seemed to get their information from the internet. 'Half the customers in libraries nowadays are using the computer anyway, not reading a book. There won't be any beady-eyed, middle-aged, battleaxe librarians to come charging over to you with her finger pressed against her lips and threatening to throw you out on your ear if you don't stop talking.'

'Besides, we've already chosen the spot that we want,' Steven told him crisply. 'On the second floor, in the general fiction section at one of the tables near a tall stand of hardback books. Don't worry, we'll show you exactly where we want you to set up, well in advance of the meet. And we want you already seated, with your back to the stand, when Chivnor shows up.'

'We'll have two beefy constables in plain clothes nearby, lolling about in the sports section. Don't worry – they'll look just like students, probably rowers or rugby jocks. Darren won't clock them,' Rollo assured him.

'More importantly, we're going to have a mike and a tiny hidden camera with live feed set up in the books behind you. A high-resolution, state of the art affair that's coming out of my new unit's budget,' Steven picked up the lead briskly. 'Both Hillary and I will be in an office nearby, watching everything. The sound and picture quality, I've been told, is so fine that it'll be almost as good as if we were right there, sitting next to you. And we'll be in direct contact with the undercover officers watching you, and if we think that anything looks dodgy, anything at all, I'll have them move in at once,' he added reassuringly. 'Don't worry – Chivnor won't get the chance to go waving his knife around again.'

'Besides, he'll know he'll get caught on the library's CCTV if he does,' Rollo said.

'It'll be as safe as having cream tea with your granny,' Steven added.

Jake Barnes fought back a grin. Right. Did he look as if he was born yesterday? Even so, he felt a lot of his fear and tension drain away. More, he had to admit, because he knew that Hillary Greene would be supervising the whole thing, than because of the presence of his bodyguards. He'd trust her judgement any day – and knowing she'd be watching gave him more confidence that he might just be able to pull this thing off.

'OK,' he said, taking a deep breath. 'When do I contact him?'

'Nothing wrong with the present,' Rollo Sale said cheerfully.

Jake swallowed hard. 'OK. What do I say?'

'Just tell him where you want to meet. Press him for the day after tomorrow, at 2.30p.m. If he can't make that, make it next Monday morning, at 10,' Crayle instructed. 'These times are the most convenient for the library staff. Only a few of them will know what's going on, and incidentally, one of the librarians at the desk will be another constable in plain clothes.'

Jake nodded.

'Tell Darren that you won't have any money on you this time. He'll be expecting you to be careful, so that won't anger him. In fact, it's good, because you want to keep him thinking that he's in control of the situation, so acting as he expects you to act will help settle his nerves,' Steven explained.

His nerves, Jake thought, fighting the urge to laugh hysterically. Instead he took a deep breath. 'Right,' he said nervously, and reached for his phone.

With a last glance at his two watching bosses, he lifted it out and began to dial Darren Chivnor's number.

In the communal office down the corridor, Hillary Greene was back and listening to Wendy and Jimmy's report of their interview with the Tyde-Harrises.

'I swear, guv, you should have seen her,' Wendy was saying. Her voice was a mixture of anger, sadness and pity. 'She was skin and bone. She looked more dead than alive.'

Hillary glanced across at Jimmy to see if the goth was exaggerating – a not unheard of occurrence – but the old man was nodding sagely.

'One of the walking wounded, guv,' he told her. 'Rebecca was their only child. And you could tell from all the photographs they had of her, that she was their pride and joy.'

Wendy sighed. 'They brought out the photo album when we started to ask about her. Baby photographs,' Wendy sighed, 'the professional sort, you know, on a rug, gurgling around a dummy. Loads as a little girl, dressed for parties and doing school sports. Then more professional shots of her when she was in her teens. She was a really great-looking girl. Could have been a model, I reckon.'

Jimmy again nodded agreement with this assessment.

'They were so proud when she got into Oxford,' Wendy said, her somewhat pixie-like face puckering in sudden pain and resentment. 'You should have heard them. How were they to know that it would be there that they'd start to lose her? That it would be there where she went off the rails?'

'Did they know any of the crowd she got mixed up with?' Hillary asked, noting the anguish in the younger girl's voice. Clearly, Rebecca's mother had touched a chord with the goth.

Jimmy sighed and produced a list of names. 'We'll be talking to them all as soon as we track down their whereabouts, guv. Along with Amanda Smallwood's nearest and dearest,' he mentioned the other case they were prioritizing. 'After that, I thought we'd hit the streets and start talking to the girls and pimps themselves, before checking out the pushers and the users. But by now, Medcalfe is sure to have put the word out that they're not to co-operate with anyone asking questions.'

Hillary nodded. She knew, as well as Jimmy, that there were always pressure points you could use. And if you were lucky, you might stumble on someone too high or strung out to be cautious. Then there were those with an axe to grind, or someone so strapped for cash that they could be open to a little persuasion. On the other hand, Medcalfe ruled by fear, and the chances were high that they would probably end up with nothing at all.

But she had no need to say as much to Jimmy, and Wendy was a bright girl. She'd soon learn.

'Oh, while you're doing that, can you add my girl to the list, too? Lydia Clare Allen. There's no point in our both covering the same ground.' Besides, rank had its privileges and it had been a long time since she'd had to pound the beat on what was almost certain to be a fruitless exercise.

'No problem, guv,' Jimmy said with a knowing grin. 'Wendy, be a luv and go and get us some coffees, would you?'

'What did your last slave die of?' the goth shot back

automatically, but she was already halfway out of the door and amenably heading towards the main lab, where the majority of the technical staff hung out, and where there was a coffee maker.

When he was sure she was out of earshot, Jimmy shifted uncomfortably in his seat, hiding a wince at the jabbing pain in his lower spine.

'She really feels sorry for Rebecca's mother, guv,' he said unnecessarily. 'And I think she's beginning to empathize with the women in these cases, too.'

'That's no bad thing,' Hillary said. 'Compassion's fine, but only so long as it doesn't overwhelm her. You'd better keep a close eye on her when you start hitting the streets. She isn't as tough or knowing as she likes to make out.'

'Guv,' Jimmy agreed. Then, in an abrupt change of topic, said, 'So what do you make of our new Super then? I noticed DCS Crayle is already starting to move his stuff out of the office, so it won't be long before we're taking our orders strictly from Rollo.'

Hillary blinked and then forced herself to shrug. Of course, she'd always known that by the end of the week, Steven would officially be gone and working at St Aldates. With her help he'd already started recruiting his team, and, if this thing with Chivnor worked out, he might find himself leading a major investigation right away.

He and his new team would need to be on their toes if they were to nail as cunning a predator as Dale Medcalfe, which meant that he sure as hell wouldn't have any spare time to see how the CRT was doing under new management. He probably wouldn't have much time for his private life, either, for the next six months or so.

Although she had known his departure was inevitable – as well as imminent – it was only now that the thought of no longer working for Steven suddenly hit her.

And a day that had already left her feeling depressed seemed to nosedive even further. For a moment, she felt her shoulders sag.

Then she gave a mental shrug.

'Rollo seems all right,' she said cautiously. 'So far, I can't see any major trouble looming. You sniff anything you don't like?' she asked curiously.

Jimmy smiled. 'Not really, guv. He seems a nice enough bloke. Not too much experience with murder cases, but then he's mainly an administrator, isn't he?'

'And as such, let's hope, not about to get under our feet too much.' Hillary grinned, then glanced at her watch. 'Well, you might as well call it a day. I'm just going to pop along and see what Steven and Rollo have set up, regarding this Chivnor thing. And I wouldn't be surprised if Jake isn't in need of a little encouraging pep talk as well. See you tomorrow.'

'Yes, guv.'

She walked to the door then paused in the entranceway and looked over her shoulder at him. 'Oh, and Jimmy?'

'Yes, guv?'

'How long do you want me to go on pretending that I haven't noticed your back's killing you?'

Jimmy Jessop blinked at her, then slowly smiled. He might have known. Nothing got past his guv'nor's eagle eyes. 'A bit longer if you don't mind, guv.'

Hillary nodded. 'OK. But get yourself to a quack sooner rather than later, yeah?' she advised him. 'You need a diagnosis and some proper painkillers wouldn't hurt. If you'll pardon the expression.'

Jimmy grinned. 'I'll put my name down on the waiting list for an appointment as soon as I can get through to an actual live person and not a recording,' Jimmy promised. 'And by the time I've done that, and got an appointment, had the appointment cancelled once or twice, and finally got to see some poor over-worked sod who probably can't speak English, my back pain will be gone. You just wait and see.'

'Isn't modern medicine marvellous?' Hillary Greene said cheerfully.

CHAPTER FIVE

I T WAS FULLY DARK by the time Hillary parked Puff in the car park of The Boat pub, and locked up. Once past the lighting provided by that establishment, she switched on her torch to walk the hundred yards or so up the narrow towpath where her narrowboat, *The Mollern*, was moored.

On a freezing, late November night, most of the wildlife was safely nestled in for the long duration of darkness, but she heard something rustle distinctly in some dead bulrushes on the far side of the canal as she moved past. Probably a moorhen, she thought, or a ubiquitous mallard. The familiar – and oddly comforting – dank, rich smell of canal water was being swept her way along with the icy breeze, and above her head, a waxing moon cast a faint silver sheen over the darkened furrows of the ploughed fields opposite.

As she reached the grey, white and gold-painted narrowboat that had been her home for so long, she felt a pang of regret that soon her homecoming would be more prosaic than this. Steven's driveway was big enough for two cars, and the front door would be only a matter of a few steps away. She sighed as she carefully stepped onto the back of her boat, and then reminded herself that, on a cold, wet, windy night, she might very well be glad of that.

Refusing to let the gloomy mood that had beset her all day

get the better of her, she went inside, shrugged off her coat and made her way to the tiny galley, tuning in the radio to a sixties station, and singing along to The Hollies. Steven should be back in a couple of hours, and she had a steak to grill, and potatoes to bake.

And after that, well, who knew?

The next morning, she was up and dressed by nine. Steven had been gone for at least two hours by that point, but instead of heading into the office, she consulted her notes instead, and then headed directly into Oxford.

After all, her team didn't need her to stand over them, watching to see that they did their jobs properly, and she wanted to catch some of Jasmine Sudbury's friends before word got around that her case had been reopened. Being forewarned meant being forearmed, and she wanted to get as much done as possible before the grapevine did its worst.

According to Jake's parents, Jasmine's best friend from her school days, 'before she started to go off the rails', as they'd put it was a girl by the name of Cathy Underhill, now Mrs Cathy Pryce, who managed a charity shop in Summertown.

Hillary found the shop easily enough in the upmarket Oxford suburb, but quickly discovered that a parking space couldn't be had for love or money – no great surprise in Oxford. Eventually she parked in a side street where the double-yellow lines had worn so thin they'd become well nigh invisible. Also the fallen autumn leaves covered any evidence that she might be illegally parked – OK, *was* illegally parked. But she felt confident enough to risk it. Mind you, before she walked away, she took several photographs of her car and the innocent-looking roadside with her mobile phone camera, just for a bit of insurance. If she should return to find a parking ticket, she might feel bloody-minded enough to challenge it in court, just for the satisfaction of giving the traffic wardens – and the city council – something to chew over.

In the charity shop, one old woman was sorting assiduously through the winter coats on one rack, and a tall, lanky student with more tattoos than body piercing was rifling through the book section. The woman behind the counter was obviously an unpaid volunteer, for when Hillary murmured discreetly in her ear that she needed a word with the manager, she was shown behind a curtained alcove to where a set of narrow, twisting steps lead up to a tiny top-floor office.

Cathy Pryce was a big-boned, rather fleshy woman with an astonishingly pretty face, who looked surprised to find someone from the police service tapping on her door. Once she'd explained her mission, however, her big china blue eyes became rather pensive, and as she watched Hillary take the seat she'd offered her, began to play somewhat distractedly with one of her locks of long, curly black hair.

'Jas?' Cathy said, rocking her swivelling chair back and forth a shade restively. 'Good grief, I haven't thought of Jas in years.' Then she flushed guiltily. 'Sorry. I should have, I suppose. I mean, I heard that she'd dropped out of sight, and all that, and that never bodes well, does it? But I hadn't really ever thought of her as missing. Not, you know, really *missing*. As in ... well, that she might have run into serious trouble.'

The office was tiny and cramped, overflowing with unsold stock and filing cabinets, with barely room to contain the single desk and two chairs that comprised the furniture. Cathy was dressed in thick, misshapen but warm-looking black woollen trousers and an outsize, faded grey sweatshirt bearing the name of some sporting team or other. Hillary doubted that her job could pay much, and she presumed that both garments had probably been donated stock that had stubbornly refused to shift.

'Is there a reason for that?' Hillary asked mildly. And when the younger woman looked at her, clearly puzzled, clarified, 'For your not being really worried about her, I mean?'

'Oh. Right. Because she was the sort of girl who was always well able to look after herself, I suppose.' Cathy paused then gave a shrug and a half smile. 'When I heard that she hadn't been seen around for some time, I just assumed she'd gone off to the smoke, or maybe abroad.'

'But with the lifestyle she was leading,' Hillary slipped in casually, 'you must have wondered?'

Cathy frowned, then sighed heavily. 'I know. And you're right – you hear such awful things about women in her position, being so vulnerable and all. Addicts and … well, doing the job she did. But, somehow, I just never believed that something really bad could happen to Jas. I suppose it was because Jas was always so … you know …' She spread her hands, clearly struggling for words. 'I don't quite know how to put it. She wasn't bossy, as such, but she was always the leader of the gang, type of thing. She was always someone who was more likely to get *up to* mischief, rather than become a victim of it. Like, at school, there was this group of us, yeah, six or seven altogether, and after school, we'd drift off and just do whatever it was that Jas wanted to do. Go shopping, hang out round the supermarket, see if we could scam some booze. Go to the park, smoke. Go to the gym and leer at the boys boxing and give them a hard time.' Cathy gave a laugh. 'Hell, I never realized before how reprobate teenage girls could be.'

Hillary laughed. She'd been a copper for nearly thirty years. There wasn't anything about teenage girls that she needed telling about. 'So Jas was always top dog,' she clarified.

'Yeah, that was it. Always – and not just with us. With teachers and other adults too, she had a way of … I don't know. Getting her own way. And it wasn't just because she was the prettiest of us, or had the best bling. Although she was plenty smart, she wasn't the brainiest of us, either. That would have been Jenny Buswell.' Cathy's face suddenly softened. 'I wonder what happened to Jen?'

Then she gave a quick shake of her head and looked across at Hillary wryly. 'Sorry, you want to know about Jas, right? What was I saying? Oh yeah, she was top dog all right, but mostly because she was always the one with the most vim, you know? She was always vital and full of energy and ideas. And she just … I don't know … *expected* things to go her way – and so they just seemed to. And she was by far the bravest of us. I remember once, this new shade of nail polish came out – some pop star had "designed" it or whatever. And Jas…. Well, sorry to say, she dared us to go and shoplift a bottle each from Debenhams. Of course, we all said we would and we piled on the bus into town, but we all bottled out.'

'But not Jas?' Hillary guessed.

'No,' Cathy laughed. 'Jas nicked one not just for herself, but she kept on going back until she'd nicked one for us all. She could have swiped a half a dozen all in one go, to cut down the risk, but she insisted on doing it one bottle at a time. Just to prove that she could.' She shook her head, looking suddenly sheepish. 'Sorry,' she added. 'I know you're the police and all.'

'Civilian now,' Hillary said. 'And really not in the least worried about a shoplifting incident from some dozen years ago.'

'Would it be that long ago?' Cathy obviously did a bit of a mental arithmetic, then winced. 'Where does the time go?'

'So, at school, she was a bit of a rebel?' Hillary said, keeping her firmly on track.

'Oh yeah. She was dead charismatic was Jas. We all danced attendance round her,' Cathy laughed, 'sort of competing to please her. You know, looking back, we were really sort of pathetic. Dreaming about growing up and marrying some rock star or other. Or getting to London and doing something that meant we'd be regularly flying off to New York or Milan. Becoming something "big" in the world. Didn't really matter what sort of "big" it was. For instance, Jenny wanted to be one of them women entrepreneurs who make their own millions and get on Dragon's Den. Brenda wanted to be a fashion model. She was skinny enough for it, but had buck teeth…. Sorry. Going off on a tangent again. Let's just leave it that we were all full of the usual teenage girl guff. I think we all knew, deep down, that it was just fantasy. That most of us would end up getting married, getting a regular job and paying off a mortgage and all that. But you know, I reckon most of us reckoned Jas might actually pull it off.'

'Because of her brother, you mean?'

'Who? Oh! The luscious Jake,' Cathy said, suddenly grinning wildly. 'Bloody hell, I haven't thought of the luscious Jake in years!' she said, shaking her head. Hillary's lips twitched, and she wished she could share this little gem with Wendy later. No doubt she'd have made good use of it in order to make the boy wonder's life a misery for weeks to come. But of course, she mustn't know what Jake had been up to.

'We were all in love with *him,* truly, madly, deeply! How could we not be?' Cathy swept on. 'Not only was he a dream to look at – tall, dark and handsome, and with those wonderful green eyes. Dead unusual that – green eyes. But he was also just the right age. Just older enough than us to make him seem super-cool and adult, but not so old as to be gross.'

'And, of course, he got rich,' Hillary added dryly.

Cathy laughed and clapped her hands. 'Oh hell, yes. Lucky sod, making all that money so young. Naturally, we all panted after him. But he was strictly out of bounds,' she added, giving a small sigh of regret, even now.

'Oh?'

'Oh yeah. None of us dared make even a pass at him. He was strictly Jas's property. And she'd go mad at anyone she caught trying to poach on her turf.'

'Her brother?' Hillary probed delicately. 'A bit off, that, wasn't it?'

'Oh, he was never that. I mean, not her *real* brother. I mean, her mum was married to his dad.... Or was it the other way around? No matter – they weren't related by blood. So it wasn't incest. Ugh! What a horrible thought that is!'

'So, although she moved in with Jake and his mum when she was little, and she grew up with him, she never actually thought of him as a brother?'

'Oh no. Even when we were little girls, I mean like eight or nine, going to parties, she made it clear that he was special. Her special boyfriend.'

'Ah.'

Cathy again spread her hands and laughed. 'I know. Sounds precocious, right? And she probably was. But even later, when we were all well into our teens, she always told us that she'd end up marrying him one day – that they had this agreement. And that they were only waiting for her to grow older, so as not to shock the parents. Then, once she'd left school, she'd be off, helping him spend all that cash. No wonder we were so in awe of her. And envious? Bloody hell, the green-eyed monster ate us all up.'

'So what actually happened?' Hillary asked thoughtfully. 'Where did it all go so wrong?'

'What? Oh. I dunno. Well, I do. When we hit sixteen, we all sort of ... scattered. Some of us stayed on and did our A-levels. Jen went off to a different college to do some course that would get her into uni. Brenda and the others left and got jobs. And of course, by then, Jake had already gone off to uni and simply wasn't around any more. Or worse – when he did come back, he'd either be talking about some girlfriend or other.'

'And Jas? How did she take that?'

'Jas ... I dunno. She never really talked about it. Besides, like I said, around then we all drifted apart. Jas, I think ... yeah, she left school as soon as she could, but she didn't get a job. At least not that I heard, she didn't. But then, she didn't need to, right?

Not with money in the family, and I dare say being a lady of leisure suited her.'

If there was any real resentment in her voice, Hillary couldn't detect it. 'And you got married, and now work here,' Hillary said with a smile. 'And Jas.... What do you think happened to her?'

Cathy sighed and began to look uneasy again. 'Well.... You know. I heard she began to get into a bit of trouble. Nothing really major at first, and I thought it was just Jas being Jas – drinking a bit too much, then experimenting with drugs and getting in with a wild crowd. By then, though, I was working in a solicitor's office. Just temping. I was a world away from all that sort of thing.'

'So you never ran into her, out and about in town?'

'No. No, I didn't. I heard.... Well, rumours. About her ... you know ... becoming a call girl. I couldn't really believe it at first.'

'Why not?' Hillary asked casually. Only her eyes, watching Cathy intently, gave away the true depth of her interest in the younger girl's reply.

'Well ... it just didn't seem likely somehow.' Cathy frowned then waved a hand vaguely in the air. 'I mean ... you know ... being paid for sex. It was so ... yucky. So tacky and down-market and not like Jas at all. Jas always dreamed big, you know? The biggest of us all. And she had a way of getting what she wanted, like I said before. Of being in charge. And being a call girl.... Well, that's sort of opposite of all that, isn't it? I just couldn't imagine her doing it, you know?'

Hillary nodded. 'But drug addiction changes everything,' she said. 'Addicts will do anything for their next fix.'

Cathy paled and audibly gulped. 'Yes. I suppose it does. Oh, hell ... I really don't like to think about her like that.' She swallowed hard.

Hillary felt bad about bringing the younger woman down, but not so bad that she was about to give up her questioning.

'Did she ever approach you for money?'

'Blimey, no! And I wouldn't have had any to give her, even if she had.'

'Do you know of anyone who actually kept in touch with her, after the school years, I mean?'

'Not really. Not any of our crowd, anyway.'

Hillary sighed. 'Did you ever notice her around town, with a man, perhaps?'

'No. But then, I wouldn't, would I?' Cathy gave a small sad smile. 'I mean, Jas was the type to be at the best nightclubs, bars, restaurants, those sorts of places. I was just a struggling secretary. And later … well, if she really did fall that low…. I suppose the places she ended up were….' Cathy again went pale. 'Well, they weren't the places I would have even known about.'

'OK, fair enough,' Hillary conceded. 'Did you ever hear any-thing on the grapevine about her? Anything you think I should know?'

Cathy smiled and looked around her at the tiny office. 'What grapevine? My world consists of my husband, a baby we're trying to conceive, and our little rented maisonette in Headington. I'd be the last to know anything.'

Hillary smiled, thanked her, and left.

She was pleased to note that the VW's windscreen was free of any nasty, official little notices as she got behind the wheel to head off to the next of Jas Sudbury's friends. Not a schoolmate this time but another good-time girl whom Rosemary, Jake's mother, had put her on to.

In the early days, Cheryl Murray had often been seen at many of those nightclubs, bars and fancy restaurants that Cathy had mentioned, and sometimes in the company of Jas and the rest of the crowd who tended to go anywhere there were drugs and money.

According to Jake, who'd done the bulk of the computer

work in tracing his sister's friends' current whereabouts, Cheryl had eventually married a retired Costa Con. She now spent her time city hopping her way across Europe, shopping, gambling and partying, and was currently visiting the UK in order to attend her little sister's wedding at the weekend. And the sister of the bride was forking out for a top London hotel reception for friends and family. And was currently booked in at the penthouse there.

So it was time to do a little gate crashing, and see just what Cheryl could remember of the good old days.

Whilst Hillary Greene headed for the bright lights and the pomp and circumstance of one of London's finest hotels, Wendy and Jimmy were in Oxford, trawling down a side street at the back of a bus station, chasing shadows.

And as they did this, in another part of the city, Darren Chivnor was sitting in his parked car and thinking furiously about public libraries, money, and his boss's bad moods.

He'd just dropped off a member of minor foreign royalty at one of Dale's best cat houses and was vaguely watching the man's bodyguard, who was walking around the grounds of the large desirable residence and trying to look like he might be a gardener. Given the dreary day, the dormant state of much of the shrubbery, and the ill-fitting business suit that did little to disguise the bulge of the concealed firearm under his armpit, he wasn't having much success.

But that was his problem.

Darren had problems of his own.

It had been another of Dale Medcalfe's enforcers who'd first alerted Darren to the fact that the old Bill were doing a review of missing women, since Darren hadn't heard it on the local television news bulletin, and rarely read the local papers. He tended to like the peace and quiet when he was driving around in his motor, since dealing with upset and uppity whores all day gave him a pain, so the radio also tended to stay off. Besides, the whine of the DJs as well as people wheedling and whining, and trying to explain to him why they hadn't made this payment or that, gave him earache.

But the big boss *had* been paying attention, and it hadn't taken long for the word to filter down from the top. Nobody was to talk about the missing women and it was Darren's job, along with a few others, to make sure that everyone knew it. Which was why he was going to have to spend the rest of the day making sure that everyone got the message.

All of which left Darren feeling decidedly antsy. Dale, always paranoid and ever vigilant, was going to be even more alert until he was sure that any danger was long past.

So he was going to have to be very careful indeed.

Of course, it could just be a coincidence that Thames Valley had announced that they were looking into their old missing persons case files just after Barnes had made contact with him. And part of him could almost believe it. After all, Jake Barnes was only a civilian, and shouldn't have the clout necessary to affect policy, but then again, he was rich, and their poster boy for the Big Society. If he said jump, he couldn't see the coppers saying no.

So when he'd got the call from Barnes asking to meet in the Central Library, of all places, he'd almost told the bastard to sod off. Yeah, he was curious and he wanted that big pay-off. After the sweetener in cash that he'd already been given, plus the real bonus of that good-quality fake ID, he could almost taste Jake Barnes's promised reward. The thought of it was tantalizing. After all, a cool million was on offer. The thought of it made his palms itch.

Then again, a fortune was no good to you if you weren't alive to spend it. And Dale had made it clear – he didn't want any of the girls or other assorted pond life talking to the coppers about the women who'd disappeared. Not that there had been that many – Dale and the rest of his fellow gang members ran a tight ship. But accidents happened. Drugs got misused. Some Johns got a bit too slap-happy.

And bodies had to get buried deep, out in the woods, where nobody would find them.

If only Darren didn't have such a nasty, sinking suspicion that Jake Barnes was going to want to know where to find one of them, in return for all that cash.

And if that was so, then things could get very tricky indeed. Because very few people knew where any of the bodies were buried – and Darren himself only knew of two. And Dale was going to take it very hard – very hard indeed – if the coppers started digging up even one of his previously buried little secrets.

The heat would be on – a bloody forest-fire worth's of heat.

Of course, there might be ways around even that, Darren thought now, watching out of his rear-view mirror as a traffic warden strolled casually past the entrance to the street, but kept on walking.

He could still take the millionaire's money and give him what he wanted, but he'd have to lie low and carry on working for Dale for a good long while before he and Lisa could eventually move away without casting suspicion on themselves. Maybe years. And he'd have to come up with some good cover story for his leaving, even then.

It was risky. Very risky. And Dale wasn't at all certain that he wanted to take that risk. If anything happened to Lisa, or his mum and brothers....

So he'd go to the meeting and find out just what it was that Barnes wanted. What did he have to lose in that? He could always say no. And he might be worrying about nothing. Barnes might be after something altogether different, something that he could safely deliver without bringing down the wrath of his boss.

But if it turned out that he did want to know about one of Dale's buried secrets.... Well, he would have to think very carefully about that.

Of course, by far the best course would be to wangle the cash off him first somehow before giving him whatever it was that he wanted, and then turn Barnes into a buried secret of his own. That way, he wouldn't have to worry about crossing Dale and he and Lisa could just move quietly abroad without any hassle.

But that probably wouldn't be easy. Barnes didn't accumulate all that wealth by being stupid.

Darren sighed as he spotted the traffic warden making his way down the street from the opposite direction now, and started up his motor, nodded across at the patrolling bodyguard, and pulled away.

At least he wouldn't be kept on tenterhooks for long. The meeting with Barnes was all set for tomorrow afternoon. In the bloody library! Darren snorted with mirth at the thought of it, and cheerfully waved to the traffic warden as he passed by.

The poor old sod looked wet and cold and miserable. As well he might. For all that the Christmas lights and decorations were already beginning to appear in the shops, there was very little cheer to be had in an English winter. And the thought of living abroad in the sun with Lisa, and lounging around a big blue swimming pool, felt so good it almost hurt.

'I think I know that girl,' Wendy said in an appalled little voice, as they stepped into a dingy little café not far from Gloucester Green bus station. 'I do. Bloody hell – I went to school with her!' she hissed at Jimmy. She sounded shocked, scandalized, fascinated and upset all at the same time.

Jimmy, whose feet were throbbing, merely grunted. They'd been doing the rounds for nearly four hours now, and his back was killing him. Hillary was right – he was going to have to go to the quacks. Ignoring it wasn't working – whatever the problem was, it clearly wasn't going to go away on its own. He'd have to take another couple of aspirin with his cuppa.

He glanced around the place with a jaundiced eye, automatically clocking the slim pickings. Already a so-called rag-and-bone merchant had spotted him and was sidling away from his table and making for the door. His speciality, Jimmy remembered from the old days, was fleecing the elderly of their knick-knacks, paying peanuts, and flogging them at antique markets for eye-watering prices. But Jimmy wasn't interested in him. He was on the hunt for Medcalfe's people.

But so far today, and just as predicted, nobody knew anything about anything. They hadn't heard, seen, overheard or guessed anything, about anyone. For all the pathetic women they'd talked to, their aggressive pimps, sad little junkies and just ordinary members of the public who'd happened to be in the wrong place at the wrong time, nobody was willing to say anything. Which meant the word was already out.

But as with anything, of course, there had been a few very minor and probably insignificant exceptions – a girl so addled on drugs that she'd obviously forgotten she was supposed to be deaf, dumb and blind, had mentioned something about one of Hillary's cases – the Lydia Allen girl. Nothing at all helpful, but he'd nevertheless pass it on to the guv'nor when he could. And one pimp, a newcomer and probably not yet sufficiently plugged in to know how truly terrified he should be of Dale Medcalfe, had been a bit too loose with his lips and confirmed that Lydia Allen had had a rep for liking the student boys.

Which, again, was hardly news.

But apart from that, they had nothing at all to show for all their hard work. Now he'd come to the café more in order to get a hot cup of tea and rest his bones for a bit, as much as because he knew that some of the more downtrodden, down-market trade liked to use this spot as a vantage point. Many of the girls sat in the windows and watched the London buses coming in, on the eagle-eyed lookout for a middle-aged businessman down for a conference, and maybe willing to play away.

And indeed, as he'd pushed open the door, he'd had to step briskly aside for one of them, who all but raced out after a man with a suitcase, who'd just got off a National Express coach.

That was the point at which Wendy had hissed so dramatically in his ear.

Now he looked across to where she was looking, and saw a girl who looked at least a decade older than his companion, with lanky brown hair, bruised-looking hazel eyes and the familiar, skeletal frame of the dedicated crack cocaine addict.

'That's Julie Pym. I'm sure of it,' Wendy said again. 'She was in my class for History. And French. I always thought she was going to be a chartered surveyor! We always ragged her about that. What the hell's she doing … like this?'

Jimmy, who had believed that nothing could distract him from the twin throbbing agonies that were his lower extremities and the dull ache in his back, found he was wrong. That did it all right.

'A *chartered surveyor*? Why a chartered surveyor?' he asked. It was not, in his experience, a career choice many women coveted.

'Oh, her dad was one,' Wendy said cavalierly as they stepped up to the counter and ordered two teas and a Chelsea bun for Jimmy. 'Oh no, she's seen me. What do I do?' she hissed.

Jimmy smiled and grunted. 'This isn't a tea party at Buck House, lass. No need for social embarrassment here. We go and talk to her. That's what we're here for, isn't it? See if she knew any of our missing women.'

Wendy paled, but managed to smile wanly and nod. 'Right. But … oh shit, what's *happened* to her? Last time I saw her was at our school leaving do. She'd got the grades to go to college and do a course. And I swear she was all set to get engaged to some bloke in the same company her dad worked for.'

Jimmy sighed and paid for their order. 'Well, you can always ask her about all that as well,' he said, more gently. Sometimes he forgot just how young and inexperienced his trainee actually was. 'What was her name again?'

'Julie. And I can't ask her *that*,' Wendy muttered under her breath. But it was too late. Jimmy was already heading to the table where Julie and two other girls, similarly old before their time and also as thin as blades of grass, were sitting. All three turned to look at them suspiciously.

And Wendy could see by the defiant and yet defeated look in Julie's eyes that her old school mate had also recognized her. And, in the next moment, would learn that she was working for the coppers.

She didn't quite know whether to laugh or cry. Or do both.

In the end though, as they began to talk, what Wendy Turnbull did, was start to get angry.

Very angry.

CHAPTER SIX

THE HOTEL IN BELGRAVIA was swanky, high-class and high-maintenance, which made it a perfect match for Cheryl Murray. In the lobby, a vast Christmas tree was in the process of being tastefully decorated in gold and silver. And the hand-blown glass baubles alone, Hillary had guessed, probably added up to more than her yearly stipend.

In her early thirties, but managing to look a decade younger, the wife of the now apparently retired bank robber, had long, sable brown, artfully waved hair and perfect make-up. Wearing an Italian designer label trouser suit in a stunning caramel colour, matched with a silk-shot amber blouse, she looked back at Hillary with a mixture of caution, interest and distaste.

At first, Cheryl hadn't been inclined to speak to her. No doubt entertaining the constabulary had never been particularly high on her agenda. Which, given her circumstances, was perfectly understandable. But after Hillary had approached the main desk and shown the receptionist her ID, she had finally managed to convey – through the scrupulously polite hotel employee – that she wasn't going to go away. And so, finally, Cheryl had conceded to her request for a 'friendly chat'.

Perhaps she didn't want her parents or soon-to-be-wed sister to know that the police had come calling, and was anxious to give Hillary what she wanted in order to send her on her way as quickly as possible. For, whilst marrying a very successful crook had definitely been financially advantageous, it probably also had its drawbacks. Especially when it came to trying to make sure that social occasions such as weddings, went off without any embarrassing hitches.

Which was why Hillary was now sitting in a swanky suite and sipping blissfully fine, ground and brewed coffee. And doing her best to ignore a delightful biscuit selection that the wasp-waisted woman seated opposite her was also ignoring but probably with more ease.

'So this is just about Jas, yeah?' Cheryl said cautiously, and not for the first time. Big brown eyes watched her nervously, as if suspecting a trap. It was clear that she was used to having to defend her choice of spouse, and it had taken much of Hillary's time so far in convincing her that she was not interested in her bank-robbing, thieving husband.

'Yes. We're reviewing our missing person cases, and Jasmine Sudbury is one of a number of people we're following up on,' she repeated patiently. 'I understand you used to know her, back in the day?'

At this, Cheryl gave a vague smile. Clearly she was happy enough to answer questions that were apparently innocuous, for she leaned back in the chair a bit and gave a small sigh. Her shoulders relaxed just slightly. But Hillary wasn't fooled. There was a definite air about the beautiful brunette, which spoke of someone who was used to taking care of number one. First, foremost, and always.

'Oh yeah, I knew Jas all right. We hung out at the same clubs and that for a while. Knew the same people, went to the same parties and what not. So we ran into each other often. Well, we could hardly avoid it, could we? The scene was so tiny – Oxford was always a bit of a backwater. That was why I was only there for a short while. I preferred London and left for there as soon as I could. I needed a bigger venue, you know?'

'But Jas was pretty much a fixture on the Oxford scene?'

'Oh yeah. She was having a high old time. A real party girl, was Jas. And she really liked stringing along the fellas too. You know, making them dance attendance on her? I think she liked that.' Cheryl's eyes gleamed for a moment, but whether in respect or envy, Hillary couldn't quite make up her mind. 'I always thought it was a bit of a power trip for her. You know, making men fight over her.'

'Wealthy men?'

'Oh yeah. Well, I mean, they paid for everything – the drinking, the dining, the dancing, the gambling, the … recreation.'

'Drugs?' Hillary put in.

Cheryl shrugged and smiled. 'Oh, I dare say. But I never did that sort of thing,' she said with a perfectly straight face.

'Of course not,' Hillary agreed, also keeping her own face perfectly straight. 'But Jas did?'

'Oh yeah. I could see she was really starting to get into it. I warned her, mind. Don't think I didn't,' Cheryl said, trying to look concerned, but somehow merely looking puzzled. 'I mean, I told her straight – doing a line or two at a party is one thing. But getting really hooked?' She shook her artful, lush head of hair. 'That's a mug's game. But you know some people just won't be told.'

'She thought she could handle it?'

'Oh yeah, but of course, she couldn't. Nobody can, can they? That's why I was so careful.'

Hillary could believe it. If anyone was able to look after her own skin, it was this woman.

'So Jas started to … spiral down?'

Cheryl sighed and gave a what-can-you-do shrug. 'She started mixing and matching, experimenting. Getting into all sorts of trouble.'

'She was a real wild child?'

'Oh yeah. I reckon her family really screwed her up.'

Hillary blinked at this sudden, but apparently genuine observation, and quickly hid a wince. When writing up her notes later, she was going to have to be very careful indeed to ensure that Jake didn't get access to them. The man already had enough on his plate to cope with, without an extra helping of guilt.

'Oh? What was the problem, do you think?' Hillary asked, careful to keep her voice casual. 'Were her parents too straight-laced? Trying to keep her on a short leash? Or was it the other way round and they just didn't give a damn?'

Cheryl shrugged, clearly bored by the subject already. But then, Hillary got the feeling Cheryl was quickly bored with any subject that didn't have Cheryl at the centre of it.

'Oh, I dunno,' she said crossly. 'She had a stepmum of course, and I thought at first that that might be at the back of it. I mean.' Cheryl waved a vague hand in the air, and the huge diamond ring on one of her fingers caught the overhead lighting and shot off prisms of rainbow colours. 'Who wants a stepmother? It's so naff, right? Who can be doing with it?' She paused, frowned slightly, then shrugged. 'But apparently Jas got on all right with her. From what she said, anyway.'

'It was her father who objected to her lifestyle, then? Did he ever cause her any real trouble?'

Cheryl shrugged. 'Well, he wasn't happy about it, I dare say. But I never clapped eyes on the bloke and Jas never complained about him.' Suddenly her lips twitched in what was definitely a not very nice smile. 'No, I reckon it was her brother that caused her the most angst. He was certainly the one she talked about the most.' For a moment Cheryl frowned, looking almost interested. 'None of us could never make out whether she loved him or hated him. To hear her talk he could be the greatest thing since sliced bread – you know, he made a lot of money young, apparently.' Cheryl looked briefly chagrined. 'All us girls wanted to meet him, since to hear her talk he was as gorgeous as George Clooney, but younger. Well, you can imagine what we were all like. All us young girls, anxious to hook a big fish,' she laughed. 'But Jas knew what we'd have done, so she kept him to herself. She was savvy like that. Really savvy. She wouldn't ever invite him to any of the parties we went to. But sometimes she'd bad-mouth him something rotten – said he was a liar, and a cheat and a real let-down.' Cheryl shrugged. 'But that was just Jas. She never was exactly consistent.'

'You heard what eventually happened to her?'

'What? About her going on the game, you mean? Yeah, I did. Mind you, I was in London by then. I'd just met Larry.'

But Hillary wasn't interested in her great romance with her gangster lover, and kept her firmly on track.

'Did that surprise you? Jas becoming an escort?'

'Nah, not really. You get a drug habit, you need to pay for it. How else is a girl gonna do that?'

'But her family had money,' Hillary pointed out. 'Didn't you expect them to come through for her?'

Cheryl frowned, clearly never having considered that. She thought about it for a moment, then shrugged. 'Her *brother* had money. Not her parents, so much.'

'Even so. Surely he'd have kept her in funds. From what you said, it sounds as if they were close.' From what she'd learned from Jake, Hillary knew that he'd been too wise to help his sister feed her habit. But Cheryl wouldn't have known that, and for all her unattractive, self-serving attitude, she had clearly been an observant and intelligent onlooker. And she desperately wanted to know what her take on it all had been.

Cheryl sighed. She was fidgeting about on the chair, clearly wishing that the interview was over, but Hillary wasn't in any hurry. Instead she just looked back at her, patiently waiting.

Cheryl sighed again and forced her mind to the task in hand. After a moment's reflection, she said slowly, 'You know, I don't think Jas would have been keen on that. On asking her brother for help, I mean.'

'Oh, *come* on! A junkie won't turn down any source of income if it means ensuring the next fix,' Hillary said scornfully.

'Oh yeah. I dare say. When it got really bad,' Cheryl instantly conceded. 'But in the early days, when I knew her, I got the feeling that she'd rather crawl over cut glass than ask her gorgeous, rich brother for anything. You ask me, she was a bit ...' Cheryl twirled a finger around her temple. 'You know, a bit twisted up about him.'

Hillary felt herself tense and forced herself to look casual. 'Give me an example.'

Cheryl shook her head. 'It's hard to explain. I mean, like you know they weren't really related or anything. Not by blood – and yet they grew up together like a proper brother and sister, but the look in her eye when she talked about him sometimes made me wonder what was going on in her head.'

Hillary nodded. Now she was definitely going to have to make sure she locked up her notes somewhere safe. And she'd better not keep them on a computer file, either – Jake was a little too handy with the old hacking skills for her liking. From now on, it would be hard copies only. If Jake ever got to read the sort of stuff that was being said about someone he regarded as his little sister, he'd probably need the services of a good shrink for months to come. If not years.

'She fancied him, you mean?' Hillary said bluntly.

'Oh yeah. Like crazy. Real love-hate shit, stuff like that.'

'Do you think they were an item?' Hillary asked, curious to hear an outsider's view on the siblings. She herself had no doubts that any romantic relationship between them could only have existed in Jasmine's head, but she felt the tension creeping back into her gut as she waited for Cheryl's verdict.

'Oh no. At first I thought so, but as I got to know Jas better, I changed my mind.'

Hillary discreetly let out a long slow breath of relief, and said mildly, 'She was a liar then?'

'Oh yeah. Totally – she was good at it, too,' Cheryl agreed with a casual grin. 'But it wasn't that so much. I mean, we were all liars in our own way – everyone on the scene was the same. Men lied about being married. Girls lied about not having had boob jobs done. It was just how it was. It's like we were all playing a role – which is more art than actual lying, right?'

Hillary blinked, but wisely remained silent.

'And Jas did it as well as anyone. No, it was just…. I got the feeling she was … I dunno. Too excitable. Too ambitious. Too …' Cheryl paused and then shrugged. 'I dunno. I can't really explain it. I just steered well clear of her. She was like a train wreck about to happen, you know? Fascinating to watch, in a sick kind of way. But not something you wanted to get in the way of.'

'So you weren't surprised when she went missing?'

'Until you showed up, I didn't know that she had,' Cheryl shot back. 'I was in London by then, like I said. I lost touch with the old gang.'

In other words, Hillary interpreted quickly, they were no longer of use to her, and thus were of no consequence.

'Did you know Dale Medcalfe?' Hillary asked brutally, and instantly Cheryl's face closed down. A shutter seemed to almost physically slam down behind the big beautiful brown eyes. It didn't take a genius to see that the question bothered her. A lot.

'Sure, I knew who he was. But I never had anything to do with him,' she said coldly. 'He was dangerous. I kept well out of his way. In fact, one of the reasons I wanted to get away to London was to avoid him and that gang of thugs of his. No way was I going to be recruited by him! He had a way of not taking "no" for an answer. Is that what happened to Jas? He got his paws on her? Poor cow.'

Hillary nodded. And sighed. Curiously enough, she believed Cheryl when she said she'd avoided Dale Medcalfe and his outfit. With anyone else, she might have thought that they were lying. After all, the kind of life that Cheryl had been leading back then was almost guaranteed to ensure that their paths would cross regularly. But Cheryl was clearly the sort of girl who'd had her big, brown, and savvy eyes wide open, even back then, when she was nothing more than an ambitious teenager. And she'd obviously quickly learned how to navigate the shark-infested waters without getting bitten.

Time to try a different tack. 'Was there anyone back then that Jas was particularly close to?'

'What? A boyfriend, you mean?'

'Boyfriend, sure, or any female friends?' Hillary wasn't fussy.

'Nah. Jas had a lot of men on a string, like I said, but I think with her, she was totally strung up on big brother. So that pretty much ruled out any real significant male in her life. And Jas just wasn't the kind to share with other women, you know? I mean, she was friendly enough with the girls on the scene, but she was never the type to share secrets or get all girly and BFF with anyone.'

Hillary sighed. Great. Another dead end.

'So you have no idea who she might have turned to – for a place to crash, or for someone to lend her a helping hand if she really needed it?'

'Nah. Sorry.' Cheryl Murray opened her big brown eyes extra wide. 'We just weren't that kind of crowd, you know?'

Hillary did.

Back at HQ, Wendy and Jimmy were back in the communal office and busily typing up reports on their fruitless trawl of Oxford's mean streets. Wendy, it had to be said, was faster on the keyboard than the ex-sergeant. But it was Jimmy who noticed Hillary first and looked up as she poked her head around the door.

'Hey troops, how's it going?'

Jimmy grunted. Wendy sighed.

'Like that, huh?' Hillary said with a grin.

'Oh, guv, all those poor girls,' Wendy said, leaning back in her chair and glaring at Hillary balefully. As if everything wrong with the world was all her fault. 'I never realized how … well … normal they are.'

Hillary blinked and gave Jimmy a puzzled glance. The old man grinned.

'Wendy ran into one of her old school pals, guv,' he explained succinctly.

'Ah,' Hillary said neutrally.

'Yeah. I mean, I thought girls got trapped into that sort of thing,' Wendy swept on. 'You know, they grow up in care and so don't have any support system in place to help them when they hit eighteen. And when times are hard economically, they can't get work and fall victim to sweet-talking pimps. I know as well, from what I learned at uni, that a lot of them have learning difficulties, or long-standing alcohol or substance abuse problems to begin with. I just didn't realize that they could be like … well … like …'

'You and me?' Hillary put in helpfully. 'But you, especially. Young, healthy and reasonably intelligent. And from what anyone would say is a normal, happy, working-class family home?'

The goth flushed unhappily. 'It's not that I think I'm better than anyone else,' she began, but Hillary held up a hand to ward her off.

'I understand. And I know what you mean.'

'But why can't anybody *help* them, guv?' Wendy said, sounding angry now rather than defensive. 'I've been chatting to them all day long, and none of them want to be doing what they're doing. The pimps take practically all the money off them, they can't afford to rent even a basic sort of place. And half of them are off their heads, or ill.' She shuddered suddenly and looked on the verge of tears.

Hillary regarded her steadily for a while. 'Do you want to be reassigned?' she asked quietly.

Jimmy looked back up from his typing at this, his glance going between the youngster and his boss, his old eyes curious, concerned, but assessing.

Wendy too looked up. Her mascara was so black and thick it gave her panda-like eyes, but if they were bright with tears, they slowly hardened.

'No, guv, I'm fine,' she said.

Hillary continued to look at her steadily for a while, then her lips twitched a little in approval. You could say what you liked about the goth, but there was no denying she had spunk.

'OK then. Tomorrow, you need to get out and do it all over again: different neighbourhood, different faces, same shit.'

Wendy's black-painted lips firmed into a grim, straight line. 'Yes, guv.'

Hillary nodded. 'OK. Carry on with the report then.' She looked up and across at the old man, and jerked her head towards the left. 'Jimmy – a quick word in my office.'

'Coming, guv.'

In her office, she slumped down behind her desk and gave him a weak smile. 'Our girl is growing up.'

'Yeah. She's gonna be a good one, guv. I'm just not sure she's the right fit for us, that's all.'

Hillary nodded. She too had doubts that Wendy was copper material, but it was up to Wendy to come to the same conclusion. No doubt time would sort it all out.

'OK, I've just had a word with someone who knew Jas Sudbury back when she was a wild child,' Hillary began, and quickly filled him in on the interview. When she was finished, she added, 'From now on, I'm going to type up the notes on Jas straight onto a memory stick and print off hard copies. I don't want Jake hacking into our hard drive and learning all sorts of stuff that is going to mess with his head.'

Jimmy nodded, looking grave.

'And when I've done that, I'm going to give you a copy of everything I've got on her so far – the interview with Jake's parents, her old friends, the lot. I want you to take a second look at it for me. See what you think.'

'Guv?' Jimmy said. He was willing enough, but looked slightly puzzled. He'd never known Hillary Greene ask to be second-guessed.

As if sensing his uncertainty, she grinned wryly. 'I just want a second opinion, that's all,' she said carefully. 'A second pair of eyes on it won't hurt.'

In truth, she wanted to see if Jimmy – as old and seasoned a hand as herself – got the same reading on things that she did. She hoped not. She might, after all, be worrying about nothing. She might, just possibly – be adding up two and two and getting five.

But she didn't think so.

Jimmy looked at her thoughtfully for a long moment, then slowly nodded. 'OK, guv. And how *is* Jake doing? I haven't seen him around much. The two bosses seem to have him well in hand.'

Hillary smiled. 'By the end of the week we'll be down to just the one boss,' she reminded him. Although she knew it was coming, it still felt odd to her to realize that Steven would no longer be the man she reported to. She shook off the thought angrily and forced herself to concentrate on the matter in hand. Jimmy needed to be kept in the loop if they were to avoid any snags. And she'd long since determined that business and personal issues were to be kept strictly compartmentalized.

'But yes. They're arranging for him to meet with Darren Chivnor again,' she swept on. 'This time, though, he'll be properly covered and we'll have eyes and ears on him at all times.'

Jimmy whistled through his teeth. He didn't need telling this could be a risky strategy. With a clever thug like Chivnor, you couldn't afford to be lax. It only took the blink of an eye for a concealed knife to be whipped out and buried in someone's ribs.

'You think anything will actually come of all this?' he asked a shade sceptically.

'Who knows?' Hillary said. 'Medcalfe's been around a long time. Plenty of coppers have tried to topple him and failed. And Steven hasn't even got his own team up and running yet so the whole thing has got a flying-by-the-seat-of-our-pants feel to it. The timing could hardly be worse. On the other hand, this opportunity with Jake and Chivnor is too good to miss. And you know what they say about looking gift horses in the mouth. We'll just have to wait and see what develops.'

'When's the meeting?' Jimmy asked.

'Tomorrow afternoon. So none of us senior management will be in,' she said, with a definite twinkle in her eye now. 'You'll just have to hold the fort for a couple of hours. Keep Wendy out of trouble.'

Jimmy grunted.

'So, did you and Wendy get anything at all from your day of pavement pounding?' she changed the subject.

'Not a lot, guv. Everyone's being as tight-mouthed as the proverbial aquatic bird's rear end. Medcalfe's obviously got the word out already to play dumb. We just got one or two useless titbits on one of your cases, actually. Lydia Allen?' He related what little he'd learned, and Hillary nodded.

'Yeah. That ties in. Her mother said that she had this fantasy about meeting a wealthy student,' she sighed. 'So it makes sense that she would have specialized in the colleges. A lot of Medcalfe's girls would have been taught how to target the wealthy male students – especially the ones from overseas. They tend to be more impressed with that sort of the thing than our home-grown lot – or so Vice tell me. I'll start checking that aspect out when I get the chance.'

Mentally she added it to her to-do list. 'Right now I'm off to see her former flat-mate. According to her mother, they didn't get on.'

Jimmy nodded. 'Anyone we know?'

'According to Vice, she's gone on to be something big in the S&M scene. A proper madam whiplash, from what I can tell. A real specialist.'

Jimmy grinned. 'You get to meet the most interesting people, guv.'

'Wanna come with me?'

Jimmy patted his chest over the area of his heart. 'Not sure I could stand the excitement, guv,' he grinned. Then he stood up and all but yelped as a spasm of pain shot up his back.

Hillary shook her head sorrowfully and theatrically tut-tutted.

Jimmy said something unprintable under his breath, and left.

And, after dealing with her emails and typing up her report on the Cheryl Murray interview, Hillary did the same.

This time, she drove towards the Oxford suburb of Osney Mead. And if the ageing Volkswagen thought that this was a definite comedown after his brief interlude parked under the cherry trees of Belgravia, he kept it to himself.

Sasha Yoo's address turned out to be a flat in a large Edwardian house in a leafy lane overlooking the canal locks. In winter, the residential area looked smart and well-kept. In the warmer months, Hillary realized with a slight jolt of surprise, it would probably look major-league pleasant. The surrounding gardens belonging to similar houses were all large and full of planting, and even in the dark, November street-lighting, the evergreens shone lushly. In daylight, there might even be some rural greenery showing elsewhere, since they were on the edge of the city.

As she climbed out of her vehicle and looked around, she

noticed the great number of parked cars meant that most of the area's inhabitants were at least two-car families, speaking even more conspicuously of comfortable lifestyles.

Which rather begged the question. What was an escort girl doing living here?

From the files, she knew that it was not the same address as the one she'd once shared with Lydia Allen before her mother had reported her missing. And had Sasha Yoo not still been known to Vice, Hillary would have assumed that the girl had got out of the game and had found herself a wealthy sugar daddy.

As she approached the house, she noticed some minor signs of wear and tear. The paint could have done with a little touching up on the windows and the main door. And the gardens, although full of laurels, weren't particularly tidy, and some hardy weeds had sprouted up on the paved path to the door.

As Hillary made her way to the main entrance, she noted that in some of the neighbouring houses, with December only two days away, some people had already put up colourful Christmas lights. And, on one or two doors, holly wreaths festooned with red ribbons had also been hung.

Hillary scowled at them. It was one of her pet hates, how Christmas seemed to be forced down her throat earlier and earlier nowadays. Shops started stocking up in September for pity's sake, and the citizenry was gradually being cajoled into getting excited about the so-called season of goodwill practically before the clocks went back. And all because the retailers were anxious to get you to part with your money. To buy presents and gifts for relatives and friends you hardly ever saw at any other time of the year, and which they probably neither wanted nor needed. Let alone appreciated. And then there was the price hike in chocolates, which really made her see red!

She forced herself to stop channelling her inner Grinch and rang the bell. Nothing happened for quite some time, then a female voice came over the intercom. It sounded sleepy, wary, and curious.

'Yes? You sure you got the right address, love?'

Hillary blinked, rather wrong-footed by the friendly question and then instantly sensed eyes on her – of the non-human variety. Knowing that somewhere in the porch entranceway a camera had to be on her, she kept her face obstinately angled forward, and even dipped her chin a little. Not that it mattered if her face was seen or even recognized. It was just a copper's instinct to be cautious.

'Yes. I'm here to see Sasha. Sasha Yoo,' Hillary said firmly.

'Of course you are, love,' the voice now sounded knowing and warm. Almost amused. And Hillary knew why. Whoever was on the other end of the video screen was assuming she was a customer. The truth had finally dawned.

Hillary was standing on the doorstep of an old-fashioned knocking shop.

For a moment, she wasn't quite sure whether to be amused or insulted. Being taken for a pervert on the search for a bit of female-on-female S&M action wasn't exactly the highlight of her day so far. Or even her week come to think of it. On the other hand, it did have entertainment value. She could imagine Steven, for one, laughing his socks off when she told him about it later.

'You know the way?' the voice asked as the door was buzzed open.

'Of course,' Hillary lied nonchalantly, and slipped inside.

If the exterior of the house lacked any obvious signs of recent upkeep, the same could not be said of the interior – which was both eye-catching and luxurious. In an odd, almost touching way. For the nostalgia had been plastered on so thick she could almost taste it at the back of her throat. The hall tiles were of the traditional black and white kind, and the wooden banisters leading upstairs were ornately carved, depicting mainly acorns and grapevines. A tall grandfather clock ticked ponderously in one corner – and was telling the right time, too. The original stained glass windows had been retained, as had a large crystal-drop chandelier hanging from an ornate frame.

And everywhere there was red. Full-length red curtains at the windows and, used as draught-excluders and for added privacy, at the internal doors. Ornate and curvaceous ormolu chairs were upholstered in fat upholstery in matching crimson. On the walls were prints of naked women wearing nothing but strategically placed feather boas and come-hither coy smiles. One almost expected to see Queen Victoria's naughty son, the Prince Regent, come sauntering down the stairs with a scantily clad beauty on each arm.

The only note that looked out of place was a display cabinet full of metal and leather. Metal chains. Handcuffs. Leather riding crops. Leather face masks with zips where the mouth should be. And instruments that looked like they belonged in a medieval torture chamber.

'Oh my,' Hillary murmured to herself as she walked past the offending articles and headed for the stairs.

She hadn't quite reached the top when a door down the landing opened. Onto a lushly, red-patterned carpet (that looked to Hillary's eyes like a genuine antique Axminster) a tall Asian girl stepped out. She was totally eye-catching at nearly six feet tall, and had a slender, almost boyish figure that was currently clad in a tight-fitting leather body suit cut high on the thigh and low at the bust. She wasn't particularly well endowed, but large brass studs, carefully positioned, drew the eye – and presumably the mind – away from any sense of disappointment. Her hair was truly amazing – long, jet black, shimmering straight as water and falling very nearly to her thighs. She stood in the doorway, flicking back impatiently a strand or two of that amazing hair, her black eyes watching Hillary with a narrow, cold look.

'I don't know you. You have no appointment.' The accent was totally English, but the staccato and slightly awkward delivery of the statements sounded distinctly oriental.

Play acting?

Hillary smiled and held out her ID.

Sasha Yoo glanced at it, sighed elaborately, sneered and then reluctantly beckoned her inside.

And instantly, Hillary felt the hackles on the back of her neck stand to rigid attention. A cold hand seemed to press against her lower back and for a second she had to fight the urge to run. This sensation, near paralyzing as it was, wasn't totally new to her, and by force of will, she was able to keep her expression neutral and carry on walking. But she was now on high alert.

Because she had experienced what she was feeling now only a handful of times before in her life. And always it had warned her of real and present danger.

She'd first felt it when still in uniform and she and her partner, a twenty-year veteran, had been called out to what had seemed to be a routine domestic – a woman with a black eye, a drunken husband. And, as it turned out, a seriously out-of-his-head-on-cocaine lodger who, for some reason, had decided that he wanted to kill someone. Copper, landlord or landlady, it hadn't appeared to matter. And when he'd suddenly popped up from behind the sofa where he'd been sleeping off his fix, she'd taken one look at him and felt what she was feeling now. Luckily, her partner had been a big man and had been able to subdue him – with the help of not only Hillary but, as it turned out, the husband and wife as well. It had been Hillary's first lesson of how someone crazed on drugs seemed to acquire near super-human strength.

The same feeling had engulfed her years later, when she'd had to visit a mental patient in a secure facility. Although there had been no physical violence on that occasion, Hillary's skin had almost literally crawled.

And finally, about ten years ago, she'd experienced this same atavistic sense of apprehension when she'd been interviewing a member of the public about a brutal rape. They hadn't brought that rape home to the man who'd raised her hackles, but years later, he'd been convicted and sent down for life for murdering his sister.

And now the feeling was back.

So as Sasha Yoo shut the door behind her, Hillary Greene was already turned to face her, and balancing lightly on the balls of her feet. She carried no weapons of course – she wasn't permitted to. And she was aware that her heart was beating slightly too fast, and that the sudden tension she felt was making her feel slightly sick. But it was too late now to remember the reason why coppers should always go about in pairs. Besides, even if she *had* had Wendy or Jimmy with her, she'd be more worried about taking care of them and ensuring their safety, rather than on relying on them to help her out. Wendy would have been too young and innocent to know how to help defend herself, and Jimmy, who'd certainly know how, and would probably be getting the same vibe as herself, would be too old. And with his current back pain, too frail.

Sasha had very good body tone, and her biceps on both arms looked remarkably firm. Here was a woman who liked to keep fit. Was maybe into martial arts? And who certainly knew how to wield riding crops and whips all right. And, unless Hillary's internal radar had lost it completely, was a stone cold psychopath.

'So what do the coppers want this time?' Sasha drawled with a playful smile. She was wearing dark red lipstick and had small, charming white teeth. But whilst they smiled, her eyes had a flat, reptilian coldness to them that made Hillary's mouth go dry.

'Just a few routine questions, Miss Yoo.' Hillary forced herself to sound polite and unimpressed. She might have just walked unknowingly into a spider's den – and a black widow at that – but she was no unwary bluebottle. But she wasn't sure if she could take the girl in a straight fight – although she'd give it a bloody good go if she had to. So that meant playing it smart.

And talking her way out of trouble.

And the obvious way to do that, Hillary told herself calmly, was to appeal to the madam whiplash's own sense of self-survival. Because she surely had one – anyone who had managed to survive the kind of life that this woman had, must have.

'We're looking into some old missing person cases,' she carried on smoothly.

According to Jimmy, Dale Medcalfe had already put out to the word to all his minions that the coppers were nosing about and that they were to keep quiet about anything and every-thing. And reminding her opponent of that fact would also remind her that her boss wouldn't be happy if she drew atten-tion to herself by attacking a copper.

She saw something – a flicker of disappointment perhaps – flit briefly across and behind the black, flat-eyed stare and sensed, rather than saw, the girl give some sort of inner shrug.

And Hillary felt her accelerated heart rate calm a little.

'Oh?'

The Asian girl, parodying boredom, tossed her head and turned towards a liquor cabinet, walking on four-inch high black heels to the drinks tray, and it was only then that Hillary felt able to take a brief look around her and suss out her sur-roundings. Her eyes went first to the only other egress from the room – a large sash window that looked out over the street below. It, not surprisingly, had a pair of long red velvet curtains framing it. There was a large four-poster bed in one side of the room – complete with manacles attached at all four bedposts. The quilt – surprise, surprise – was made of red silk.

'Drink? The brandy's good.' Sasha Yoo waved a crystal

decanter at her teasingly.

Hillary smiled, wondering if the sash windows opened, or had been painted shut. Just in case. 'No, thank you. I understand you used to room with a girl called Lydia Allen?'

'Never heard of her,' Sasha said, so quickly that her first word almost overlapped Hillary's last.

'Strange. You and she worked for the same boss.'

'I'm self-employed.' Again, the response was lightning fast. Sasha poured a large measure of what did indeed look like a very good quality brandy into a bulbous glass and took a sip. She sighed elaborately in pleasure, then began to prowl the room restlessly, watching Hillary with an amused smile that did nothing to reduce Hillary's blood pressure. As she walked, she reminded Hillary of one of those big cats you sometimes saw at the zoo – a natural-born predator. She practically wafted and oozed decadence.

And suddenly, Hillary got it.

This whole set-up must be aimed at high-end patrons, with a really sick, sexual deviancy. Men with money would pay highly to live out a fantasy like this. The old-fashioned brothel, set in a period house, in a smart Oxford suburb. And knowing that there were all those normal plebs out there, going about their dreary, day to day lives with no idea what went on behind these walls. What a kick that must give them. And the over-the-top interior design, right down to the fake gas lamps that she'd noticed in the hall and on the landing, all added to the show, feeding the fantasy.

And then of course there were the girls – top quality, professional, and specialist, like Sasha. No doubt, in other rooms, Medcalfe had installed girls who'd take the whippings and beatings rather than give them out. Along with other girls who liked to dress up as nurses, or strict school ma'ams, and who knows what else.

It was the sort of house where anything went, and people

could forget themselves and go over the top. It was the sort of house where a girl could get killed.

'Lydia's mother seems to remember you well,' Hillary said, watching Sasha closely, and she gave a mental nod. No doubt the brandy was the real deal – VSOP, aged, and pricey. The gentlemen who called on Sasha would expect nothing but the best. No doubt it was all included in the bill. As were the cigars Hillary could see, spilling out of an antique humidor set on a glossy mahogany side table.

'Don't know the lady.' Sasha yawned extravagantly. 'Now, if you don't mind, I have to finish getting ready. I'm going to a fancy dress party,' she mocked, indicating her apparel with a sly hand. 'You don't think I dress like this all the time, do you?'

Hillary sighed. She was in no mood to play the straight man to Sasha's comedienne.

'When was the last time you saw Lydia Allen?' she asked, careful to keep her voice neutral and flat.

'Never saw her.'

'I'm told she preferred students. Did you and she go to any particular college in search of marks?'

'Never been interested in academia.'

'Did she have any regular John that she was afraid of? Someone who strayed into your preferred territory perhaps?'

Sasha Yoo's eyes flashed. 'Don't mistake me for some simpering little victim, Mrs Policeman Plod. I dish it out. I don't take it.'

There was real venom in the voice now, and the long, red-painted nails holding the brandy schooner suddenly tightened. And for a second, Hillary seriously and unashamedly contemplated making a run for it to the door.

With every moment that passed, it was becoming more and more clear to her that this woman was seriously disturbed. It was no act – these teasing, taunting, mood swings. It probably hadn't been for some time. Just when had the lines become blurred for her? When had she stopped being a woman playing a role, and genuinely toppled over into madness? One thing was for certain – having the services of a genuinely volatile madam whiplash must play really well for the more radical end of Medcalfe's clientele.

She supposed that, in one way, this could only play to Dale Medcalfe's advantage. She could well understand why his clients with the most severe wish for domination and subjugation would flock to someone as damaged and dangerous as Sasha – a woman who genuinely hated the world, and probably men in particular.

But that could be a dangerous game. If she ever lost control, a John could end up seriously hurt – or even dead. They'd surely have to keep a close eye on her....

And then Hillary could have kicked herself for being so slow. All along she'd sensed something artificial about the way Sasha Yoo was reacting to her presence. And now, suddenly, she understood why. The room was wired for sound and vision. Somewhere, one of Dale's minions would be watching and listening to everything that went on. Ostensibly to make sure that Sasha didn't cross the line with her Johns. But who knows? Perhaps they regularly videotaped what went on in this building. The potential for blackmail had to be almost boundless.

So that meant that Sasha was playing to the unseen audience, as much as to her. Which was all she needed to know.

'What do you know about any of the other missing girls, Sasha?' Hillary asked.

'Don't know any missing girls.'

'Amanda Smallwood?' she tossed out the name of one of Jimmy's cases. 'A mother of two small children. They miss her and want her back.'

'Oh, boo hoo.'

'Jasmine Sudbury?'

'Sounds like the name of a chocolate bar.'

'Rebecca Tyde-Harris?'

Sasha yawned again, but not before Hillary had seen the tell-tale tightening of her shoulder blades. Now that, Hillary thought with a brief flare of elation, had been a palpable hit.

'You're boring me, Mrs Policeman Plod. Why don't you go away now?' She gave Hillary a dismissive flick of her red-painted nails and walked casually to the window and looked out. The way she did it, so openly, told Hillary that the glass had been specially treated so that no one outside could see in.

'Tell me about Dale Medcalfe,' Hillary said then, just for the hell of it. Because now, she was sure, she was in no immediate danger. Sasha wouldn't dare attack Hillary with her minders looking on. In fact, she must be too busy showing her boss's watcher what a good girl she was being by towing the company line, to care much about Hillary at all.

'Don't know no Mr Medcalfe,' Sasha replied airily and tossed off the last of the brandy before sauntering back to the liquor cabinet to pour another.

Hillary wondered how many she could drink before she even started to feel fuzzy-minded. She guessed it would be quite a few.

Hillary, like most people, didn't like being frightened. It made her angry, and made her feel ashamed. And right now, she wanted some pay back for the nasty time she'd just been through. Which was very human of her, but which could also, in this case, prove to be very useful. Because now she needed to see just how dangerously unstable Sasha Yoo was. Since it might just prove to be useful to them somewhere down the line.

So she smiled gently. 'You like watching men writhe and squirm, don't you, Sasha?'

The tall young woman froze for an instant, then casually lifted her glass and took a sip.

'That's what they pay me for,' she admitted casually.

'Nothing illegal in that, Mrs Policeman Plod. We're all consenting adults here. You want me to give you a stroke or two with my favourite riding crop? On the house?' she purred.

Hillary smiled. 'Maybe later,' she said, pleased to see that her flat-voiced response momentarily surprised and non-plussed the other woman. 'I suppose they all have a safe word, though, don't they?' she carried on, making her voice sound thoughtful and just a shade regretful. 'When they want you to stop?'

Sasha went very still.

'That must be very disappointing for you. Because of course, you *do* have to stop. Don't you, Sasha? That must be so frustrating for you.'

'It's time you went now,' Sasha said, walking to the door and opening it.

And Hillary silently agreed with her. It *was* time she went. Besides, she'd learned all that she needed to know. And she knew when it was time to stop pushing her luck. And from the look of bitter and ravaging rage that she could see on the Asian girl's face, now was definitely the time to stop pushing.

'Thank you for your co-operation, Miss Yoo,' she said sweetly, as she swept past.

Once outside, she walked back to the car on legs that felt decidedly spongy, and wasn't surprised to discover that she was shivering violently. It took her a moment or two to unlock the car door and after she'd done so, she all but fell into the driver's seat.

For a moment, she simply sat and breathed. She felt sicker than ever. For a moment, she wanted nothing more than to get out her mobile and call Steven, just to hear his voice. Just to be reassured that all was still well.

But the moment passed. It had been a long time, after all, since she'd needed her hand holding. That wry realization steadied her somewhat, and slowly, the sick feeling receded. She leaned forward and turned on the engine, hoping for once that the heating system would work quickly.

And as her toes started to defrost, she forced herself to review the last half an hour or so.

What, exactly, had she just learned from all that?

That Medcalfe was running a high-end knocking shop was no real surprise. But Sasha Yoo's borderline crazy personality was. The madam whiplash was obviously a big earner for Medcalfe, but for how much longer could he keep on running her before she did something really crazy? Or was it possible that he didn't even know about her? Oh, he must have some idea that she was cracked, but perhaps he hadn't realized just how badly. It was not as if he'd have reason to talk to her face to face much, as Hillary just had. Indeed, he might not even have talked to her at all since setting up the place. He'd have lower-ranking members of his organization to see to the day-to-day running of the place, and the collection of money. And how likely was it that any of *them* would be mental health experts?

Thoughtfully, she put the car into first gear and drove carefully through the dark streets back towards HQ. She wasn't quite sure, yet, where all this might be leading, but she had a feeling that they might just have had their first big breakthrough.

'And how do you think this will help us?' It was actually Rollo Sale who asked the pertinent question, some twenty minutes later. She, Steven and her new boss were sitting in his office and Hillary had just given them a complete run-down of her findings so far. Needless to say, it was her last interview that had gained their attention the most.

'I'm not sure, sir,' Hillary responded honestly. She was now back to her old self, and was showing no signs of having been shaken, although she noticed Steven was watching her closely, as if sensing her mood. It both worried and thrilled her how well he seemed to know her. 'But at the very least, I think she's a weak link in Medcalfe's armour. None of his immediate gang will ever grass on him because they know the consequences if they do. And all his girls are junkies and too fragile to be of much use to us, but a genuinely crazy person.... Well, they can be unpredictable.'

'She's hardly likely to give him up without some serious persuasion, though, is she?' Rollo said. 'And it's not as if we have anything on her.'

'I'm not saying that we have, sir,' Hillary said patiently. 'I just think that it might be a good idea to bear her in mind. If something does break later on, as a result, say, of Steven's future work in trying to crack Medcalfe's organization. She might just be a useful wedge in helping to make the break even wider. And she genuinely hates men, and the life she's leading, of that I'm certain. If she gets the chance to stick the knife into Dale... well, I wouldn't be surprised if she wasn't just crazy enough to do it. After all, Dale relies on fear and intimidation to keep people in line. But ...'

'But someone insane might not fear very much,' Steven finished the sentence for her.

Hillary shot him a swift, appreciative look. 'Exactly. And let's not forget, she's a loose cannon in other ways, too. One of these days I can see her really overstepping the line with some punter or other, and really doing him some damage. And then Medcalfe either has to get rid of her or Sasha herself might do a runner before he gets the chance. Either way, it could be the catalyst we need. And if we can persuade her it's in her best interests to come running to us... Who knows?'

Hillary was a realist. It was possible Steven could spend years in his new job before making any real dent in the problem. Which meant you had to think long-term.

'I'm just saying, once you've got your unit up and running properly, sir,' she said to him now, 'keep her in mind. I think, somehow, somewhere along the line, she might be a potential gold mine for you.'

Steven nodded. 'Thanks for the tip. But for now, you're to stay away from her,' he ordered crisply.

Hillary smiled. 'No argument here, sir,' she said, with some feeling. Normally she wouldn't have liked the idea that he was being protective of her. It implied that he didn't think she could do her job. But right now, she was glad that someone cared if she kept her skin intact or not.

'It's no wonder Diana Thompson didn't like her,' Hillary mused. 'All those years ago, before her daughter went missing, she met Sasha and sensed something off about her, even back then.'

Rollo shifted slightly on his chair. The speculation about Sasha Yoo was interesting, but as far as he was concerned, it was very much a back-issue. It was time they got on to more important things.

'About young Jake's meeting with Darren Chivnor tomorrow,' he began firmly, and Hillary straightened and listened attentively, as between them, her two bosses filled her in on the arrangements in place for their rendezvous at the library.

CHAPTER SEVEN

That night, Steven Crayle returned to his own house. It was late, and he hadn't wanted to disturb Hillary on the boat. Besides, both of them were keyed up about the meeting tomorrow and sleep was going to be hard to come by, even without the challenges of them both cramming into Hillary's narrow bed on the *The Mollern*.

As he showered tiredly, he found himself pondering the years that might lie ahead. At the moment he was working flat out making sure that the transfer to the new job and the new set-up in St Aldates went smoothly. And it was a dead cert that he was going to be working hard for many more months to come as he struggled to get the new unit up and running.

Hillary had been instrumental in helping him pick out potential new members for what he hoped was going to be a proficient and tight-knit team. Although a lot of officers had expressed an interest in working for the new initiative, very few would in fact make the grade. Having Hillary's experienced eye, not to mention access to her wide-ranging network of contacts when it came to helping sift the wheat from the chaff, was proving invaluable.

No doubt about it, to have her as a life partner was a massive bonus for any ambitious man. Just take the case in point. Only a month ago, Commander Donleavy had made it clear that

Steven's job was to clean out the sewers – and taking down the big players would certainly do that. And here he was, not even fully in the saddle yet, and already, thanks to Hillary's efforts, he might already have a halfway decent shot of taking down Medcalfe. Of course, Jake Barnes's unexpected input had started the ball rolling, but he was relying on Hillary to help him use the situation to at least give him a starting point in his coming war with the criminal kingpin.

There was more to life than work, though, and as he slipped into his cold and empty bed, he lay for a moment staring at the ceiling.

Hillary had been happy when she'd told him that she had managed to rent a year's mooring rights on the canal just a hundred yards or so from where he now lay. Indeed, from the back bedroom of the house, they'd be able to see *The Mollern* once the narrowboat was in situ. And as she'd said, it would be an absolute doddle for her to move home. There'd be no need to hire a van and hardly any extra costs would be involved. She'd simply moor up practically at the bottom of his garden, and move, bit by bit, over a week or so.

And then he wouldn't be lying in this large bed all alone and she'd have the chance to get used to the luxury of all the space his large and comfortable home provided for them. And as much as he loved spending weekends on the boat with her, and the odd overnight stay, there was no getting away from the fact that the narrowboat could feel a bit confining.

Not that he'd ever been so stupid as to tell her that, knowing how well she and her home seemed to fit one another.

But wasn't that part of the problem? He stirred restlessly on the bed, turning over and sighing grimly at the early hour depicted in green lighting on his digital alarm clock. Hillary clearly had no intention of selling the boat. And she had bought only a year's mooring rights which meant that they were going to start their new life together with Hillary having the safety net provided by having her old home moored, literally, within her sight. And just what did that say about how much confidence she had in theirs being a long-term relationship? Or was he just being oversensitive? Was he asking too much in wanting her to be as committed to their partnership as he was? Was he just being a big girl's blouse by feeling so worried by the fact that she had refused to marry him, and opting to co-habit instead? Or was he right to be concerned?

Steven sighed and rubbed a tired hand across his face. He knew that the ghost of her past marriage still haunted her – and who could blame her? And he'd always known she had trust issues with men. How could she not have? He had been so sure that he could cope with that.

But what if he couldn't?

He muttered an angry oath to himself and turned his back on the alarm clock and determinedly closed his eyes. He was not going to mess things up by being too demanding. He was not going to crowd her, or do anything to make her uneasy. He loved her too much.

And perhaps, there, right there, was the real thorn in his flesh.

And yet didn't they say that in all relationships, there was one who did the loving, and one who was loved? And if that was truly the case, then he was just going to have to accept the fact that he wanted and needed her more than she did him. And not let any stupid, macho bullshit get in the way of their happiness.

Having sorted that out, Steven closed his eyes and tried to go to sleep.

On board *The Mollern*, Hillary Greene slept soundly. She'd gone to bed early, knowing that she was going to need to keep her wits about her and keep her eyes sharp for Jake's meeting tomorrow afternoon, and she wanted to feel refreshed and alert.

Before that meeting, she wanted to talk to Lydia Allen's step-father. Although Lydia's disappearance was almost certainly down to her working life as one of Medcalfe's girls, that didn't mean that she could blithely ignore any other avenues; a pretty young girl with a disgruntled stepfather causing family tension was a situation that couldn't be overlooked.

She had no idea that her lover was, at that moment, lying awake and tormenting himself with doubts about her com-mitment to their relationship. And if she had, she'd have been astonished by what he was thinking.

The next morning she awoke early and pulled on a warm pair of dark, bottle green corduroy trousers, matching it with a cream cable-knit sweater and a dark green jacket. The colours suited her dark chestnut cap of hair perfectly, and she applied a light green eye shadow to her lids, and the merest brush of a dark plum lipstick. Then she pulled on a pair of serviceable, flat-heeled black boots with a reinforced toe-cap. Not that she was expecting trouble exactly, but she felt, psychologically, that she needed to be prepared, just in case Darren Chivnor turned rough.

And besides all that, after that nasty interview with Sasha Yoo, she felt the need to boost her confidence and remind herself who was in charge. It wasn't often a low-life unnerved her to the extent that the Asian woman had, and it had left her feeling wrong-footed and uneasy.

It was still near dark as she stepped off the boat, since in early winter, morning light wasn't always that easy to come by. She stepped onto the towpath and felt the treacherous crunch of frost underfoot. Cautiously, she tested the frozen puddles for ice. And sure enough, her foot started to slide out from under-neath her, and with a sigh she reached into her bag and turned on her torch.

As she did so, something plopped distinctly into the canal

right beside her, and her torch spun quickly that way. And she was just in time for the beam of light to illuminate the sleek brown fur and leather-like tail of the large brown rat that was swimming energetically across the icy water. For a moment she watched as the rodent swam competently towards some old bull rushes and disappeared.

She smiled.

She had no problem with rats.

As her dad – a countryman through and through – had often said, there was nothing wrong with a sleek, healthy, brown country rat. They were not the same creatures as the black city rats, and when he'd caught one on his allotments and shown it to an eight-year old Hillary, she had, in fact, thought the bright-eyed, whisker-twitching creature thoroughly enchanting.

Now she walked towards the pub car park without turning a hair and fished inside her bag for her keys.

Hillary had long since learned that the human was a far more obnoxious creature than anything that had fur and a tail.

According to her research notes, Danny Thompson, Lydia Allen's stepfather, worked at a recycling plant in east Oxford, and it was to this industrial site that she drove after first checking in briefly at HQ.

Steven had looked a little hollow-eyed, she'd thought, and Jake was clearly keyed up about the meeting that afternoon, so she'd left them to it, reassuring everyone concerned that she'd be back in plenty of time to oversee the meeting at the Central Library later that day.

The first thing she noticed about Danny Thompson's place of work was the proliferation of seagulls and crows. They seemed to be everywhere. The next thing was the distinctive odour, closely followed by the noise of the machinery that sorted and crushed the things that society discarded every day. She had no doubts that recycling was the way to go, and she kept reminding herself of this as she made her way to a two-storey, concrete-grey office block that was almost exactly the same colour as the sky.

The last day of November was threatening rain that might just be cold enough to turn to snow, but at the moment the clouds were simply lying overhead in a menacing, gun metal grey blanket.

Inside, however, the offices were mercifully warm and oddly cheerful, sporting prime colours on the corridor walls, which were littered with photographs of smiling men and women sporting fluorescent orange coats and yellow hard hats.

A cheerful, large woman in the first small outer office gave her directions to Danny's office further back, looking curious, but not offensively so, when Hillary produced her ID card.

Danny Thompson turned out to be a tall man with a muscular body that was just starting to turn to fat. He must be in his early fifties, Hillary guessed, but still had a head of thick blond hair and pale grey eyes. A good-looking specimen, his jaw was impressively square, and he looked puzzled by her ID, but invited her to sit and at once offered her a mug of coffee which she accepted.

Hillary very rarely turned down coffee.

As she sat, she did some swift mental calculations. When Lydia had been in her mid-teens, this man must have just turned forty or so. Just a few years into his new marriage, would he have found a young teenage girl tempting? Or was she doing him a disservice? The trouble was, Hillary tended to think of people as guilty until they were proven innocent. It was something she always remembered to keep in mind, but never particularly worried about.

Now she smiled at Danny Thompson and crossed her legs elegantly. He noticed, but still seemed more puzzled than anything.

Briefly she explained who she was, and what she did for the

CRT, and concluded amiably, 'We're currently taking another look at your stepdaughter's case, sir.'

'Oh. Yeah. Diana did mention it. That you had been round to the house, I mean. She was right upset about it. Anything that reminds her of Lydia brings her down. Well, obviously.'

He had a slightly nasal voice, with something of an accent. Not quite Birmingham, but from that way somewhere.

'I'm sorry, Mr Thompson, it wasn't my intention to cause your wife any distress,' Hillary said. And meant it.

He shook his head, and waved a hand vaguely in the air. He was sitting behind a slightly untidy desk, and had on a slightly untidy suit. He reminded Hillary vaguely of her old chemistry teacher. 'Lydia going missing was the worst thing that happened to us,' he carried on. 'And until she's found, Di won't be able to get on with her life. Not proper, like.'

'Do you have any idea where she might have gone, Mr Thompson?' she asked quietly.

Danny's pale grey eyes widened. 'Me? No. No idea. I thought at first that maybe she'd finally got some boy to take her on – that maybe they'd gone off on a jaunt together. Then, later, when time went on and she still didn't get in touch with Di, I thought … well … that something bad had happened to her. It wasn't like her to let her mum worry by not getting in touch.'

'You think she's dead?' Hillary asked bluntly, but not harshly.

Danny winced. 'Yes, I suppose I do. I don't say so, because of Di, like. I mean, a mother's got to have hope, doesn't she? Until … well, until a body's found or something. You've got to believe that she might come walking through the door, someday, don't you?'

'She was in a dangerous profession,' Hillary said, watching him closely.

Again he winced, but said nothing.

'Did you have any specific boy in mind?' she changed the subject slightly.

'Huh?'

'You said you thought that your stepdaughter might have found herself a boyfriend to look after her?'

'Oh. No. Well, that student she was so hooked on, maybe. But I wouldn't call him a boyfriend exactly. He was clearly … paying her.' It obviously caused him discomfort to have to put into words what Lydia had done for a living, and she imagined that it would have made him angry as well. Clearly Daniel Thompson had been raised in a respectable, working-class environment where prostitutes had probably never been mentioned. Well, not in front of his mum or sisters. So just how much had it hurt his vanity and sense of self-worth to have a working girl for a stepdaughter? And just how fragile was his ego?

Hillary nodded, her face showing none of her thoughts, and casually asked, 'Which student was this? The one she'd formed a relationship with?'

'She didn't tell me his name,' Danny said, then half-grunted, half-laughed. 'Well, she wouldn't, would she?'

'Why not, sir?'

'Because he was clearly embarrassed to be seen with her by a member of her family. Even Lydia could tell that. It didn't fit in with her fantasy that they were a … a normal, loving couple.'

Hillary frowned. 'I'm sorry, sir, I'm a little confused. Perhaps you could explain a bit more? Did she bring him home with her?'

'Hell, no! He wouldn't want that, would he?' Danny said with disgust. But whether for Lydia or her erstwhile beau, Hillary couldn't be sure.

'So where exactly did you see Lydia with this student?' she probed relentlessly.

'At a pub in town.' Danny sighed. 'It was like this, see. It was the work's annual do, we all get together for a slap-up meal at one of those swanky pubs on the river, you know? Di didn't come that year because she was down with some sort of bug, so I went on my own. That's when I saw Lydia. She was hanging around at the bar with a bunch of student-types. Rowers, rugby blues, I dunno. That hale and hearty, hoity-toity crowd who think that life owes them a living. You know the type?'

Hillary smiled. She did. 'Yes, sir. And one of them…?'

'A good-looking foreign lad,' Danny said. 'Dark, but not a … a … ' he paused, clearly not sure of the word he should be using. 'Oh hell, I dunno.' He gave up the effort to be politically correct with another half-grunt, half-laugh. 'Anyway, she was hardly in any hurry to introduce us, was she? When she noticed me with the others …' At this point he broke off and waved a vague hand at the premises around him. 'We were milling around in this area outside the door to the restaurant.' Danny shrugged. 'She didn't look best pleased about it, I can tell you.'

'Your wife did mention that you and she didn't get on,' Hillary probed delicately.

'Nah. She was a real daddy's girl, and she thought I had taken his place. The truth is, Trevor Allen was a right bastard. Liked his drink and liked knocking Di around. She was well rid of him. And from what Di tells me, he couldn't have given a toss about his kid. Never read her a bedtime story, took her out to the park, nothing like that.' He paused, then sighed. 'Me and Di only got together, like, long after he was gone. But Lydia still saw me as the big bad wolf who ruined her parents' marriage, and there was no talking sense to the girl. I tried, but …' He shrugged.

Hillary nodded. This was pretty much the same story as the one Diana had given her. So it was probably true, unless both of them were lying to her – which was hardly beyond the realms of possibility.

'Did you make contact or did Lydia?' she asked next.

'Huh?'

'At the pub. When you bumped into each other.'

'Oh. I did, I suppose. I said hello. Not much else. I was at the bar getting a pint – I could hardly ignore her, could I? Even though she was dressed in a skirt that barely covered her, and this low-cut top. It was clear what she and the couple of other girls with her were up to. And some of the lads looked real smug, like. They could tell that I knew what was what. Anyway, let's just leave it that it was pretty embarrassing. We both wished we hadn't seen the other. But like I said, I had to say hello, right?'

Hillary nodded thoughtfully. Just how embarrassed *had* Danny Thompson been, by that impromptu meeting? And just how angry had he felt with the handsome, young students who looked so smug?

'Your wife told me that Lydia had a plan to snare herself a rich student,' Hillary said casually.

Danny did the same snort-laugh thing again. His eyes, she noticed, roamed the office restlessly, rather than settle on any one thing. 'That just goes to show, doesn't it, how naïve she was? As if some foreign lad with plenty of money was ever going to think of her as anything other than disposable rubbish.' He looked out of the window at all the crows and seagulls and his own kingdom of rubbish.

Hillary nodded. 'It must have been hard. Seeing your daughter in a situation like that.'

'Stepdaughter,' Danny Thompson corrected at once. 'I've got a boy and girl by my first wife, and my Celia is a nurse. Works up at the Churchill. In radiology.'

There was definite pride in his voice now.

'Nurses are angels in my opinion,' Hillary said gently. 'And they don't get paid anything near what they should do.'

Danny nodded. 'Too damned right.'

'So Lydia must have been a disappointment to you?'

145

Danny shrugged. 'I tried. Di tried. But she just went her own way. Couldn't be told anything. You know how it is?'

'Yes,' Hillary said heavily. 'This student that she seemed to be so fond of, you sure you didn't get his name?'

'Quite sure. Only it was clear, like, that they knew each other real well. I mean, that they'd been ... together quite a number of times. The other girls with her seemed to divide their time and attention throughout the whole group, but Lydia and this one lad stuck together. Like he owned her or something.'

Hillary nodded, and listened to her alarm bells ringing loud and clear. For one thing was for certain – Danny Thompson must have studied the young people very closely that night, and over some period of time, to notice the dynamics of the situation. And he obviously hadn't liked the thought of Lydia being bought and owned by the 'good-looking, dark-skinned foreigner'.

'Do you have any idea what college this lad went to, Mr Thompson?'

'What? No, why should I?'

'Well, I know you said she didn't introduce you to him, but was he wearing something that gave you some hint as to where he was studying? Or what subject? Often students, especially athletic types, wear T-shirts with their college crest or names on them – some kind of sporting affiliation.'

'Oh. Yeah. Right....' He paused, clearly thought about it for a moment, and then began to nod. 'Yeah, you're right. They do. But I don't think he was wearing a college sweatshirt or anything. But I heard them talking about some big cricket match. And the lad she was with had done well.... Hold on. Yeah, one of the others was joshing him like, saying how his college never won any silverware so there was no need for him to be so cocky. Hell ... what college did he say...?'

Hillary waited patiently, but without much hope, but for once, her pessimism was unwarranted. There was nothing wrong with Danny Thompson's memory. Or at least, not when it came to remembering details about his stepdaughter.

'St Bede's. That was it,' Danny said, snapping his fingers in triumph. 'He was from St Bede's College.'

Hillary made a note of it, thanked him, and went on to ask a few more questions, but he wasn't able to add much more. He'd never seen Lydia again after that occasion and had no idea what might have happened to her.

But on the drive back to HQ, Hillary couldn't help but wonder just how much Danny Thompson had resented his stepdaughter's way of life. It had been clear that he had some serious issues with it.

But just how serious had they been?

Jake was in the canteen with Rollo Sale, but felt too keyed up to eat. However, very much aware of the new boss's eyes on him, he was being careful to act cool, and so forked a small morsel of quiche Lorraine into his mouth, and forced himself to swallow it.

Rollo ate his own chicken salad sandwich with not much more enthusiasm. In his straightforward career, he hadn't been the senior investigating officer on many cases where an undercover man under his command had to meet, in a public place, a known and dangerous criminal and he was feeling nervous. Distinctly so, since so many things could go wrong. All of which meant that he'd spent much of last night tossing and turning and thinking about all of them – much to his wife's annoyance and concern.

Roland Sale thought of himself as a good and experienced police officer, but he was also an innately honest one, and that included being honest with himself. And right now, he was very willing to concede that he was glad that both Acting Chief Superintendent Steven Crayle would be there, and in the background Hillary Greene too. As a superior officer and one who was – technically at least – still the commanding officer of the CRT – at least for the next three days – if anything *did* go wrong, he knew that Steven would take the flack, which might not have been very noble of him, but at least it had enabled him to get *some* sleep.

And as for Hillary Greene, he had no trouble acknowledging that she could almost be considered an old hand at this sort of thing. Her own career had been far more varied than his. She not only had a medal for valour, but had also been shot in the line of duty. And even after retiring and coming back to work for the CRT she had, along with the old but canny ex-sergeant Jimmy Jessop, confronted and disarmed a seriously deranged stalker.

So no doubt about it – if anything did go wrong at the public library later, she was a good ally to have by your side.

He sighed now as he finished his sandwich, and hid a smile as the young man opposite him tried to eat a few more bites of his own meal. Whilst Rollo understood and appreciated the effort that Jake Barnes was making to appear cool and collected, he was, nevertheless, still miserably aware that Barnes was very much a civilian. Not even a fully-fledged copper. And one thing was for sure. If anything bad *did* happen, and for some reason Darren Chivnor let loose with a knife and Jake, or even worse, another member of public was hurt, the media would have a field day.

It helped a little to know that the library staff had been well briefed, and that long before the meeting was due, all members of the reading public would have been asked to leave the room in question. And that, after Chivnor had arrived, no other readers would be let in. Even so, Chivnor had to enter and exit via the main doors, and there was no way they could cordon off the lobby without arousing his suspicions. So at some point he was bound to rub shoulders with unsuspecting members of the public, coming and going, most probably on the main staircase – and even though it was hugely unlikely that Darren would suddenly go berserk, the thought was enough to give him ulcers.

And to think that he'd thought applying to be head of the CRT would be a nice, reasonably challenging but ultimately stress-free way of winding down his career. Ah well. Rollo gave a small, wry smile.

Still, once Steven's last few days in harness at the CRT were over, and this particular case was passed over to him and his new team to continue and conclude, he was hopeful that things would quickly settle down.

All things considered Rollo had a feeling that his new posting was going to suit him well enough. The more he worked with Hillary Greene, the more he came to like and respect her. And he could certainly see why both Commander Donleavy and Steven rated her so highly.

And he had no problems with Jimmy Jessop, either. Like most senior men, Rollo Sale appreciated a good, experienced sergeant. And even though his colleagues might consider working with old and formerly retired coppers hardly ideal, Rollo didn't have any issues with it.

Of course, the inexperienced kids that CRT was also forced to work with could present problems. He wasn't quite sure what to make of the young woman who came to work looking like an extra from a horror film, for instance. But, by and large, they were always going to be Hillary's problem anyway. It was part of her remit to see if any of the young volunteers might make decent coppers and to try and keep them out of trouble and usefully engaged even if it became clear that they weren't.

Rollo sighed once more, glanced at his watch, and nodded. 'Right then. We'd best be off,' he said briskly, but with an encouraging smile for the clearly nervous multi-millionaire. 'We want you in position a good hour before you're due to meet Darren. Just to do a few system checks and make sure that the security arrangements are all that we asked for.'

Jake swallowed hard, but nodded. 'Yes, sir.' He felt sick, and wished he hadn't eaten even the few bites that he had. He didn't want to let Hillary or the rest of the team down by messing things up now. Above all else, though, he was miserably aware that within a few hours he would probably know what had happened to his sister.

He wasn't sure just how well he would be able to cope if the news was to be as bad as everyone thought that it might be.

Hope wasn't the last thing left in Pandora's box for no reason and he couldn't help but feel, stubbornly and against all the odds, a vague but persistent belief that maybe, just maybe the news might turn out to be good.

After all, there was just a chance it *could* be good. Right?

An hour later, Hillary, Steven and Rollo were all seated in a small office just across from one of the public library's reading rooms, and were concentrating intensely on the monitor that was sitting on the plain pine desk in front of them. A group of secretaries and clerks had been made temporarily homeless in order to accommodate them, and a sound and digital recording expert sat at another smaller desk, earphones on and concentrating on the live feed coming in from the room opposite.

The security arrangements that Rollo had mentioned had all been inspected and found adequate. The reading room was now littered with people, but two of them were library staff who'd volunteered to man the desk, and the rest were all plain-clothes police officers. As Jake had been assured, three of them were young and fit, thickset men, bearing the legend of an Oxford student rugby team on their sweatshirts. And all of them were armed with concealed tasers, a weapon that was still somewhat controversial, but given Chivnor's record with a knife, had been sanctioned for use by the top brass.

The surveillance experts had already been in and had set up a truly excellent operation. Tiny cameras had been placed on the surrounding shelves, and one had been concealed in the spine of a book resting on the table where Jake Barnes was currently sitting, pretending to read a newspaper. This camera was capable of extreme close ups and was giving them a clear picture, in full colour that was also being recorded. Watching it, Hillary was glad to see that she could see every detail of Jake's face. Even the fact that he was sweating slightly. It wasn't the state of the young man's nerves that interested her, but the fact that the quality of the picture was so fine that she might just as well have been sitting at the table herself.

The closest she'd ever been to Darren Chivnor was one night over a week ago, when she'd seen him coming out of a gent's toilet block in the park on a dark and cold night. On that occasion, he'd had a knife in his hand, and she had seen him largely in profile.

Now, hopefully, in this one-on-one meeting, she'd be able to get a proper feel for the man they were dealing with. And to do that she needed to be able to read his body language, watch his face, his eyes, and listen to his voice.

Beside her, Steven was thinking much the same thing. One of Hillary's many talents, he well knew, was her prowess in the interview room. She had a way of getting quickly into a suspect or witness's mind and drawing out information from them before they were even aware of what she was doing. She was also very good at reading characters, and could probably ace a psychology course, should she ever decide to take one. All her knowledge had been learned on the job and, right now, he could feel her almost quivering at his side, like a whippet on a racecourse just waiting for the trap to open.

He glanced across at her, noting the glitter in her beautiful, sherry-coloured eyes, the calm but tense set of her shoulders, and felt a pang of pride and desire lance through him. He wanted to reach out and touch her hand, but of course, he didn't. It wouldn't have been appropriate.

On his other side Rollo Sale looked pale, but composed. He could tell Sale wasn't one hundred per cent happy with the scenario, and he could sympathize with him. Not yet a month since accepting the job, he was having a proper baptism of fire. So much was riding on this meeting. If Jake blew it, any hopes of getting close to Medcalfe's gang went up in smoke, but if he got it right, who knew where having a hook into one of Dale's most trusted lieutenants might take them?

The radio over by the technical officer's table suddenly crackled into life, and everyone tensed as a WPC's voice rattled off the news that the suspect had just been spotted entering the building.

Jake wasn't wired for sound, of course, since they'd agreed that Darren Chivnor would definitely be on the look-out for any tell-tale signs – and might even demand that Jake allow him to pat him down. Consequently, Jake had been ordered to wear a tight-fitting T-shirt and jeans, and to wear his jacket open, with the inner pockets fully exposed. Since the area surrounding Jake had microphones galore, it wasn't necessary that he should wear any equipment.

Each one of the pseudo rugby players was wearing a small earpiece, which allowed the news of Chivnor's arrival to be relayed to them, and one of them now gave Jake the pre-arranged signal to warn him that the meeting was imminent.

On the monitor, Hillary could actually hear the slight intake of breath Jake gave, and she nodded in approval. Good. She really could hear and see every little thing.

'Let's just hope he remembers your briefing,' Hillary said softly to Steven, who nodded. They were all very much aware that Jake was the wild card here – as a civilian consultant, he had had no formal police training at all. But that didn't mean, of course, that they hadn't all done their best to give him a crash course.

'He should be OK,' Steven said, with more confidence than he felt. 'Rollo and I rehearsed him for practically every situation we could think of. And he knows just what we need to get from this meeting. Besides, he's motivated.'

'Even so, a lot of it he'll have to play by ear,' Rollo put in. 'And he'll need to react to circumstances as and when they materialize.'

Hillary nodded and made a mental note. Her new boss was a cautious man. And probably a bit of a pessimist as well. Neither of which was necessarily a bad thing. Merely something to bear in mind and pass on to Jimmy later. In her job, keeping an eye on the criminals was important, but sometimes, keeping an eye on your boss could be even more so.

Every copper worth his salt knew that both of them could mess you up just as badly.

'There he is,' she heard Steven say beside her, and her eyes scanned to a second monitor on the desk, this one keyed in to the library's own CCTV system. And sure enough, just coming through the main doors was a shaven-haired young male, wearing dark denims and a leather biker's jacket. Even from the relatively poor quality of that particular footage, Hillary could make out the almost compulsory dark patches that told her he had some sort of tattoo on the back of his neck. It probably went all the way down his back. Her concentration was more on the jacket, though. Bulky and loose fitting, he could be hiding an arsenal under there.

As he headed towards the stairs he looked around. Carefully, slowly, and making a thorough job of it, he missed nothing. And she was glad that they had decided that they wouldn't have any undercover officers in sight at this point. Furthermore, if he was already this alert and eagle-eyed, she was even more relieved that they'd decided to keep the number of officers in the reading room to a minimum of six. And that the other three officers concerned were all female.

One was a middle-aged veteran from the thief-takers squad. Famous for looking like a grey-haired and eminently mug- gable little old lady, she was currently standing by a display stand of books with a shopping bag in one hand, and a pair of reading glasses in the other. She was a black Dan in some- thing or other, or so Hillary had heard, and rumour had it that the station house boxing champion went in fear and trembling of her – as apparently did most of the Alsatians in the canine unit.

The other two officers were much younger women, and were sitting at a table nearby, surrounded by books and taking notes. In Hillary's opinion they looked like they were studying too hard and too diligently to look like real students, but she doubted that Darren Chivnor would know the difference.

The rugby players instantly went into their role-playing as a group of slightly too-loud jocks, bored with study, and now grouped behind the back of the bookshelves, out of sight of the library staff.

Apart from these, the room was deserted. Unusually so. They were all banking on the fact that Darren wouldn't realize how busy the Oxford library normally was, and that on a wet, cold, grey winter's afternoon, the dearth of readers wouldn't strike him as odd.

At his table Jake shifted slightly, turned the page of his news- paper, and then looked up.

On the CCTV monitor, they could all see that Darren was now poised in the entrance way to the door, and was looking around. He spotted Jake fairly quickly and Barnes slowly folded and put away the newspaper, careful (as he'd been instructed) to make sure that it in no way impeded the view of the minia- ture camera hidden in the book.

'And here we go,' Steven said tensely.

Over by the table the technician made sure that the digital

feed was safely recording every image and capturing every sound.

Everything now relied on Jake Barnes doing his part.

Darren approached the table slowly, looking around, noting the two members of the library staff going about their business at the desk, not even looking up as he passed. To the right, by a large bookstand, some dumpy woman was turning the plastic shelves around, picking out the occasional book and reading the blurb. He could also hear some male jocular voices talking about 'the state of the pitch' coming from behind some bookshelves.

Two tasty-looking girls were sitting down four desks away, studying hard.

He nodded briefly at Jake as he approached, noting that the millionaire was sweating and looked distinctly nervous. This suited him just fine. A quick glance told him that he wasn't wearing any nasty bits of wire under his tight shirt.

Not that he was really expecting any trouble. He had a nose for people lying to him, and he was ninety-nine per cent sure that when Jake Barnes had first approached him, he was flying solo. There had been something reassuringly amateurish about it.

Now he pulled out a wooden, plastic-padded seat in bright orange and sat down.

'Sorry about the last time we met up,' Chivnor said at once, saving Jake from having to make the opening gambit. What Jake should say at the very beginning of their head-to-head had been the cause of some serious discussion.

'That's all right,' Jake said at once, heartily relieved to find that his voice hadn't come out in some sort of a comical, Monty Python-like squeak.

'Like I said, I thought that guy who walked in on us the last time was someone I knew. I had to make it look good. I never would have cut you.'

Jake nodded and forced himself to smile. He supposed, in the world that Darren inhabited, that sort of sentence was almost normal. But this was all good. Steven had said that Darren would probably start off nice and easy. After all, he wanted to get his hands on the money that Jake was offering, and to do that, he would want to try and put Jake at his ease.

So far, everything was going according to how they'd planned it.

Over the past few days, both Steven and Rollo had taken him through a series of possible scenarios, and it was now just a question of seeing which ones panned out, and to follow the formula they'd set up for each one.

So, Darren had apologized, he'd accepted it, now he had to move on, but not too fast.

'I guess, in your position, you can't be too careful,' Jake said amiably.

In the room opposite, Steven nodded. 'Good,' he said softly to Jake's video-screen image. 'Keep yourself sympathetic and understanding. Make him feel you're on his side.'

'Too damned right,' Darren said, and leaning back in the chair slightly, gave a brief smile. 'So, this is where you finally tell me what it is you're after, yeah?'

In the other room, Steven drew in a sharp breath. 'Woah! That was quick. We thought he'd beat about the bush a bit more first.'

But Hillary shook her head. 'No. It makes sense. He's going to want to keep this as quick as possible. He doesn't want to run the risk, however slight, that he might be seen with Jake, and besides, right now, he's almost eaten alive with curiosity and impatience. For weeks now he's had this tasty carrot of serious money dangled in front of him, and he wants to find out just what he has to do to get it.'

'Let's just hope it doesn't throw Jake,' Rollo muttered.

On the video screen, Jake blinked but rallied quickly.

'OK. Why not?' Jake licked his lips, probably in an unconscious gesture of strain, and took a slow breath. 'Like I said, it's got nothing to do with your boss, or crossing him, or grassing on him or anything like that,' he said, as per his instructions. Both of his bosses had drummed it into him that he needed to make Darren feel comfortable with what he was going to be asked to do, and by far the easiest way of accomplishing that, was to reassure him that his own skin wouldn't be in jeopardy.

'Glad to hear it,' Darren said, glancing back at the library staff manning the desk. One of them was busy on the computer whilst the other was swiping the bar code on the back of a book under a scanner that was emitting a bright red light.

Darren turned to look at Jake again. 'So, wassup then? What do you want?'

'I just want to find my sister, Jasmine Sudbury,' Jake said bluntly.

Darren Chivnor went very still indeed.

In the small office, everyone tensed. But Jake had done only what he'd rehearsed. Once Chivnor had asked the question, he was not to beat about the bush. He was to give him all the information he had as quickly as possible, before Darren could have time to interrupt. So he swept on quickly, 'Her name is Jasmine Sudbury, and she—'

'Jas?'

Darren repeated her name sharply, and in the office, Hillary Greene moved imperceptibly a little closer to the monitor. Her eyes were fixed on the young thug's face.

And she was sure of what she saw.

Surprise. Followed by … what was that? Relief? Followed by a flash of … amusement?

'You want to know where Jas is?' Chivnor repeated. But now he sounded slightly confused. 'But I thought …' He began, then abruptly stopped speaking. His eyes narrowed thoughtfully.

'He's suspicious,' Hillary said tensely, her voice suddenly sharp in the silent room. Rollo Sale had gone slightly pale, and by her side, Steven had tensed, too.

'I know,' Steven said. Then added quickly, 'But I don't get it. Why? Why should that make him suspicious?'

But Hillary was hardly listening. She thought she had a pretty good idea why. But right now, she was more intent on watching Jake. Everything depended on what he said next.

'Stay focused, Jake,' she whispered to the monitor. 'Keep it together.'

But Jake *was* feeling a little flustered. Of all the possible scenarios that he'd gone over with his two bosses, this hadn't been one of them. Chivnor was supposed to either deny ever knowing Jas, or fob him off, or maybe even tell him flat out what had happened to her. What he wasn't supposed to do was look at Jake as if he were barmy.

For a moment, he felt frozen, not sure what to do. Or say.

But, luckily, Chivnor saved him the need to come up with something.

'Just a minute. You said Jas is your *sister?*' Chivnor asked. 'But her last name's not Barnes. So what are you trying to pull?' His tone was slightly aggressive now, and there was no doubting that he was definitely on edge.

'No. Technically, she's my stepsister,' Jake said, trying to calm his heart-beat, which he could hear thundering in his chest. 'But her dad married my mum when she was only little, so we grew up together, like a real brother and sister, you know? She's Jasmine *Sudbury* because that was her mum's name.'

And trying to get things back on track, he quickly launched into the pre-prepared speech he was supposed to give. 'I know Jas worked for your boss a while ago, but a couple of years ago she just dropped out of sight. I figured either you, or someone in your outfit would know where she went. Or what happened to her. And I'm willing to give you a cool three-quarters of a million for proof of her whereabouts.'

There, he'd got the sum of money quickly into the conversation, just as Steven and Rollo wanted.

And sure enough, at the mention of it, Darren Chivnor's eyes glinted greedily and he leaned forward in the chair. 'Not enough,' he said at once. 'Besides, you've said before that a million was on offer.'

And slowly, Jake began to relax. He wasn't quite sure what that little stumble had been about earlier, but now he was back in familiar territory. Steven had told him that Darren would almost certainly demand more money – that it would be an almost automatic reflex. Which is why they'd chosen the sum they had. Because it made Jake's natural come-back sound both natural and reasonable.

'OK. I'm willing to make it a straight million, but only if and when I actually set eyes on her in person.' He launched into the response perhaps a little too quickly, for in the office, Hillary shook her head.

'That sounded too quick and too rehearsed.' Rollo picked up on it at once, unknowingly rising a little in Hillary's estimation. For whilst it was clear that her new boss might be a tyro at this sort of thing, it didn't mean that he was slow off the mark.

Luckily though, Darren Chivnor was too excited by the thought of all those zeros to notice Jake's surprisingly quick and seamless response.

'And that's all?' Chivnor asked, once again with some suspicion. 'You just want to know about Jas?'

'Yes. That's all,' Jake said. Then swallowed hard. Now came the hard bit. 'I'm not a fool, I know that Jas might well be dead, but if she's some Jane Doe in a morgue somewhere, or has already been buried in an unmarked grave, I need to know that as well. And you won't get any of the money until I have DNA proof of her identity.'

And having gulped out that challenge, he could only stare at the skinhead opposite him and wait for him to either deliver a crushing blow, or to make his day.

Was Jas dead, or was she, against all the odds and by some miracle, still alive?

But in the event, Darren Chivnor did neither.

Instead he simply stared back at Jake for a good few seconds, a mixture of bafflement, uncertainty and something else warring on his face. Clearly he was doing some major thinking. And Hillary Greene, staring at that face on her screen, thought that she might just know what it was that he was thinking so hard about.

And if she was right, Jake Barnes's world, and that of Jasmine Sudbury's parents, was about to implode.

'I have to think about this,' Darren said at last. 'I'll be in contact, yeah?' And suddenly he pushed the chair back and walked away.

Taken by surprise, Jake got up and started to follow him. And in the office opposite, Rollo, Hillary and Steven all said, "No!" almost simultaneously.

Back in the reading room, it was almost as if Jake could hear them, for he suddenly jerked to a halt. But it was common sense that had told him that it would be stupid, and potentially dangerous, to go after the skinhead.

Helplessly he watched Darren out of sight, then slumped back into his chair. Emotionally drained now, he suddenly felt exhausted.

Although he'd been alternately dreading and looking forward to this meeting, he had at least been sure that, once it was over, he'd finally know what had happened to his sister.

Now he felt only a sense of crushing disappointment.

He looked up as Hillary, Rollo and Steven walked towards him. They'd left the office only when the CCTV had confirmed that Darren had left the building.

'You did well,' were Steven's first encouraging words.

'Yes, well done,' Rollo Sale confirmed.

'But he didn't tell us anything!' Jake wailed. If he hadn't been so upset, he might have realized that Hillary Greene was unusually silent.

And that she wasn't quite able to meet his eye.

CHAPTER EIGHT

BACK AT HQ IT was starting to get dark, and as they all trooped into Rollo's office, Hillary walked to the main window and stared up. There she could just about make out the lights that were starting to come on in the car park, shining with a faint orange glow on the vehicles parked beneath them, playing havoc with their colours.

As she watched, just above her at pavement level, a set of size ten boots stomped past, and a cigarette was illegally dropped and trodden on. Bloody litterbug, Hillary thought with a grin. The trouble with working from the basement was that it made her feel like a mole sometimes, or one of those forest creatures that lived perpetually under leaf litter. The thought of herself as some busy little dung beetle scuttling about in the dark and trying to deal with all of the dung that life seemed intent on dropping on to her head, made her lips twitch.

With a sigh, she told herself to stop waxing so damned philosophical, and tuned in to the voices going on behind her.

'At least he didn't turn you down flat, that's the main thing.' It was Rollo who was currently doing the talking, but even with his upbeat take on things, it was clear that Jake wasn't feeling anywhere near so optimistic.

'But why didn't he just tell me what happened to her?' he demanded. 'Or at the very least, say if she was alive or dead?'

From the way the sound of his voice moved, Hillary could tell that he was pacing restlessly up and down.

Over at his desk, which was his for the next two days only, Steven wasn't watching Jake at all. Instead, the outgoing Acting Chief Superintendent was watching Hillary Greene. She had been unusually quiet and he wasn't at all sure that he liked the carefully cultivated, neutral look on her face. In his experience, when Hillary Greene got enigmatic it was time to sit up and take serious notice.

So what had he missed? Because something in Jake's little talk with Darren Chivnor had set her inner sniffer dog quivering.

'He was interested in the money though, wasn't he?' Jake demanded. 'I mean, you could tell he was really anxious to find a way to get it.'

At which Rollo Sale snorted. 'Of course he was! Who wouldn't be?' the older man said scornfully. 'But you have to remember, he's a cautious bastard – working for someone like Medcalfe, he has to be. He knows more than anyone just what happens to those who run foul of his boss. He just needs a little time to think things through and sort out all the angles, that's all. Don't forget, the last thing he said to you was that he'd be in touch.'

Jake turned to look at his other boss. 'Sir, do you think that's all it is?'

Steven took his eyes from the woman who was shortly to become his live-in partner, and focussed on Jake's unhappy face.

'Yes, I do. And stop beating yourself up. You followed the instructions we gave you as well as any trained officer could have done. All in all, Superintendent Sale is right – the meeting was a success.'

'You don't think then, that he didn't say anything because he doesn't actually *know* what happened to Jas?' Jake asked the question that haunted him the most. 'I mean, Medcalfe's got quite a few lieutenants in his gang and he could have assigned any one of them to deal with Jas's situation. Whatever that was,' he added quietly. 'And there's no guarantee that he would have known the details. Is there?'

The two senior men exchanged a quick glance. Both of them had a pretty good idea why Darren hadn't simply leapt at the bait and spilled his guts then and there.

And Jake, who was nobody's fool, not only caught the look that passed between his two bosses, but also noticed that Hillary Greene, the one person in the room he trusted more than any other, was keeping conspicuously quiet. Not only that, she was staring out of the window with her back firmly to the room, as if distancing herself from what was going on.

He swallowed hard. 'OK, so what am I missing?' he asked helplessly.

He pointed the question at Hillary's turned back, but it was Steven who felt compelled to tell the young man what everyone was thinking but nobody was actually saying.

'Jake, if Darren *could* have taken you to your sister then and there, or even told you where to find her ...' Steven began, then hesitated as he tried to think of a gentle way of finishing the sentence. Realizing that there wasn't one, he shot Hillary's turned back a brief, worried glance, then continued, '... then he probably would have done so – or at least, confirmed that he could do so. That is, *if* she were still alive and working for Medcalfe, and *if* he could have been sure he could collect the money before giving up what he knew.' Steven sighed. 'And don't forget, he's had a lot of time to figure out a way to make sure that he gets his money before giving you what you want. So once he knew what it was you were after, it would have taken him only moments to figure out how he could play things.'

Jake blinked. 'So the fact that he didn't ...'

Steven heard Rollo shift uncomfortably in his seat, and

spread his hands silently.

'You think it proves that she's dead,' Jake finished flatly.

Rollo Sale coughed slightly.

Hillary Greene, neck craned right back, continued to stare silently out of the window. It had started to rain. No – actually, from the glimpses of white flecks that she could see drifting down in the rays of the orange-coloured street lamps, it was beginning to sleet. December had come in meaning business. Who knows – perhaps this year they'd even have a white Christmas.

'It seems the most likely answer, yes,' Steven said softly behind her. 'And Chivnor knows full well that if she *is* dead, he's going to have to be very careful about having you discover her remains.'

Rollo sighed and took up the baton of educating the youngster. 'Look at it from his point of view, Jake. He can hardly lead you wherever she is without implicating himself in murder, can he? Or maybe even worse from his point of view, in implicating his boss in murder. And that's the last thing he's likely to do, because he knows that if he drags Dale into this, he can forget about getting twenty years to life in a cosy little cell somewhere at Her Majesty's pleasure – he's likely to end up dead himself.'

'So what are you saying? That this has all been a waste of time?' Jake wailed.

'No. Of course not,' Steven put in quickly. 'Like you said, he *wants* the money. By now he can practically taste it. And he's obviously got a certain amount of low cunning. He didn't get to rise as far as he has in Medcalfe's outfit without having more than his fair share of brains. He's just got to think of a way of giving you what you want without risking his own skin, that's all. And that may take him a little while to come up with something – or not – depending on the circumstances.'

'Either way, you've just got to be patient now,' Rollo chipped in. 'He'll call you, don't worry about that. He won't be able to resist the thought of that million quid, believe me.' He sighed. 'Look, I know you wanted more from this meeting,' he conceded, 'but if you stop and think about it, Jake, you'll see that that was never really very realistic.'

Jake dragged in a ragged breath, then his shoulders slumped and he sighed in defeat. 'OK. I've got to go and phone my parents. They'll be expecting … well … something.'

'Then tell them that things are progressing well. That you're much closer to the truth now than ever before,' Steven advised. 'But they, like you, are going to have to be patient a little bit longer.'

Jake nodded, glanced across at Hillary, who was still watching the fall of rain and snow above her, and opened his mouth to say something. Then he obviously thought better of it and instead turned and left.

Once the door had shut behind him, Rollo groaned. 'The next few weeks are going to be hard on him,' he predicted. 'We *have* got eyes on Chivnor, haven't we? Just in case he takes it into his head to go and check out wherever they got rid of the body.'

Steven nodded, although he thought it highly unlikely that Darren would be so accommodating. Then he said quietly, 'Hillary?'

But Hillary merely turned away from the window and began making her way to the door. 'I need to check in with Jimmy and Wendy. I asked them to do some legwork for me this afternoon on the Lydia Allen case.'

It wasn't until she'd almost got to the door that Rollo Sale realized that he'd missed something – something that Crayle had clearly picked up on. Because as she reached for the door handle, Steven said, a shade more sharply, 'What? What is it? What's going on?' And he clearly wasn't asking about the Lydia Allen case.

Hillary looked across at him, seemed to hesitate for the briefest of moments, then shook her head. She didn't feel comfortable putting her neck on the line before having enough facts to back up her theories. Not even for Steven.

'It's like Superintendent Sale said, sir,' she murmured blandly, 'the next few weeks are going to be hard on Jake. We'll have to keep a really sharp eye on him.' And that was as much of a hint as she was willing to give.

And with that, she opened the door and slipped out. Back in the communal office, she wasn't surprised to see that both Jimmy and Wendy were back from their afternoon's fishing expedition. Outside it was now fully dark, and probably perishing.

'Anything?' she said, by way of greeting.

Jimmy, caught in the act of dry-swallowing two aspirin, nodded, but obviously wasn't in any position to speak, so it was Wendy who answered her.

'We think his name is probably Kyle Karastrides, guv,' she said.

For whilst she and the others had been overseeing the meeting between Jake and Darren, Hillary had asked Jimmy and Wendy to see if they could discover the name of the student that, by all accounts, Lydia Allen had been so taken with just before she went missing.

'First we got a list of students from St Bedes for the years in question,' Jimmy took over, 'deleted the women and the Anglo-sounding names from the mix, and ran the rest of them past her mother.'

Hillary nodded. 'Did Diana recognize any of the names?'

'No, guv, but she confirmed that Lydia *had* seemed to think that marriage might be on the cards in the near future – which had to be wishful thinking on her part, I dare say, but we had to check it out. So next we ran the list through various databases, but very few of them got married here in the UK during the timeframe we're talking about. Two were arrested on minor charges, one died, and three applied for British citizenship. Of course, if she did run off or elope overseas with one of them, then that might be why her mother hasn't heard from her in all this time.'

Hillary sighed. They both knew how likely that was. Fairy tale endings, where the call girl with the heart of gold actually ended up marrying her rich, handsome foreign prince only happened in Hollywood films. Or really bad literature.

'And it's gonna be one hell of a job trying to track down the current whereabouts and married status of all the foreign students now that they've either gone back home or scattered to all four corners of the globe.'

'Right.' Hillary winced just at the thought of it. 'Don't even try to bother. So why do you think this Kyle fella might be the one then? I can't see any dean or bursar of an Oxford college giving you the names of past students who liked to dally with the local paid talent.'

Jimmy actually snorted with mirth at the idea, then bit back a yelp as his heaving shoulders and ribs made his lower back suddenly flare up again.

'No, guv,' Wendy said. 'It was one of our street contacts who came up with the name.'

Hillary cocked an eyebrow at Jimmy. 'Street contact, huh?' she said, trying to look and sound impressed by the way the goth nonchalantly threw out the term. This time, Jimmy was wise enough to merely content himself with a grin.

'Yeah. One of the girls who knew Lydia said she was bragging about marrying this rich Greek guy,' Wendy said.

'Apparently he was a bit of a regular on the circuit, and he wasn't quite as much of a one woman punter as Lydia thought,' Jimmy put in cynically. 'Imagine that!'

'Gasp, shock, horror,' Hillary drawled, leaning against the doorframe. 'So a lot of the girls knew him then – in the Biblical sense?'

'Seems like it, guv.'

'Though to be fair, Cindi-with-an-I *did* say that Kyle was fairly smitten with Lydia,' Wendy put in. 'And that they did go around a lot – far more than was usual.'

'And was this Cindi-with-an-I pretty sure of his name?' Hillary asked, amused. Although the question was addressed to Wendy, she was actually looking at Jimmy, who was far more likely to have had a good reading on Cindi-with-an-I's reliability, than Wendy. He nodded slightly in confirmation.

'Oh yeah, guv,' Wendy sailed on. 'From what she said, he was quite a looker. Tall, dark, handsome and very polite. Not one to forget, she said.'

'Polite?' Hillary echoed, surprised. Whilst that wasn't exactly a new one on her, it was rare in Johns.

'Yes, guv.' Wendy nodded vigorously, her black hair flying across her cheeks. 'Cindi-with-an-I said he had lovely manners – all the girls remarked on it. He claimed he learned them from his Turkish grandmother.'

'How nice for him,' Hillary said.

Jimmy grinned. Wendy perked up. 'And guess what, guv? Even better, Cindi reckoned she'd seen him still around town. Like, recently.'

Hillary blinked, thought about it for a nano-second, then nodded. 'Doing a post-doctorate, is he?' She glanced across at Jimmy, who nodded.

'Guv. We got back in touch with St Bedes. This time they didn't mind telling us that Kyle Karastrides is doing a DPhil in Modern History.'

'Got an address?'

'Yes, guv. In Jericho. Apparently Mummy and Daddy have enough money, in spite of all the financial upheaval going on back in the old homeland, to provide their son and heir with a nice little two-up, two down overlooking the canal.' As he informed her of this, Jimmy ripped off a page from his notepad and handed it over.

Hillary glanced at it and then outside. 'It's getting late. I'll talk to him first thing tomorrow. I doubt he'll be out of bed before ten. Well done, you two. Wendy, you'd better get off. It's sleeting outside, so drive carefully.'

'Guv.'

Hillary waited until she was gone, then took her still-warm seat and filled in Jimmy on the meeting at the library.

When she was finished, she watched a shade pensively as the old man started going through his usual ritual of clearing up his desk before getting off home himself.

'Anything on your other case yet – Amanda Smallwood?' she asked.

Jimmy sighed. 'No, guv. It's got the feeling of a no-hoper to me,' he confessed.

Hillary grimaced. Sometimes you got a case that you just knew in your bones you weren't going to crack. It didn't mean you stopped trying.

'Hard luck,' Hillary said, with genuine sympathy.

She continued watching him for a moment, and he was just locking his desk drawer when she said quietly, 'Jimmy, did you read my notes on Jasmine Sudbury yet?'

Jimmy looked up, desk key in hand, and met her level gaze. 'Yes, guv.'

'And what do you think?'

For a moment, her right-hand man said nothing. Then he shrugged. 'I reckon I'm thinking much the same thing as you are, guv,' the canny old ex-sergeant finally said cautiously.

Hillary slowly let out her breath. 'Ah,' was all she said.

She'd been afraid of that.

Overnight, the sleet had turned to rain before stopping altogether. The clearing skies had then dropped the temperature like a stone, which meant that Hillary found herself skating, rather than driving, into work the next morning.

In Kidlington, the Christmas lights had been put up in the main shopping area, which meant serious seasonal shopping was now well under way, so she made sure to catch up on her paperwork in the office before heading in to Oxford. That way, she avoided the worst of the rush hour traffic.

Not that there was much traffic in Jericho at that hour.

Kyle Karastrides's house showed that all four windows were not only firmly closed, but had the curtains still drawn across them to keep out the cold, grey day pressing against the glass. As she'd predicted, the postgraduate wasn't exactly a lark.

She had to ring the bell three times before there was any sign of life. Eventually, she heard the shuffling sound of footsteps coming down the stairs and the door opened.

On the threshold stood a very handsome man just approaching thirty. He had dark wavy hair, coal-black eyes, a neatly trimmed goatee beard and skin the colour of milky coffee. He smiled instantly on seeing her, displaying a fine set of white teeth, and giving every appearance of being delighted to see her. Hillary had the distinct feeling that it was his default setting when meeting any reasonably attractive and hitherto unknown woman.

'Hello?'

'Mr Karastrides?'

'Yes.'

Hillary flashed her ID and the smile instantly faded. Instead, an unmistakable look of fear replaced it, flashing across his face quickly, but never quite managing to disappear altogether.

Hillary felt her inner copper's bell clang clear and strong, and had to remind herself that the student's reaction might mean nothing particularly significant. It was a sad fact, but lots of people from different cultures regarded a visit from the police as something to be dreaded and feared – whether they had a guilty conscience or not. Indeed, in some countries a visit from the authorities inevitably meant automatic incarceration – or worse.

But Hillary didn't think that Greek citizens had any reason to feel particularly downtrodden or wary of people flashing badges.

'As you may have heard in the media,' Hillary swept on from introducing herself by giving him an encouraging smile, 'Thames Valley Police are currently re-investigating cases of missing persons.'

Kyle Karastrides nodded and swallowed. 'Er, yes, I think I heard something about that. I read about it in the *Oxford Times*.' He was dressed in black silk pyjamas and a black kimono-style dressing gown intricately embroidered with red, gold and silver Chinese dragons. This he pulled a little closer around his lean body and definitely paled even further.

'Perhaps we could discuss this inside, sir?' Hillary asked, careful to keep her voice cheerful and casual. 'It's a cold day, and you're letting all the heat out.'

'Oh, yes, of course. But I'm not dressed, as you can see.'

Hillary smiled. It was clear to her that Mr Karastrides definitely didn't want to invite her in. Which was interesting. But again, perhaps not necessarily significant. Perhaps it was time to apply just a little pressure and see what happened.

'I can wait for you to get dressed sir,' she said helpfully. 'But your name has come up in one of our investigations. If you would prefer, we can continue this conversation down at the police station. But at the moment, we're just making preliminary inquiries that can probably be cleared up in a few minutes.'

'Oh, I see. Well, in that case. Er, please come in.' He stood back into a tiny hall, and indicated a door to the left. 'If you'd like to make yourself comfortable,' he offered nervously, and indicated the stairs behind him. 'I'll go and get some clothes on.'

'Thank you, sir.'

The living room she entered was small and painted a neutral shade of off-white with a hint of apricot. Generic black leather and chrome furniture was pushed against the walls, and in the centre of the room, an Ikea coffee table played host to last night's left-over pizza and a couple of empty cans of larger. A large flat-screen television and stereo system both looked top-of-the-range.

Hillary glanced around quickly, but could see very little by way of personal items. No photographs of his mum and dad, or any particular lady. Nor were there any magazines, or even books. Which was odd for a student engaged in writing a thesis. Perhaps he wasn't trying too hard? She certainly got the impression that the young man was well entrenched here.

In record time Kyle was back, dressed in a pair of old blue jeans and a baggy white sweatshirt bearing a pithy saying that had been all the rage about five years ago. He nervously indicated one of the chairs for her to use, started to sit down himself, then abruptly shot up again.

'Oh, please forgive me, would you care for some tea?'

His English was perfect, and spoken with almost no hint of an accent.

'Thank you, sir, but I won't if you don't mind. I had a large cup of coffee before leaving Kidlington.' Hillary smiled. She noticed he waited until she had sat down before sitting himself.

So Cindi-with-an-I was right when she said he had lovely manners. Garnered from a Turkish grandmother, according to Kyle. But from what little she'd been able to find out about Kyle Karastrides from Wendy's research, his family in Greece were all strict Orthodox Christians. And she felt, for a moment, woefully under-prepared and ignorant of other cultures. It wasn't often Muslims married out of their religion, so did Turkey have a Christian community? Is that how he came by his mixed heritage?

Hillary guiltily shrugged off her insular-related deficiencies. It probably wasn't relevant, she consoled herself. But what definitely *was* relevant was the fact that Kyle's family, had they known about it, almost certainly wouldn't have approved of their oldest son and heir dallying with ladies of the night.

She knew from Wendy's notes that Kyle had three sisters, but no other male sibling. And she rather thought that that might count for a lot in Kyle's family. Was that why so much money had been spent on his education? And were the restrictions that were almost certainly imposed on him whenever he went home, the reason why he was clinging on to Oxford, way past the time when his parents might reasonably have expected him to go home and take over running the family business? Which, if her memory served her right, was some sort of import export company specializing in antiques, pottery and various other types of crafts.

But it was time to stop speculating, and set about finding out what, exactly, was causing the good-looking young student such angst.

'So, the case we've reopened takes us back, almost to the day, to December 2012,' Hillary began calmly. 'A young woman called Lydia Clare Allen disappeared. She was a known working girl in the local area.'

In his chair, the history student was sitting very tense and upright, and listening politely. But he went yet a shade paler still.

And Hillary could well understand why. He knew that she knew that Lydia was a prostitute and that he'd paid for her services. Which, for a young man with his upbringing, was almost certain to engender both embarrassment and humiliation in equal measure. And perhaps all the fear that had been emanating from him had nothing to do with any guilt he might feel, or knowledge about her fate, but everything to do with worry that his parents might get to hear about his relationship with her in the first place.

After all, if he should find himself in disgrace, he was almost certain to be recalled home. And unless she'd missed her guess,

Kyle Karastrides was a man who very much wanted to hang on to his freedom for as long as he could. After all, a man in a foreign country, far out of sight and out of mind of his loving family, could often find himself so many interesting things to do.

'At that time, you'd have already completed your BA Degree at St Bedes and would just have started on your DPhil.' She helpfully jogged his memory, since he didn't seem to be in any hurry to add anything to the conversation. 'I believe you knew her, sir?' she finished flatly. She deliberately phrased it more as a statement than a question, and was careful to keep her voice business-like and non-judgemental, since she didn't want to have to go through the rigmarole of him denying it. She wasn't in the mood for any coy denials from the Adonis in blue jeans. Besides, like everyone else, she found pointless hard work extremely tedious.

Kyle, finally realizing that he wasn't going to be allowed to be merely a passive onlooker any longer, shrugged and gave a little-boy-caught-out smile. It was charming. He looked like a little puppy caught out peeing on the best Axminster. And Hillary had no doubt that a lot of women melted at the sight of those dark chocolate eyes of his.

'What can I say, er, Detective?' He shrugged winsomely. 'I was young, and she was pretty.' Clearly, in the panic of finding a representative of the law on his doorstep, he'd either not registered her name, or else had since forgotten it.

She didn't take offence at this. Nor did she help him out by repeating her name and the fact of her civilian status. The more wrong-footed he was, the better she liked it. Instead she nodded smoothly. 'Of course, sir. But I understand that you and she … how shall I put it? That you were rather a regular of hers?'

Kyle laughed. It was an abashed, modest laugh. He looked, if anything, even more adorable. And Hillary was sure that beneath all that charm, he was now utterly terrified.

'Well, like I said. She was very pretty, and had a very fetching way about her. And I ... well, I suppose I was rather young for my age. I'm not a very sophisticated person, Detective,' he admitted appealingly. 'What can I say? She bowled me over.'

'So you saw a lot of each other?'

Another graphic shrug and appealing smile.

'It must have been expensive.'

His smile faltered a little. 'Oh, well. Money....' He spread his hands. 'She had her ... er ... handler ... what do you call them...?'

'Pimp, sir,' Hillary supplied dryly.

'Yes. Whenever he was around, she was always nervous. I think she was afraid of him.'

'Yes, sir, the girls usually are,' Hillary conceded tartly.

So, he was offering up her pimp as the most likely culprit for her disappearance, was he? Interesting. Of course, in reality, a pimp was the last person to damage the merchandise since it meant a loss in his earnings. Unless a girl did something really stupid of course, in which case a beating was usually administered. But not, as a rule, anything more fatal than that. A dead girl earned no money, after all. So when prostitutes ended up dead or missing, it was usually a John, or drugs, that were at the heart of it.

Time to apply a bit more pressure.

'So you *were* close?'

'Well, as close as can be expected, under the circumstances,' Kyle finally admitted reluctantly.

'Really, sir? We've been talking to her associates and they all say that you and she were something of an item.'

'Oh, I wouldn't go so far as to say that.'

'No? I believe Lydia even told her mother that she thought that marriage might be on the cards.'

'What? No!' Kyle jerked forward in his chair. 'No, that was never ... my family would ... No. I'm sorry, but it's ridiculous.

A girl like that ... I never promised to marry her. Never,' he repeated emphatically.

Hillary took a long, quiet look at the young man in front of her. Without doubt, he was now seriously agitated. Which wasn't particularly surprising.

'Tell me, sir, what did your friends think of it?' she asked. She threw the unexpected question out because she wanted to take him off guard – which she certainly did. But also because she wanted to remind him that his version of events wasn't the only version she had access to. 'Your flatmate for instance. What was his name again...?' She in fact had no idea who Kyle's closest friends might be, but she was betting that he had no reason to know that.

'Mike? He ... er ... never really liked her. In fact, he thought I was being a bit of a mug, isn't that the expression?' Kyle answered the question automatically, as people tended to do if the truth had been startled out of them.

Hillary made a pretence of checking back through her note-book. 'Ah, this would be Mr...?'

'McIntyre. But Mike left Oxford right after he graduated. I believe he's managing an estate up in Scotland somewhere. Surely you're not bothering my friends with this nonsense, Detective?' He did his best to sound indignant and scathing, but fell somewhat short.

She looked at him coldly. 'A young girl in such a notoriously vulnerable profession, disappearing without trace or any word to her friends and family isn't our idea of nonsense, sir,' she reprimanded.

'Oh, no, of course not. That's not what I meant,' the young Greek backtracked at once. His knees were going up and down now as his feet tapped the floor in an unconscious habit that indicated real stress. 'Of course, it's very serious. Very bad. I never meant to make light of it.'

Hillary allowed herself a small nod. 'Quite so, sir. So I take it that you were very worried when Lydia dropped out of sight?'

'Yes, naturally,' Kyle agreed, but was back to being very cautious again. 'But nobody knew where she'd gone. I asked around, and one of the other girls thought she might have gone to Paris. Someone, apparently, had said that there were ... er ... opportunities over there.'

'I doubt her pimp would have just let her go gadding off overseas, sir,' Hillary said, knocking that bit of rubbish on the head right from the start. But it was again interesting. First he put the pimp in the frame. Now he was floating the theory that Lydia had been lured overseas. He seemed mighty anxious to steer Hillary away in a direction that didn't lead back to him. But was that merely self-preservation on his part – a conservative young man's instinct to deflect scandal, and thus indicative of nothing particularly sinister? Or was it down to something else entirely?

'Oh. No, of course he wouldn't,' Kyle said unhappily in answer to her sardonic observation. 'I didn't think of that. But the truth is, by then ... well, things were fizzling out between us. They'd run their course, I suppose you could say. I was growing up a little.' Again he shot her the winsome smile. The one all but guaranteed to turn female knees to jelly. Unfortunately for the Greek Adonis, however, Hillary's cartilage was practically made of stone.

'So she'd served her purpose then, sir? You were tired of her?' she interpreted.

From being pale, Kyle promptly flushed an ugly shade of dull red. But whether it was anger at her unequivocal question, or shame because of the truth that lay behind it, was hard to tell.

The young man quickly hung his head and shrugged. 'I was very young,' he repeated in a small voice.

Yes, Hillary mused. He probably was. Growing up in a confined and religious household, she was perfectly willing to believe that the eighteen-year-old boy was probably very naïve and innocent when he first arrived in Oxford. But naïve enough to fall in love with a working girl? Now that she simply couldn't swallow.

Yet he'd admitted to being smitten with Lydia. And Lydia, desperate to grab her prize of a rich, handsome student, must have realized that Kyle was by far her best shot. And yet Lydia would have had a working girl's often cunningly good instincts, plus a solid grasp of human psychology. So she'd have quickly summed up the hold his family had on him, and the fact that they'd hardly welcome someone like her into their family with open arms.

So why had she been so confident that they were going to get married?

Unless … Hillary gave a mental nod. Yes. That made sense.

'Pregnant, was she, sir?' she asked quietly. 'And, since you two were so exclusive, did she claim it was yours?'

Kyle Karastrides's head shot up and his dark brown eyes widened on her. His jaw went slack.

'Very awkward that, sir,' Hillary sympathized, as if he'd just verbally confirmed her guess. 'After all, it was hardly likely to be yours, really, was it? And it's not as if you can trust a pros-titute in something like that, after all. And even if by some chance it *was* yours, you could hardly take her home to your parents, could you? What did she do? Threaten to tell them? Insist on a DNA test? Did it all get a little too real for you, sir?'

'What? No. I don't … look, this has gone on long enough,' he blustered. 'I've tried to co-operate with your investigations, but if this is the way you're going to go on …' He got to his feet. 'I think I must insist you leave now. And if you want to speak to me again, I shall have a solicitor present, I think.'

Hillary nodded and slowly rose. She knew her exit line when she heard it. 'Of course, sir,' she said pleasantly. 'That is certainly your right. Thank you for your time.' She smiled at him calmly, and couldn't resist one last little probe. 'You've been most informative.'

And yes. There it was again. That flicker of real, sick terror.

Hillary allowed him to show her out without saying another word, but she was already reaching for her mobile, even as she set off down the back streets in search of where she'd finally managed to find a parking space.

'Hello? Wendy? I want you to get on the computer right now. Drop whatever else it is you're doing.' As she walked the narrow pavements, dodging the ever-present shoppers and cyclists who preferred the pavement to the road, she was thinking furiously. 'Find a current contact number for me for a Mr Michael McIntyre if you can. No – not the comedian. He was a student with Kyle Karastrides. According to Karastrides, he's now a resident somewhere in Scotland. Oh yes, and I might need to talk to Cindi-with-an-I myself at some point.'

'OK, guv,' Wendy said, on the other end of the line. 'But Cindi might not be happy talking to you. I kind of promised her that she wouldn't have to talk to anyone senior, like.'

Hillary shook her head and sighed. 'It's never a good idea to make promises you can't keep, Wendy,' she advised sagely and uncompromisingly, and hung up.

As Hillary Greene slid behind the steering wheel of her ageing Volkswagen, intent on returning to Thames Valley HQ, Darren Chivnor was busy researching how easily, in this digital age, someone could electronically transfer money out of one account and into another.

And the answer was very easily indeed.

And as he closed down his laptop, he was grinning widely. He could scarcely make himself believe it. But before the week was out, he was going to be a millionaire! It was actually going to happen.

When he'd met up with Barnes yesterday at the library, he'd almost expected it to be yet another disaster. Maybe Barnes had been lying all the time and he'd have his copper friends there to arrest him. Or perhaps he'd try and threaten to turn him in to Medcalfe if he didn't just tell him what he wanted to know. Maybe the money on offer would only turn out to be something like a measly fifty grand after all, for all his big talk of a million. Or what he wanted would turn out to be something that Darren simply couldn't deliver.

But something.

Because in his heart, Darren found it almost impossible to believe that he could, for once in his life, get that lucky. All he'd ever known was grind, disappointment, ugliness and the same old shit, day in, day out. He'd never had a break, never got to grasp the golden, glittering prizes that sometimes seemed to swim past him, just out of reach. It was always the other guy that got it.

So when he'd sat in that bloody silly library and Barnes had told him just what it was he wanted, and was willing to play a cool million for it ... well, Darren simply hadn't been able to believe it. Which was why he'd had to bail so quickly and get himself sorted out and under control. Otherwise he might have started to do cartwheels, right then and there. He'd wanted to scream with laughter.

It was just so unbelievably easy. He wouldn't even have to worry about Dale. To think – all he had to do was take Barnes to Jas Sudbury and he and Lisa could start a new life somewhere warm and glitzy.

Again, a wide, gleeful grin split his face. Of course he had to admit that it had been a bit of a facer, learning that Barnes and Jas were brother and sister. Well – almost. Who'd have thought that? A skank loser like Jas, related to a genuine golden boy? It just went to show.

Darren shrugged, then reached for his mobile phone. One thing was for sure. He wasn't about to look *this* gift horse in the mouth.

As he began to pound out the numbers, his hands were shaking so much in excitement that he fumbled twice, and had to start again.

Back at Kidlington, Jake Barnes answered his phone. All his incoming calls were being automatically recorded now, but he was expecting to hear his mother's voice, or that of one of his friends. He certainly hadn't been expecting to hear from Chivnor so soon, so when he heard Darren's voice he almost had a coughing fit as a bit of saliva went down the wrong way.

'Yeah, Jake? It's me,' Darren began. He didn't give his name, but then Jake hadn't expected him to. Both Steven and Rollo had warned him the thug was bound to be wary over the telephone line.

'Hello. Have you had a chance to think about things?' he responded equally as cautiously, careful not to mention any specifics, as his bosses had coached him.

'Yeah, I have. And I think we can come to some arrangement. You're a bit of an IT buff, right? Well up on online banking and what not?'

Jake felt his heart start to pound. It was actually happening. Right now. He glanced up, but only Jimmy was in the office, Hillary being out somewhere and Wendy having left, muttering something about finding Cindi-with-an-I. Or had he misheard that?

'Yes, I do all right,' he admitted. Jake wondered if he should get up and go to Steven's office to warn him what was going down, but thought it might not be a good idea to get distracted. Besides, Steven could hear it all later, when he played the recording back.

'So you'll know how to transfer funds from your account to one I give you?'

'Yes,' Jake said. 'I can do that from my tablet.' And then, remembering Steven's dictates, added, 'But don't think I'd be fool enough to go with you to some lonely spot in the woods or something.' Not that Jake had needed telling *that*! There would be nothing to stop Darren from luring him to some remote spot on the promise of taking him to Jas's buried body, only to stick a knife in his ribs and force him to wire-transfer the money, before killing him and disposing of his body. 'And I'm not getting into a car with you, either,' he added. Again, the same scenario applied. 'If you want me to transfer money electronically, then we're going to have to meet up, via separate journeys. And it has to be in a public place with lots of people around.'

On the other end of the line, Darren Chivnor laughed. And he sounded genuinely happy. 'Sure, I understand,' he said, again without any apparent rancour. 'So how does Bristol train station sound? All those busy commuters – public enough for you?'

Jake felt totally nonplussed. 'Well, sure,' he said cautiously, trying to figure out the angles. 'But you don't get any money until I see Jas. You do understand that, right? I mean, I did make that clear, yeah?'

'As crystal, mate. No worries – so, tomorrow morning, ten o'clock. Meet me at the burger joint not far from platform three.' And before Jake could object, or ask any more questions, he rang off.

Back at HQ, Hillary felt the buzz even as she walked past Steven's office and into the communal area.

'What's up?' she asked curiously.

Jimmy glanced up at her and grinned. 'Chivnor's just been in touch with our boy wonder. They've arranged another meeting for tomorrow. They're all together now in the guv'nor's office, discussing the ins and outs.'

Clearly Jimmy expected her to go and join them, because he looked surprised when, instead of leaving, she walked over to Wendy's desk instead and scanned the mess of paperwork. 'I asked Wendy to track down … ah, I see it.'

Hillary picked up a slim folder with her name on it. Inside was not only a telephone number, but a print off of all the information on Michael McIntyre that Wendy had been able to find. And according to Wendy's cheery accompanying note, their Michael McIntyre wasn't related in any way to the comedian.

Instead, he was the son of a wealthy Essex pawnbroker, who'd studied Zoology and Ecology at Oxford, and was now managing a game estate in Ayrshire.

Hillary nodded vaguely at Jimmy and retreated back to her stationery cupboard. There she got on the phone, and within minutes, was talking to the man himself.

He was clearly surprised to be taken away from his trout streams and grouse and transported back in time to his Oxford days, but after a few minutes, was soon talking away quite happily. And whilst his thoughts on the odd romance between his former flatmate and his call girl paramour weren't particularly illuminating, Hillary, with a bit of deft questioning, was able to learn something more interesting by far.

CHAPTER NINE

Aᴼᴛᴇʀ ʜᴀɴɢɪɴɢ ᴜᴘ ᴛʜᴇ phone on the unknowingly helpful Mr McIntyre, Hillary leaned back in her chair and racked her brains.

Who did she know in the canine unit who owed her a favour? She reached for her old diary and pretty soon had tracked down a now retired mate from Bunko who knew the head of the unit. It turned out that the top dog man still owed him a favour, but he was happy to pass it on to her.

This rather convoluted system of bartered favours was something Hillary knew all about and was quite comfortable with. So after contacting him and promising the top dog man a favour of her own (via some computer work which would be done under the table by one of the CRT's IT people) she was granted her own wish. Which for now was off the book and might well remain so if she was just chasing a wild hare.

As she walked back to Steven's office, she had the name of an officer and his canine pal written down in her notebook and an appointment with both in half an hour's time. Which was very fast work indeed, but it was the only time slot that this particular officer and his spaniel had available.

She knocked quickly on the door and stuck her head around. She saw Steven first of course, but mindful of the changing of the guard in just over a day's time, she addressed her opening remarks to Rollo Sale. 'Sir, I hear Chivnor's made contact. Is there anything we need to worry about?'

'Come on in,' Rollo said, but Hillary, although stepping through the door and carefully shutting it behind her, made no move to approach his desk.

'Sorry, sir, but I've got to be somewhere in...' she checked her watch, 'twenty minutes. And I have to make it in time. It's not something that can be put off.'

'OK – that's fine. And yes, Chivnor *did* ring Jake a short while ago. It's as we more or less expected. He wants Jake to bring the means with him to electronically transfer the money to an account of his choosing.'

'Jake reckons he can rig it so that it'll appear that the money has been transferred, when in fact it hasn't,' Steven put in.

Hillary glanced at him, eyebrow raised sceptically. 'Really? I thought banks had pretty tight procedures nowadays?'

'So they do,' Steven said dryly.

'So won't Darren sense a rat?'

'Jake says not. And he's the IT boffin – so he should know. He did try to explain it to us – something to do with him not really contacting a bank at all, but setting up the system to make it appear as if he has. To be honest, I didn't really follow it,' Steven admitted.

'Me neither,' Rollo Sale said.

'So long as he's sure,' Hillary said. 'The last thing he wants to do is stuff it up and get on the bad side of our Darren. But what if Chivnor doesn't just rely on Jake's computer gizmo, but actually rings his bank in person, on the phone, and talks to an actual human being? If the bank official tells him the money hasn't been deposited, Jake could be in serious shit. Our Darren has a reputation of settling his anger issues with a knife, remember.'

'Don't worry,' Rollo said, just a shade nervously. 'Jake made it quite clear they wouldn't be meeting up in any remote places.

Or travelling in the same car. So there shouldn't be any opportunities for Chivnor to turn nasty.'

Hillary nodded. 'Good. And how did our Darren take all
that?'

'Remarkably well in fact,' Rollo said. 'He even suggested
a venue for the meeting that not even Jake could argue with.'
He nodded across at Steven. 'We were just discussing why he
seemed to be so OK with it, in fact. He has to have an angle –
but we haven't been able to pinpoint it yet.'

Hillary nodded. It was a good rule of thumb. Most villains
had angles. 'Where's the meeting exactly?' Hillary asked.

'Bristol train station – tomorrow at ten in the morning,' Rollo
said.

Hillary gave a small mental nod. It was just as she'd thought.
It was looking more and more as if her theory about Jas Sudbury
was on the money.

'Right,' she said simply. Because the venue Darren had
chosen made perfect sense. 'We'll all be there, I take it?' she
added, but was actually taking that for granted. 'You're arranging cover for him now?'

'All that's already under way.' It was Steven who answered
the question, but he was looking at her thoughtfully. 'We've
been in contact with our Bristol CID colleagues, and they're
talking to the transport police that cover the Bristol rail termi-
nus. They're not particularly happy about it, apparently, but
we're all agreed there shouldn't be any danger to the public.'

'No,' Hillary said. Unless …

'We were just discussing the possibility of having Jake wear
a wire,' Steven went on, interrupting the dark direction of her
thoughts.

Hillary shook her head. 'I think that's an unnecessary risk,'
she said. 'If Darren spots it, it's all over. Just drum it into Jake's
head that he's not to go off anywhere else with Darren, no
matter what incentive he offers.'

Not that she thought Darren was likely to ask Jake to go anywhere. Unless she was totally off her game, it was all going to go down at the station.

'You think …' Rollo started to say, but Hillary was already heading back towards the door.

'I'm sorry, sir, but this other thing really can't wait. I've only got a short window to get it done. Perhaps we can discuss it again later, when you've had a chance to fine-tune the details with Bristol. What time do you want us all in tomorrow?' Her hand already on the door handle, she cast a quick look over her shoulder.

'Five a.m. for a briefing. It'll take a couple of hours to get to Bristol and then we need an hour or so to make sure of the site, and that we and the Bristol lot are all singing from the same hymn sheet,' Rollo said.

'Fine,' Hillary said crisply.

And was gone.

In their office, Rollo Sale glanced across at the outgoing Acting Chief Superintendent and gave a wry smile. 'In a bit of a hurry, wasn't she?'

'Yes,' Steven agreed with a grin. 'Something must be breaking on one of her cases.'

Rollo nodded. 'You didn't push her on it, though?' he asked curiously. 'You didn't feel the need for an update?' He wasn't criticizing Steven Crayle's methods – he was just genuinely curious. Within a matter of hours now he was going to be solely in charge of the CRT and Hillary Greene was one of his major assets. And he was willing to get all the top tips he could on how best to manage her.

'No,' Steven said. 'If there was something she needed us to know she'd have said so. She's probably checking out a hunch or a long shot, in which case she wouldn't want us to know if it didn't pan out. But don't worry – they usually do. And she'll let us know as soon as she has something important, don't worry.

She's not the type who needs to grandstand.'

'All good to know.'

Steven smiled across at his replacement. The more he got to know Sale the happier he became about leaving him in charge. Naturally, he and Hillary had discussed him in some detail over the past month, so he knew that Hillary had no serious doubts about her ability to work with the man. But he felt he owed it to Rollo to give him a heads up now. The quicker he learned the ropes as far as his top investigator was concerned, the better.

'Was that the only thing you noticed about her just now?' he asked carefully. 'That she was in a hurry?'

Rollo caught his tone and looked at him for a moment. He clearly thought about it for a moment, and then slowly frowned. 'Not really. Why? What are you getting at?'

Steven smiled peaceably. 'When you mentioned that Darren was happy to meet up in a very public place, and even chose Bristol train station of all places, did she look surprised to you?'

'Well, no.... Oh.' Rollo slowly leaned back in his chair as he finally understood what the other man was getting at. Because Hillary Greene *should* have been surprised, of course. When Jake had reported to them about Chivnor's call, and they'd listened to their recorded telephone conversation, both of *them* had been very surprised indeed. For a man who knew that he wasn't going to get his money unless Jake had proof of Jasmine Sudbury's whereabouts, he hadn't seem at all worried about the very public nature of Bristol's train station. Especially since Jake, as per instructions, had made it very clear that he wasn't going to go anywhere with Darren on his own.

So why *had* Medcalfe's thug been so confident about the outcome of the meeting? Because it was clear from his tone of voice that he was one very happy bunny. And yet, he could hardly kidnap Jake from such a public place and drive off with him, could he? Nor could he threaten him to transfer the money by wielding his favourite weapon – a knife – on a concourse full of people. All Jake would have to do is yell or make a run for it.

So just how did Chivnor plan to keep up his end of the bargain, and get his money, all within sight of hundreds of commuters? That's what they had been trying to figure out when Hillary had interrupted them.

But when she'd been told about it, she hadn't so much as turned a hair. Which meant … For a moment longer, Rollo Sale thought it over. Then he nodded.

'She's not surprised because she already has a fair idea of what Chivnor's up to, right? She's one step ahead of us, isn't she?'

Steven slowly smiled. Now he was getting it. 'You'll find that she usually is,' he warned him simply.

'But how? Does she know something we don't?' Rollo demanded sharply.

But already Steven was shaking his head. 'No. She doesn't work that way. As I've already said, she doesn't make grand plays or hold stuff back in order to pull the rabbit out of the hat and play the superstar. We've all seen and heard the same things that she has. All the information she has, is in her reports. We can read them any time we like.'

'But she's put the facts together and we haven't?'

Steven Crayle slowly grinned. 'Welcome to CRT,' he said mildly.

Lucy Lockett was simply beautiful. The moment Hillary saw her, she wanted to stroke her velvet-like ears and coo into her deep brown eyes. And her handler, an eighteen-stone ex-miner with a totally bald head and tattoos ranging up his arms and neck that clearly showed his allegiance to Sheffield United Football Club, clearly felt the same way. For when she met them outside in the car park, the liver-and-white spaniel was sitting on his lap in the canine unit's mobile van, and looking up at him adoringly.

'Hello – you must be Barry?' Hillary said, opening the other side of the van and climbing up into the passenger seat.

'Yes, guv. You DI Greene?'

Hillary grimaced. 'As was. Just a civilian now … sergeant?'

'Dawes, ma'am.'

'Guv's fine.'

The dog handler grinned. Like everyone who'd worked at Kidlington for some time, he knew all about DI Greene. 'My guv said you needed a favour. Off the books, like?' He sounded vaguely curious, but not inclined to push it.

'Yeah. Well, for now. It might get official later, depending on how things work out,' she felt obliged to warn him. 'Although it's equally possible that I just might be adding up two and two and getting four, when all I should be getting is twenty-two.'

'Don't you just hate it when that happens?' Dawes said deadpan.

'So, who's your companion? And can I take her home with me?'

And that's when she learned Lucy Lockett's name, and fell under the spell of the canine's big brown eyes.

Dawes started the van and Lucy immediately jumped down into the space between the seats on the floor. Hillary was almost sure that the proper protocol was for her to be in the back, in a cage, in case of traffic accidents. But what the brass didn't see, the brass couldn't grieve over.

'Where we going, guv?'

'Just head for Cumnor Hill and I'll give you directions from there,' she directed.

'Right.'

As they set off, Hillary checked her notebook. The directions that Mike McIntyre had given her had sounded clear enough over the telephone line, but she was very much aware that she was looking for a semi-secret location nestled in the hill and woodland near a small village. And well off the beaten path. And not being a natural Davy Crockett type (she'd even been chucked out of the girl guides before she could do the orientation course) she could only hope that she'd find the place without looking like too much of a prat. Getting Barry, Lucy and herself lost could also probably be described as wasting police time. The desk sergeants alone would wet themselves laughing if that ever came out – the bastards – and would make her life a misery.

As it happened, though, they found the spot with relative ease.

It was a typically cold, wet, grey December day. Barry Dawes pulled the van discreetly off the road and a short distance down a farm track, where he could park it under the cover of some dripping ash trees. Looking out of the window, Hillary was glad that she'd chosen to don her warmest and most waterproof raincoat that morning.

'There's a selection of wellies in the back, guv,' Barry informed her cheerfully, further improving her sense of wellbeing. 'My guv'nor said that we were just going for a walk, that right? Just you and me, two private citizens, like. And I just happen to be exercising Lucy Lockett at the same time, yeah?'

Hillary smiled. 'That's it.' With budget cuts being what they were, Hillary knew that if she'd made this request official, forms would have had to be filled in and invoices paid out, and Steven would have had to OK it, and then deduct the cost of it from who knew where. And it would probably take forever to arrange. And after all that, it might well turn out to be for nothing.

Which was why Hillary preferred to do it this way.

Barry Dawes looked out at the grey lowering sky, the muddy ploughed fields, the dank, dripping trees and chill wind and grinned. 'And why not? It's a lovely day for a stroll in the park.'

Hillary grunted. Wasn't it just?

As she slipped on a pair of wellies that were only just slightly too big for her, she re-read the directions in her notebook. With the van locked up, she made sure that the locally famous hill was to the north of her, then checked to see that the spinney Mike McIntyre insisted should now be in sight, was in fact on her right – as per the ecologist's directions. As it was, she confidently pointed the way forward and they started walking towards the trees.

Beside her, Barry strode along in an easy, amiable silence, whilst Lucy Lockett, tail wagging in ecstasy, darted about sniffing rabbit trails and other such delights. At the moment, the dog was clearly in her non-working mode, and if anybody had happened to be about, they might indeed have mistaken them for a man-and-wife couple, out walking the family pet.

Only Hillary knew how far from the truth that was.

'We going far, guv?' Barry finally asked. 'Not that I mind, but Lucy and me have to be back by four for a training session. We're showing a Lab/Collie cross the ropes.'

'No, not far. And luckily, it's not a big area that needs covering, either. As a matter of fact, the site is of special scientific interest. In the summer, it'll have Oxford zoology and ecology students crawling all over it. Otherwise, it should have been left pretty much undisturbed by the general public.'

'Oh? Rare orchids?'

'No. Bats,' Hillary corrected.

'Bats, huh?' Barry said. And gave a quick look skywards.

Hillary hid a grin. 'Don't worry. They hibernate in the winter.'

Barry grinned back. 'Did I look worried?'

'Not much. It should be just up ahead, in this stand of trees. Apparently there's an old ruined folly in there somewhere, where the bat colony is.' Idly, she wondered what species Mike McIntyre had been studying. But he hadn't said, and she had neglected to ask. Pipistrelles maybe?

Learning the ins and outs about Michael McIntyre's project hadn't been a high priority for her. Instead, she'd asked him if he'd been one of the many students to study Wytham Woods, and he'd confirmed that he had been. Oxford University students were known for their research in that area. Then she'd asked him if he'd ever taken Kyle Karastrides there. But he hadn't. And from what he'd said, the woods were so well studied, nobody would go there who sought privacy anyway.

He had, however, taken Kyle with him one night on one of his other projects, to study the bats. And when he'd gone into more detail, it had been all that Hillary had needed to know.

Now as they paused on the outskirts of the small, slightly boggy stand of trees in the middle of a vast ploughed field, Hillary watched the rooks and crows circling around, cawing morosely, and shivered slightly.

It was a desolate, bleak spot.

'In here, is it?' Barry asked prosaically.

'Yes.'

She watched, fascinated, as Barry whistled his spaniel over, and gave the cadaver dog her instructions. The spaniel instantly became both alert and excited, and watched Barry intensely. When he gave the signal, the dog entered the woods and they quickly followed.

'So, how's Sheffield doing this season?' Hillary asked, as they stepped into the darker, danker gloom of the stand of trees.

'Oh, don't get me started,' Barry snorted, watching Lucy carefully as she began ranging around the ground competently. She seemed to be quartering the area in a haphazard, but thorough way. 'I went up last weekend and should have stayed at home.'

Hillary commiserated. And, following Lucy's lead, they moved on to the next area of trees. Hillary, glad of the wellies in the oozing mud underfoot, listened to a blow-by-blow of the football match, and let her thoughts wander.

Was she wasting her time here? Had she read Kyle

Karastrides all wrong? It wasn't exactly common, in a murder case, to meet a witness, peg him as your prime suspect right away, and then discover the missing victim's body all on the same day. But stranger things *had* happened.

And you had to follow your gut instinct.

But there was still Lydia's stepfather hovering around on the fringes of the case to consider. And in many ways, he was also a classic suspect, and she might well end up with …

'Guv?'

Hillary snapped her attention back to Barry. 'Sorry?'

For answer Barry merely nodded his head in the direction of his dog. Lucy Lockett was sitting down near a large fallen beech tree, her tongue lolling happily. She was watching her handler with the same adoring look as before.

And for a second or two, Hillary didn't understand what she was supposed to be looking at.

And then she did.

Most members of the public, if asked, would say that they thought a dog trained to sniff out drugs or – in Lucy's case, a dead body – would find what they were looking for and then bark to attract their handler's attention. Or maybe, if it was a pointer, to do that nose-straight-back-to-tail pointing manoeuvre so indicative of the species.

But Hillary knew that a lot of dogs, when they'd found what they'd been sent to look for, simply sat down on the spot and waited quietly.

Like Lucy now sat and waited.

And for a moment, Hillary felt a totally human sense of triumph. Yes! She'd been right all along. It paid to be brave and take chances now and then. And to be vindicated was a definite relief.

And then, the next second her heart fell, as she realized the full import of what she was seeing. And she said quietly, 'Oh, hell.'

Beside her, Barry reached into his overcoat and drew out a squeaky toy. 'Do you know who it is?' he asked quietly.

Hillary nodded bleakly.

Of course, Lucy *could* have found somebody else's buried body. And until the forensics people and pathologists were able to confirm it, she wouldn't know for sure. But given the circumstances, it had to be Lydia.

'And soon I'm going to have to tell a very nice lady just why her daughter didn't come home for Christmas dinner all those years ago,' she said flatly.

Barry Dawes sighed, then called his dog over and began to play with her with the squeaky toy. Hillary didn't object to this seemingly irreverent activity. She knew that playing with the toy was Lucy's reward for doing her job and a vital part of her training.

So as the man and his adoring canine cavorted under the dripping trees, Hillary moved away and pulled out her mobile phone.

It was time to make this official.

Over the line, she heard Steven's voice and smiled. 'Hey, it's me,' she began somewhat wearily, then began to fill him in on where she was and what she needed.

Soon, she knew, the place would be swarming with white-suited men and women whose job it was to attend the dead and catalogue the evidence, and a large tent would be erected over the spot where Lydia Clare Allen had lain all these years. There would be forms to fill in (and in the case of the cadaver dog, judiciously backdated), forensic teams to direct, and uniforms to organize in a – by now – almost certainly pointless fingertip search.

And tomorrow was an early start.

And to cap it all, it started to rain in earnest – a cold, steady, persistent dripping of water that inevitably found its way down the back of her neck.

As Hillary Greene waited patiently for the others to arrive, she watched the big man play with his happy, lovely and loving dog. The squeaks of the rubber toy sounded incongruous in the dark woods as Hillary took a stick and put it in the ground, marking the spot where a young, murdered girl now lay. And as she did so, it suddenly flashed through her head that, somewhere within this scenario, there must surely be a deep and very significant philosophical truth to be learned about the state of the human condition.

It was just such a pity that she was too damned dim to figure out what it was.

CHAPTER TEN

WENDY WAS THE FIRST person Hillary saw when she finally got back to HQ. It was now fully dark, and when she'd left the woods, the forensics team had erected lights to help them continue digging. They had found human remains before the light had faded, but the pathologist on site was being slow and thorough, and he had made no predictions about when they might expect to start getting solid answers.

But he had deigned to make a preliminary report, and the bones were probably that of a female in her mid to late twenties and with nearly all her teeth in place, getting a DNA match would be possible.

Which was enough for Hillary to be going on with.

She was on her way to Steven's office to update him and Rollo, when Wendy met her in the car park. 'Is it true? You found a body?' Her first words were rushed and excited.

'Yes.'

'Is it Rebecca Tyde-Harris?'

Under the orange glow of a street light, Hillary sighed wearily. 'Sorry, Wendy, but I don't think it is. I think it's Lydia Allen.'

The young goth's shoulders slumped. 'Of course. She's one of your cases, isn't she? If Rebecca had been assigned to you, instead of me and Jimmy, you'd have found her by now.'

Hillary put a gentle hand on the girl's shoulders. 'First of all, don't be so sure. Not every case gets solved, you know, no matter how hard you work on it. And there's not a copper around who isn't haunted by a sense of failure over some poor victim who never got justice.'

Wendy grimaced.

'Second of all, don't do yourself and Jimmy down – you're doing your best. And thirdly, Jimmy told me how tough the interview was with Rebecca's family. And it's only human that you should want to help Rebecca's mother to get closure. But you can't take the responsibility for the whole world on your shoulders. Nobody can. And believe me, it won't do anyone any good to try. Not you, not Rebecca – wherever she is, nor Mrs Tyde-Harris, either.'

Wendy nodded glumly. 'I know. I just wish we could tell Rebecca's mum and dad that we'd found her. You know?'

'I do,' Hillary said, withdrawing her hand.

'So how do you cope, guv?' Wendy asked disconsolately. 'About the ones that got away?'

Hillary smiled grimly. 'Who says you do?' she asked, then shrugged. 'You never give up, basically,' she said softly. 'I've known old coppers, retired for years, who still investigate, off and on, the ones that nag at them. And sometimes, you just have to pass the baton on to your colleagues,' she added. 'And trust that, somewhere down the line, someone else might stumble onto something that you missed.'

And then, thinking about Sasha Yoo's reaction when she'd mentioned Rebecca's name, she gave a small, grim smile. 'But don't give up on finding Rebecca just yet,' she advised her. It wasn't over yet, not by a long shot. Now that Sasha Yoo was on their radar, she wouldn't be at all surprised if Steven's new team, at some point in the not too distant future, succeeded where the CRT had so far failed.

'But me and Jimmy haven't a clue, literally,' Wendy said

bitterly. 'Nobody's talking. It's so sad, guv. These girls get caught up in stuff, and get sucked down, and there's often nobody to help them climb out. If they've been in care, they have no family, and their friends either don't understand the life, or are in it themselves, or are too scared of the likes of Medcalfe to do anything to help them,' she carried on heatedly.

Hillary nodded. 'Sounds to me like they could all do with a good social worker,' she said casually. 'Look, I've got to report in to Steven. See you tomorrow, OK? It'll probably be late in the day, though,' she added, mindful of their appointment in Bristol.

'OK, guv,' Wendy said absently.

As Hillary walked away, she tossed the young girl a quick glance, pleased to see that she was looking thoughtful. Good. Perhaps that comment about the need for good social workers would sink in.

It must have been her night for accidental meetings, because as she pushed her way through the lobby and headed down the steps into the basement of the building, she met Jimmy Jessop coming up. He was holding on to the railing with a strong hand, and wincing with every step he took.

He looked up as he sensed her presence and tried to straighten his back. He almost managed it.

'Guv.'

'Jimmy.'

'I hear the meeting between Jake and Chivnor has been set up?'

'Yes, in Bristol.'

'Need another pair of hands and eyes, guv?' he asked hopefully.

Hillary smiled. He was a game old sod. 'No, thanks, Jimmy.' If anything went wrong, and Chivnor either tried to leg it, or fight it out, the old sergeant would be in no fit state to help out. In fact, she might be too worried about him to keep her mind on the job.

And it was indicative of the closeness of their relationship that he could clearly read her mind. Because he suddenly sighed, and nodded, and said, 'I'm gonna set up an appointment to see my local quack.'

'Back's not getting any better then?' she asked sympathetically.

'No. But with a bit of luck, a bout with a chiropractor or occupational therapist will do wonders. Well that, and drugs.' He grinned widely. 'And if all that fails, hell, I'll even try acupuncture.'

Hillary winced. 'Good luck with that. Oh, by the way,' she added, as they started to pass each other on the steps, 'I've planted the seed with Wendy about the need for good and competent social workers. You might just want to keep plugging away at that for me.'

Jimmy grinned. As fond as he'd become of the young goth, he was with Hillary on this one. She'd make a far better social worker than she would a copper.

'Will do, guv,' he said cheerfully.

Hillary waved him goodnight, and continued down into the basement.

Both Steven and Rollo were still at their desks and when she tapped on the door a minute later, it was Rollo who called out for her to come in. As she did so, she noticed with something of a pang that Steven's temporary desk was now almost completely cleared. Just one more day and he'd be gone.

But it was clear that his last day would go out with a bang, rather than a lazy whimper.

'Sir,' she said first to Rollo then smiled at Steven. 'Sir,' she repeated.

'I take it your hunch paid off then?' Steven said without preamble. 'Take a seat and fill us in.'

Hillary did so. And it quickly became clear just how fast she had worked.

'So you just liked him for it, right from the off?' It was the first question Rollo asked after she'd finished her report, and it was clear he sounded a little sceptical.

Hillary shrugged. 'Not just him, sir. I didn't like the way Lydia's stepfather seemed so interested in her activities, either.'

'So why Kyle?'

'Well, sir, it was a combination of things. First, his motive was solid. If Lydia had been pregnant, or only pretending to be so, it would mean Kyle's whole way of life would be compromised. He'd have to either marry her or go home in disgrace. For a family with strict religious principles, there were no other alternatives. Either way, he might lose his funding to stay in the UK, lose his position as favoured son – who knows, might even have been cut off without a penny.'

'But you don't know that she *was* pregnant?' Rollo persisted.

'No sir, that was an inspired guess. But if you'd been there and seen the look on his face ...' She shrugged. 'And if the pathologist *does* find indications that the body in the woods had been carrying a foetus then we'll have DNA evidence to prove paternity.'

'You think it likely?' Rollo asked, as Steven simply sat quietly and listened, content to let the new man discover for himself the worth of his primary investigator.

'I think so, sir, on balance. From what I've been able to learn of Lydia, she might have been a bit of a dreamer, but she wasn't stupid. She'd have known that to catch her man she'd have to be careful and thorough. And she'd have known about his family – to them, a grandchild would be the one thing guaranteed to at least give her a shot at marrying into a wealthy family.'

'What made you suspect a personal motive at all? I mean, hadn't we all assumed that Lydia would turn out to be the victim either of drugs, or one of Medcalfe's Johns?'

'Yes, that was the presumption,' Hillary said. 'But when Jimmy and Wendy learned from the street that the only bit of

talk going around concerned Lydia, well, it was rather sugges-
tive, wasn't it?'

Rollo Sale blinked, thought about it for a moment, and then
nodded. 'Oh. Right. The fact that they were willing to talk about
Lydia, when word was out that nobody was to talk to the cops
about any girl that was down to Medcalfe ...'

'Exactly. It probably meant that Lydia's disappearance had
nothing to do with them,' Hillary confirmed.

'OK. And I get why you thought she might have been buried
where she was. A foreign student couldn't have known of many
places where he could stash a body.' Rollo nodded. 'Unless
a mate of his hadn't happened to have taken him to the ideal
spot.'

'Yes, sir. As soon as Mr McIntyre mentioned the bat colony,
and the remote nature of the woods, I realized we'd need to get
the cadaver dogs on to it.'

Rollo coughed. 'Yes. Precisely.' He needed to discuss her
roundabout way of getting *that* little problem sorted out so
quickly. Because whilst he realized that her way had been the
most efficient, it did now require a little bit of creative fiddling
with the paperwork.

'I, er, hope that things like that don't happen around here
often?' he asked mildly.

Hillary smiled. 'No, sir. Not often,' she said. And noted his
preference to do things by the book. Still, there were always
ways to work around a boss who disliked going off piste, as it
were.

'So, what's next? We pull Karastrides in for questioning?'

Hillary stirred on her seat. 'I think, perhaps, not quite yet,
sir. We need to ID the body first and inform her family. And if
the pathologist does find DNA from a foetus, and we can match
it to Karastrides, then we'll have the perfect wedge to crack
him open with. Not that I'm expecting him to put up much of a
fight, mind. He struck me as the type to crumble. Who knows,

maybe he'll even turn out to have a conscience. Killing a whore is one thing – killing your own unborn child.... Well, for a man brought up as he was, that must have been playing on his mind. I think, once he's leaned on, he'll cave.'

Steven watched Rollo Sale consider all this, then decide to rely on her judgement.

'But he might just be flight risk sir,' Hillary added cautiously. 'He has ties to not only Greece but possibly Turkey as well. I recommend you alert the border agencies. If he makes any plans to travel, we might have to act sooner than we'd like.'

Rollo nodded. 'Yes, I was just going to suggest that,' he said. Truthfully, too. And Hillary believed him. She smiled, then caught Steven's eye and the silent communication that passed between them was easy to read.

She and her new boss were going to get on just fine.

'Now, perhaps we should talk about tomorrow,' Hillary said firmly.

It was nearly 8.30 when a very nervous Jake Barnes, and a far more sanguine Hillary Greene drove into Bristol station car park and were directed to a parking space by a local uniform who'd been expecting them. In the car behind them, Rollo and Steven followed their lead.

Last night, Hillary had gone through with them everything that she had been thinking, and all that she suspected might happen today, being careful that Jake couldn't overhear a word of it. At first Rollo Sale had been uncertain, but Steven less so. In the end, they'd formulated a plan that would accommodate both Hillary's predictions – should they come true – but would also allow for a wider range of possibilities.

As per these plans, Jake now left them quickly, in case Darren had arrived early and was in a position to watch out for his arrival. The last thing they needed was for the thug to see Jake with people he would immediately sniff out as coppers.

They watched the young man make his way inside where he'd head for the café they'd previously marked out as giving him his best vantage point for the proposed meeting.

There was still more than an hour to go.

Then they made their way to the station manager's office. That individual had already arranged for their Bristol colleagues to set up shop in a small office overlooking the concourse. And it was here that they met DI Brian Taylor in the flesh for the first time. Hitherto only a voice over the phone, in person he became a lean man of average height, with thinning dark hair and a narrow, intelligent face. He shook hands briskly all around and got straight down to business, confirming that the arrangements they'd asked for were now in place.

On the platform were six officers in plain clothes. The station security cameras were now feeding into the monitor on the small desk in one corner, and they had lookouts in the car park, to spot Chivnor the moment he arrived.

For a while, the room was full of conversation, but after a while, and as the time for the meeting drew closer, the conversation fell away, leaving them in tense silence.

And then the radio crackled to life and Hillary felt a distinct sense of déjà vu from Oxford Library as a voice over the radio advised them that the target had arrived.

Over the CCTV screen, Hillary saw Jake leave his seat in the café and make his way towards the meeting point. By the window overlooking the main concourse, which had reflective glass, making it impossible for the people below to see inside, Hillary watched the busy scene. All morning, trains had been leaving and departing, and people had flocked, queued, and boarded trains. Passengers waiting for delayed trains milled about, some with suitcases at their feet that occasionally tripped unwary pedestrians. Some kids ran about, playing, eating chips out of fast food cartons, or dozing on chairs next to harassed-looking mothers.

'There he is,' Hillary said, having quickly picked up on Darren Chivnor's distinctive shaved head and tattoo-covered neck. He had clearly spotted Jake and was now heading towards him.

In the end, it had been decided that Jake needed to wear a wire, and to compensate for this, he was wearing a loose, heavy leather jacket. If the thug asked to frisk him, it would be all over. Which was a fact very much on Jake's mind as Darren approached, for he did as he had been coached, and held out his tablet conspicuously in front of him. And as Darren drew level said straight away, 'I've got the transfer all set up and ready to go.' Because they wanted Darren fixed on getting his money right from the start and greed was a very good way to divert him from suspicion.

'Great. I don't have to tell you what'll happen if you screw me over, right?' Darren said at once. His voice came over loud and clear in the office.

Jake, who had every intention of doing just that, smiled nervously and nodded. If left to his own devices, he might well have let Darren have the money – provided he found Jas, of course. After all, his original plan had been to pay the man his money. But he understood why Steven and Rollo had forbidden it. As Steven had pointed out, if Darren got his money, he'd simply disappear with his girlfriend and then they'd never have the chance of using him in the eventual takedown of his boss. And besides, as Hillary had also so pithily explained, it would stick in their craw something rotten to allow a man like Chivnor, who'd caused so much misery and pain to others, to live a life of Riley on some foreign beach.

'No worries. But I don't start tapping out numbers until I have proof of where Jas is, and what's happened to her,' Jake told him.

Darren grinned. 'Fair enough. Let's go then,' he said, turning on his heel and heading towards one of the platforms.

Alarmed, Jake trotted after him. 'I told you I'm not going anywhere with you. Not even on a train,' he added. It had, of course, been one of the scenarios they'd gone through, that Darren might try to get him on a train. It was semi-public, and he might feel safe in a crowded car. But what if it emptied?

As it turned out, however, that wasn't what Darren had in mind. 'We're not getting on a train. We're waiting for one to arrive,' he told Jake.

Jake breathed a sigh of relief, then frowned. 'Why? Who's on it? Is it someone who knows where Jas is?' he added eagerly.

Darren smiled widely. 'In a manner of speaking.'

'Who is it? A man? A John? The one who killed her?' Jake's voice sounded hoarse with emotion, even over the concealed wire.

'No, mate. We're waiting for a girl.'

In the office, Steven said softly, 'You were right, Hillary.'

DI Taylor looked at her curiously, but said nothing.

Over the wire, they heard Jake again. 'What girl? Someone Jas knew? Someone she worked with?'

'No. This girl won't have known Jas. But she soon will,' Darren's voice said.

And again, it was clear that he was amused.

'I don't understand,' Jake said, clearly baffled.

'I know you don't. But you soon will. See, every day young girls leave home. They fall out with their parents, or their stepdad starts visiting their room at night. Know what I mean?' Darren laughed.

In the room, Rollo Sale grimaced and DI Taylor said something bitter under his breath.

'Or they just have this dream of living some *Sex in the City* sort of lifestyle,' Darren swept on, his contempt obvious. 'Either way, they come all the time, fresh off the train or the bus. Looking for adventure, a glam flat, a man who can provide them with bling.'

Down on the platform, a train had just come in, and Jake stared at the people streaming out of it and shook his head. 'I don't get it. What's that got to do with Jas?'

'Wait and see,' Darren said smugly.

In the office, Rollo Sale slowly nodded his head. Yes, Steven was right. Hillary Greene had nailed it.

'There she is.' It was Hillary who spoke now, but she was still standing by the window, looking down at the concourse. 'Just approaching the platform from the other end. Wearing a dark blue skirt and jacket – she hasn't spotted them yet. When she does she might rabbit. DI Taylor, can you have one of your men move up behind her and be ready to grab her? The last thing we want is for her to do a dip and dodge act and disappear in this crowd. Have you got her?'

'Yes, I see her,' DI Taylor said, a radio in his hand. 'You're sure of your ID?'

By now both Rollo and Steven were also beside her.

'Oh yes,' Hillary said, watching the woman walking confidently towards the end of the platform. 'See the way she's watching everyone carefully. No doubt on the lookout for a young girl with a holdall and a scared or excited expression.'

At that moment, the woman turned and glanced behind her, no doubt checking to see if anyone of that description had got past her. And they could all see her face clearly now.

'Yes, that's her all right,' Steven said flatly. 'That's Jasmine Sudbury.'

On the platform, Jake saw her at almost the exact time as Steven stopped speaking, and he staggered forward. His shock was so profound that, for a moment, darkness crept in from the outer edges of his vision. It took Darren Chivnor, reaching out sharply to grab his hand, to stop him actually falling flat on his face.

'Jas?' Over the wire, they could clearly hear the disbelief and joy in Jake's voice.

'Yes. Now, about my money,' Darren said. He started to haul Jake around, clearly intent on standing over him as he made the transfer. 'You said you needed proof. You've seen it. Now I want my money.'

But two things then happened in rapid succession.

Jasmine Sudbury, alerted to the sudden and awkward movement ahead of her, turned her head and saw first Darren Chivnor, whom she instantly recognized, and then her brother, being held firmly by the arm. And her pretty face, as Jake's had done just a few moments before, went deathly pale.

The next instant, she turned to run. As she did so, a tall, thickset young man behind her reached out and grabbed her and said loudly, 'Miss Jasmine Sudbury? I am arresting you on suspicion of solicitation and living on immoral earnings. You don't have to say anything …'

Before he could finish, Jasmine Sudbury started struggling and swearing.

And Darren abruptly released Jake and walked quickly away.

Up in the office Rollo Sale said at once, 'Stop him. DI Taylor, have your men hold him.'

In the same moment, Hillary said urgently, 'No, sir. Let him go.'

DI Taylor, caught in the act of rising the radio to his face to give the order, glanced at Rollo for instructions.

'Sir, if you pick him up, Medcalfe will hear about it within the hour, and then Chivnor will end up dead in some ditch somewhere. And you won't be able to hold him anyway – what can we charge him with? And if we're to have any chance of bringing down Medcalfe, we need to have Chivnor still in play. Right now, he hasn't got his money, and he'll be desperate to get it, so we can still use his connection to Jake. If we arrest him now, we lose all that.'

Taylor glanced between them impatiently. 'I need an answer,' he said. 'Chivnor's still in sight but we'll lose him once he's outside.'

For a moment, Hillary and Rollo stared at one another. She was right, and they both knew it. The question was – what was her new boss going to do about it? Hillary had known many superior officers who would countermand her now, just out of sheer pride.

Rollo's eyes flickered for moment, then he looked at Taylor. 'Stand your man down,' he said. 'Let Chivnor walk. We know where he'll be. We can always pick him up later.'

Rollo nodded at Hillary but he didn't thank her for preventing him from making the mistake. But then, she didn't expect him to. Or need him to. He was the officer in charge, and had the right to maintain his status in front of the others. And she was no prima donna – she didn't need her feathers stroking.

But as their eyes met, she gave the barest nod, and saw him give the barest smile in return.

And both were content.

'Right,' Taylor acknowledged, and turned his attention back to the screen. His man was dragging a now quiet and mutinous Jasmine Sudbury towards the exit. Another officer was escorting an arguing Jake back towards the offices.

'Jake's going to have a lot of questions,' Steven said. 'He must be feeling as if he's been hit with a bloody great sledge hammer right about now.'

Hillary sighed. 'He's going to feel a lot worse than that before all this is over,' she predicted grimly.

They took Jas to the local nick, where they all met up briefly in DI Taylor's office to discuss strategy.

'You know we won't be able to hold her for long, right?' the Bristol man said. 'Once she demands her brief, and she will, she'll be out in a couple of hours.'

Steven nodded with a sigh. 'Then we'd better be quick,' he looked at Hillary. 'I'll start off, and see how it goes.' Hillary nodded. Steven then glanced at Rollo. 'You all right observing?' There would be a room with a two-way mirror where the Superintendent could watch and listen.

Rollo nodded briskly. 'Sounds fine to me.'

Jasmine Sudbury looked up as Steven and Hillary entered the room. Slouched in the chair, she looked a little shorter than the five feet seven that Hillary knew her to be. With a short dark cap of glossy dark brown hair and blue eyes, she was attractive enough. Only a second look revealed the cold hard glint in the eyes and the white tension lines around her eyes and at the corner of her mouth – a mouth that was now curving into a somewhat cocky little smile.

'So, what's going on? And what's all this rubbish about immoral earnings?' she demanded.

Steven and Hillary both took seats, and the recording was started with the usual preliminaries. Steven opened the file in front of him and speed-read it. DI Taylor had managed to get together an impressive amount of detail on Jas, considering the short notice he'd been given.

'It says here that you live in a very nice flat in Clifton, Miss Sudbury,' Steven began mildly. 'With a lovely view of the bridge, or so I'm told. Those sorts of views don't come cheap.'

Jas sighed and studied her nails, which were painted a bright pink. But underneath the insouciance Hillary could sense her tension. She could also tell that the other woman's mind wasn't really focused on the charges against her. And it wasn't hard to guess what – or rather who – had distracted her.

'I got a good deal,' Jas said with a smile. 'I knew the estate agent. You know what I mean?' she smiled suggestively.

'Oh, please.' Steven sighed. 'Tell me what you were doing at the train station this morning.'

'Catching a train. What else?'

'Which train?' Steven pounced. 'Tell me the destination, number and time of departure.'

Jas's eyes narrowed.

'Come on, if you were really catching a train you would know where to and when it leaves. What train was coming in, or due, at that particular platform, Miss Sudbury?'

Jas studied her nails in silence.

Steven nodded. 'I thought not. You were there to pick up girls, weren't you, Miss Sudbury?'

'You think I'm gay?' Jas laughed and ran her eyes insultingly over Steven's face and form. There was something cold and ugly in her eyes, and Hillary was glad that Jake wasn't being allowed anywhere near this. At the moment he was being debriefed by a member of Brian Taylor's team in an office a couple of floors above them, and he wasn't going to be let within a country mile of his sister.

'So what if I am?' Jas shrugged. 'If I remember rightly, that's no longer illegal in this country.'

'No. But procuring underage girls for the purposes of prostitution is,' Steven said. 'Come on Jas, don't play games. You're a smart girl.' He knew, as well as Hillary, that they needed to find the right buttons to press, and quickly.

'Sure I am,' Jas said. 'That's why I know all this is a crock of shit. You really wanna make me say it?' Jas laughed again, and in a fairly decent James Cagney impersonation, added, 'You ain't got nothing on me, copper, see?'

She started to push her chair away.

'Now …'

'Sit down,' Steven snapped.

But Jas kept on rising. And Hillary, beneath the table, nudged her leg against his. She knew why he wasn't getting anywhere, and she had a bloody good idea how she could change that. It was time to try another tactic.

'Were you surprised to see your brother this morning, Miss Sudbury?' she asked mildly.

As expected, the intense blue eyes immediately fixed on her. Slowly, Jas sank back down and shrugged. 'Jake? Yeah, but so what? I haven't clapped eyes on him for years.'

Her gaze was mocking, the words nonchalant, but there was something in her voice that sounded as if it was echoing in a deep well. Which was encouraging.

Hillary nodded. 'Since you walked away from your family without a word. Leaving them all to wonder and worry. But they shouldn't have, should they? A girl like you – tough as old boots, right? Managed to get clean, and a whole new career, too.'

Jas shrugged. 'They never cared for me. Besides, Jakes's mum wasn't even my real mum anyway, and my dad … well, he's a loser.'

'And so's Jake,' Hillary said, allowing contempt to sound in her voice.

Instantly, Jas's eyes flashed. 'He's not! He's a millionaire twenty times over!'

Hillary shrugged. 'He's still a loser,' she deliberately goaded. 'What do you think he was doing with Darren Chivnor? You did recognize Chivnor, didn't you?' Hillary taunted.

And beside her, she could feel Steven tense slightly.

When he'd silently handed over control of the interview to her, he'd known that she would have a plan, or had seen an opening that he'd missed. But he hadn't expected her to go quite so improvisational on him. And whilst he was happy to trust her, and see where she was going with all this, he rather suspected that, over in the observation room, Rollo Sale was probably having kittens about now.

'Yeah, I know Darren,' Jas said cautiously.

'Back when you were in the life, in Oxford, yes?' Hillary propounded. 'One of Medcalfe's girls, weren't you?'

Instantly Jas tensed. And so did Steven – and again, with

good reason. They'd both agreed beforehand that mentioning Dale Medcalfe would be bound to shut down Jas faster than anything else could do. And whilst they might have hopes of eventually using her to gain insight into Dale and his organization, they knew it would take a lot of patience to coax anything even remotely worthwhile out of her. So why had Hillary just chucked that particular grenade into the mix?

'Screw you,' Jas said. 'I ain't saying nothing about Dale.'

'No, I understand that,' Hillary said smoothly. 'And there's really no need for you to. We already know that you started off as just one of his regular girls. Got into some trouble with drugs. But instead of all that bringing you down, you were strong enough to rise above it, weren't you, Jas? Worked your way up, in fact. Came to the big man's attention. So much so in fact, that he eventually set you up in your own gig down here – trolling for new talent, helping to run one of his houses.' Oh, yes, Brian Taylor, once he knew where to look, had been very thorough.

'So of course you're not going to rat on your boss,' Hillary continued, sounding weary and bored now. 'As Acting Chief Superintendent Crayle here just said, you're a smart girl.'

In the observation room, both Rollo Sale and DI Taylor were on the edge of their seats, waiting to see where Hillary was going with this. Because even Taylor, who didn't know her well, could see that Hillary Greene was clearly in charge of that room.

'Unfortunately, though, we were talking about your brother, weren't we? And he's not as smart as you, is he?' Hillary gave a shrug of her own.

Jas was now sitting up very straight in her chair. And wasn't smiling at all.

'What do you mean?' she demanded sharply.

Hillary laughed lightly. 'You're still not asking the right questions, Jas,' she taunted, her voice mock-reproving. 'The question you should be asking is this. Just what was my dear brother Jake doing with the likes of Darren Chivnor? And if you don't like that one, perhaps you should ask yourself another. Why is a man as important as an Acting Chief Superintendent so interested in one of Dale Medcalfe's top lieutenants? And why have we been keeping such a close eye on one Mr Jake Barnes?'

Hillary leaned slowly forward in her seat, and over the table top speared the young girl with her eyes. 'Because when you start getting answers to those questions, you'll understand just what a loser your brother truly is.'

Jas slowly went pale. 'Oh shit. What did he do?' she whispered.

Hillary laughed. 'What didn't he do?' She turned to Steven and gave a rueful shrug. Steven, playing up to her, spread his hands in a where-do-we-start gesture. He had no idea what was happening, but he knew a cue when he heard one.

'Well, for a start, he began by trying to find you the old fashioned way,' Hillary began. And started to sweat slightly. Because she knew she had to be careful now. Very careful. She needed to play Jas just right – and one miscalculation on her part could bring about disaster.

But of one thing she was sure – Jasmine Sudbury both loved and hated her stepbrother in equal, twisted measure. And from all that she'd learned about her from friends and family, it was clear that everything the girl had done with her life so far, had revolved around her feelings for him. The whole sorry catalogue of her teens had been an attempt to get him to notice her. Leaving home all those times had been done solely so that he would find her and bring her back. Forcing him to worry about her. Think about her. Look after her. But through it all, he'd never stood up and done what she so desperately wanted.

He'd never claimed her as anything other than his little sister.

And so had come the years of self-destruction, culminating

in her most cruel revenge. Going missing without making contact. Not caring that her father and mother would suffer. Caring only that her brother would.

And it was only by tapping into Jas's mixed-up, angry, destructive and passionate nature that Hillary could hope to make her forget her fear of Dale Medcalfe and his retribution and over-ride her instinct for self-preservation.

If only she could channel it just right.

'When you dropped out of sight, he hired a PI firm to find you,' Hillary carried on with a small, ironic shrug. 'I don't know why he bothered, personally, but he obviously thought you were worth it. Anyway, they failed, of course, because as we know now, you *wanted* to disappear. Not because you were dead, or had come to grief as everyone feared, but because you wanted to enjoy your new life. A life where you were the one who had all the power for once – a life where you got to live in a swanky apartment and wear nice clothes. After all, if your brother could make his fortune, why not you? And you liked that taste of the good life that Jake showed you all those years ago, didn't you? The holidays abroad. The flash cars.'

Jas stared at her. 'What's all this got to do with Jake now?' She was clearly not going to be distracted, which meant that Hillary was on the right track.

Further encouraged, she ploughed on. 'Jake's PIs learned enough to know that you'd been part of Medcalfe's stable. And when you disappeared, Jake thought Medcalfe was responsible. And guess what?'

Jas's blue eyes widened. 'Oh shit,' she said again.

'Exactly,' Hillary said, nodding emphatically, and again allowing contempt to creep into her voice. 'The fool was so determined to find you, so stupid as to think that you actually mattered, that he was willing to risk everything to find out what had happened to you. And to try and bring Medcalfe down for it,' she said. She'd begun by flattering Jas's monstrous ego, naturally. But she also knew that it was important to reinforce the possibility that Jake might secretly, romantically, love her after all. That was what Jas had always wanted, and to validate her hopes and dreams by acknowledging them could only reinforce her fantasy.

Which was vital. Because the more convinced she became that Jake might possibly love her in the way that she craved, the more likely she was to want to save his neck.

'Can you believe it? The stupid idiot thought that just because he got lucky with some penny ante dot com business, and then invested it in a real estate market where even a fool couldn't lose money, he believed he had the balls to take on someone like Medcalfe!' Hillary shook her head in disgust, and before Jas could protest, ploughed on. 'Which is where Chivnor comes in. Jake approached him for information. Darren, needless to say, saw an opportunity to make some big money and took it. Mind you, he damned nearly knifed your brother once, in an Oxford park. And still the fool was so desperate to find you that he gave him another chance. Now how's that for devotion?'

'Did he hurt …' Jas began urgently, then shook her head. 'No. Jake was obviously all right.'

'Sure he is. Well, for now,' Hillary laughed. 'Mind you, I don't know how long *that'll* last,' she snorted scornfully. 'Chivnor's been feeding him information for months,' Hillary lied smoothly. 'Just dribs and drabs, rumours about your whereabouts, your old Johns, that sort of thing. Bleeding him for tens of thousands, the mug. But today our Darren was going for the big score. Unfortunately for him, we've been keeping our eye on Medcalfe for years, and so we know from our sources that Dale has started to get wise as to what Chivnor's been up to,' she lied again. 'And you know Dale doesn't like his thugs getting independent minded. And when he found out that Chivnor was speaking to a civilian consultant at Thames Valley…' Hillary broke off as Jas gave a gasp. 'Oh, did I forget to mention that

Jake volunteered his services to us coppers?'

'Oh, the fool!' Jas hissed.

Hillary laughed again. 'Haven't I just been telling you that?' she jeered. 'He had some idea that he could hack our systems in his crusade to try and get you back. So, anyway, that's basically where we're at now,' she concluded, with a huge yawn. 'And you know Dale. He won't take this lying down. Right about now, I imagine he's putting your brother and Chivnor straight at the top of his shit list. And we all know what happens to them, don't we, Jas?'

Then she shrugged.

'Still, I don't suppose *you* care what happens to him. He's not even your real brother, is he? Not blood, I mean, so—'

'Shut up, shut up, SHUT UP!' Jas screamed, lurching to her feet, the chair skittering away behind her. 'You don't know nothing, you horrible old bag!'

Steven made to move, but Hillary put a warning hand on top of his. So they sat in silence for a while as Jasmine Sudbury paced about the room like a caged tigress.

By now, Steven, who thoroughly appreciated her play, was holding his breath. As was Hillary. Eventually though, Jas picked up her chair and brought it back to the table and sat down in it.

Then she looked at Hillary with a small, tight grin.

'Don't think I don't know what you're up to, you bitch,' Jas warned her venomously. 'You just want me to help you bring down Dale. And I can do it, too. I've kept my eyes and ears open all these years, and I know more than just the business stuff.'

In the observation room, Rollo Sale drew in a heavy breath. 'Bloody hell ...' he whispered under his breath.

'But why should *I* risk *my* skin?' she demanded. 'Many coppers before you lot have tried to bring down Dale and crashed and burned. And if you try and fail ... I'll end up dead,' she said bleakly.

She was right. And Hillary debated strategy for a bare fraction, but instinctively knew that now was not the time to lie. Or to play games. Now was the time to go straight for the jugular. 'And if you don't help us bring him down, Jake'll end up dead. You know it, and I know it. Have you really thought about that?'

'I've lived without him all right these past few years,' Jas stated. She sounded almost proud of the fact. And Steven Crayle felt his heart sink. She was just too cold. Too arid. Too far gone to reach. Why should a heartless wretch like this care for anything but her own precious skin?

But Hillary had no intention of admitting defeat.

'So you have,' she said softly. 'But then, you've always known that if you wanted to, you could see him again whenever you liked. Just get in your car and go park outside his house and get a glimpse of his face. Or you could pick up the phone, dial his number and hear his voice.' She leaned forward on the table, her voice sad and mesmerising now. 'But once he's dead and gone, Jas, he's dead and gone. You won't be able to torment him, or make his life miserable. And any chance that you could make him love you – really and properly love you – will be dead and gone as well. A dead man can't do anything, Jas. Except moulder and rot.'

Slowly she leaned back in her chair and shrugged. 'It's up to you,' she said, casting the final toss of the dice. 'Do you really want to kill him, Jas?'

For a long, long moment, Jasmine Sudbury glared at her. Then her eyes flickered. A brief spasm of some deep, dark emotion crossed her pinched, white face, and then she ducked her head.

'What do you want me to do?' she asked sullenly.

When Hillary left the interview room a while later, Rollo was feeling like a limp dishrag. Steven was busily getting down on tape everything that Jasmine Sudbury knew about the outfit she worked for. Which seemed to be a lot. And as head of the new unit charged with cleaning out the sewers, it was clear that his first task of bringing down Dale Medcalfe was suddenly looking a whole lot more likely.

Hillary nodded at Brian Taylor as he passed her in the doorway, then joined her new boss by the two-way mirror.

'When he's finished, I'm going to recommend that he brings in Sasha Yoo as well,' Hillary said. 'I'm sure that she has vital information about the Rebecca Tyde-Harris girl. And if she thinks that Jas is talking, she'll scent blood in the water. Which might just be enough to shake something loose.'

'You really think that she hates Medcalfe enough to turn state's evidence against him?'

'I do. Plus, I think she's as mad as a hatter.' Hillary thought back to Sasha Yoo, and her flat with the hidden, watching cameras. And contemplated all the violence the woman had inflicted on others over the years. And shuddered. 'And don't forget, we still have Chivnor on the hook. He didn't get his money today, and if Steven and Jake can convince him that there's still a chance he could get his hands on it – especially if he thinks there's a good chance Medcalfe really will be going down ... just think what damage *he* could do.'

Rollo sighed. 'Steven's going to have to be very careful. That's an awful lot of balls to juggle in the air. And Medcalfe won't go down without a fight.'

Hillary nodded soberly. 'I know.'

'Do you think Jake will still want to help us anymore?' Rollo asked curiously. 'Will he be in any mood to co-operate, given all this?' He nodded towards Jasmine Sudbury, who was in the midst of spilling some very ugly truths indeed.

Hillary sighed. 'I hope he will,' she said quietly. They'd need him to keep playing Chivnor.

'Well, at least she's still alive. He was so sure that she was dead so ... this is a bonus. Right?'

Hillary shrugged helplessly. Was it? She supposed so – of a kind. But she wasn't sure. From what all that the witnesses had said about Jas, and from what she'd slowly gleaned of her personality, Hillary had begun to peg her as being more likely to turn out to be a villain, than a victim. Something that Jimmy Jessop, after reading her notes, had also discerned. But she doubted that such a thought had ever crossed the minds of those closest to her.

Now, one thing was for sure – the boy wonder and his parents were going to have to face up to some very hard home truths and find a way to cope with some brutal new realities in the near future.

It was two days before Christmas when Hillary Greene walked to her narrowboat mooring in Thrupp for the last time. It was a sharp, cold day, with a clear blue sky and the nip of frost in the air.

Steven, now working of out St Aldates, was neck deep in the Medcalfe affair, and wouldn't be there when she arrived at his home. *Their* home, now. Nor did she expect him to be. She, more than anyone, knew just how much the job would consume him, and his time, for the foreseeable future. And neither of them would have it any other way. Besides, she was no young blushing bride and hardly needed to be carried over the threshold – metaphorically or otherwise. She would just moor her boat and then start unloading her stuff, and proceed to move into her new home, and her new life, with no mess and no fuss.

At least *her* professional life was clear sailing at the moment. Kyle Karastrides, when finally arrested for the murder of Lydia Allen, had almost immediately broken down in tears and confessed, much as she had always guessed he would.

Wendy Turnbull had taken the decision to become a social worker, and had given her notice the day before. Jimmy had promptly taken her off down to the Black Bull to celebrate.

Jake Barnes and his family were still trying to come to terms with the return of Jas – and just what it all meant. And everyone could only wish them the best of luck. And Jake had not only agreed to continue helping them with Chivnor, he'd even transferred to St Aldates, in order to work more closely with Steven in bringing down Medcalfe's empire.

Yes, all in all, things were looking good.

As she approached her boat, Hillary Greene turned her mind to gentler thoughts, and found herself contemplating Christmas dinner. Her first in her new home.

Would Steven invite his grown children to come around? Or his elderly parents?

Or all of them?

Either way, she'd better get herself to the shops at some point and buy a bloody great big turkey. If she could remember just how to go about cooking one now that she'd have access to a decent-sized oven!

With a sigh, Hillary reached down and slipped free the ropes, then stepped lightly onto the back deck. With a deft twist of the ignition, she started the *Mollern*'s engine, and, at a sedate three miles an hour, gently chugged her way towards her new life.